*C. Fardoe*

## After the Shots

C. Fardoe holds a Bachelor of Fine Arts in Creative Writing from the University of British Columbia. She is the winner of the silver Medal in the 2002 Scholastic National Art and Writing Awards. Born and raised in Winnipeg, she has lived in Paris but currently resides in Vancouver, where she writes the blog *Coco & Vera*. *After the Shots* is her first novel.

# C. Fardoe

## *After the Shots*

*To my darling Tee,
I didn't kill you off in this one, sorry - maybe next time!
Love,
Cee*

*C Fardoe*

To E.C.,

because a dedication is better than a signed copy, anyway.

"It was in 1973, when a group of Basque militants assassinated Adm. Carrero Blanco. The admiral was a stone-faced secret police chief, personally groomed to be the successor to the decrepit Francisco Franco. His car blew up, killing only him and his chauffeur with a carefully planted charge, and not only was the world well rid of another fascist, but, more important, the whole scheme of extending Franco's rule was vaporized in the same instant. The dictator had to turn instead to Crown Prince Juan Carlos, who turned out to be the best Bourbon in history and who swiftly dismantled Franco's entire system. If this action was 'terrorism,' it had something to be said for it."

— Christopher Hitchens

after the shots.

## Chapter 1

Today is the day. I've decided. His theory that Euskara holds the key to Proto-Indo-European has been viciously refuted by our linguistics professor. He is angry and ashamed; gathers his things hastily when the lecture ends. The timing, his mood... I couldn't have planned the scene more perfectly.

When I see him leave the lecture hall, I hurry out in the opposite direction, taking the back door. In the corridor, I spot him immediately; he strides toward me with his head down, a thick textbook tucked under his left arm. I rush towards him, my posture square and determined. We collide in ten paces, shoulder against shoulder. He drops his textbook, the same way I did all of those years ago in the school hallway, and the look of surprise, of embarrassment on his face when it hits the ground sends my memory hurtling back to our first chance encounter.

I was fifteen. I'm older now, and more self-assured – at least, on my good days – but when I stand so near to him, I still feel my heart knock against my rib cage like it's trying to escape.

"I'm sorry," he mumbles, flustered, eyes on the ground.

We both bend down, but I'm faster. I reach the book first, and hold it back. I've played this scene over in my head a thousand times, at least once every day since the first time I lived it. I know every beat, even in reverse. "*Da ados*," I tell him gently in Euskara. "That's okay."

"*Barkatu*," he repeats himself in Euskara, his cheeks reddening. He reaches again for the book. I pull it further out of his grasp and he looks up at me, finally, pleading. Lauran Echeverria. He still has the bluest eyes I've ever seen. "Sophie?"

"I want to talk to you."

He shakes his head firmly, no and responds to me deliberately, in French, "I need that book back."

"All I am asking is one *kafea*," I tell him in Euskara, my voice equally measured. "There are things I need to say to you. If you want to leave after one cup, that's your choice. I can only ask you to come – I can't make you stay." I extend my hand to pick up his book, and the cowl neck on my sweater falls forward to reveal the scar on my shoulder. Lauran's eyes widen. He swallows. I can see his determination waiver. "One coffee," I repeat. "Please."

"Just one."

§

Lauran and I walk in silence, side by side. My old instincts tell me to reach for his hand, but I hold back, clench my fists so that my nails dig half-moon shaped indents into my palms. My high-heeled footsteps echo off the walls of the empty hallway. I'm grateful for the sound of blaring car horns and barking dogs when we step out of La Sorbonne into the cobbled street. When there are no words, Paris never fails to fill the silence.

I send a message to my brother to let him know I'll be late coming home. It's still strange, at times, to realise that he worries about me. So much has changed since we were squabbling siblings in the little *commune* that was our hometown, a sports star and his ill-behaved adopted sister.

Without discussion, Lauran and I both turn in the direction of the *Café des Éditeurs*. Starbucks is closer, but I feel like a traitor to my heritage whenever I order a coffee topped with whipped cream. The streets are faintly wet with rain, but the sky is clear. I notice the details because I am concentrating so hard on holding all of the words I want to say inside of me. They are on the tip of my tongue in a jumbled mass, and threaten to spill out of my mouth at any second. I have planned this so carefully. I can't let myself ruin it when I am ten steps away from success.

In spite of the chill in the air, we choose a table outside, under the heavy red awning. I order *café noisette*; Lauran signals to the waiter that he will have the same. While we wait for our coffee, I slip my box of *Gauloises* from my purse and offer one to Lauran. He shakes his head, still silent, stubborn. "Suit yourself," I shrug- I know he smokes- and light one. I relax as I inhale, and the collar of my sweater slips again.

Lauran shudders as it slides, a second before my scar is actually visible. "What happened to you?"

I take a slow drag on my cigarette before I respond. There is a short answer and a long one. If I give the short answer – I was shot – he will stand up and walk away before his coffee arrives. "Oh, my scar? I got that near the end of the story," I smile, maybe a bit coyly. "I'm going to start at the beginning."

"*Deux cafés noisette*," our waiter announces, obtrusively slamming our cups down on the wooden tabletop.

"How long is this story?" Lauran wants to know - but he asks gently, in Euskara, and I can see him studying the shatter marks near my left shoulder. I can see that he remembers the way my skin looked when he used to know each other, before the scar. And maybe, just maybe, that it makes him sad to remember.

I slip my sweater back over my shoulder to cover my discoloured flesh. I know that I have a chance now... And if I say the words right, they might be enough to make him forgive me. "It starts just outside of Bilbao, in Spain, in 1986. That's where I was born..."

§

Of course I've told you all of this before, but I'm sure you've blocked it out, and I hardly blame you for it; I would have done the same. I was born prematurely and dangerously underweight to a frail young girl with a blackening purple bruise around each of her blue eyes. She named me Amaia Oihane. The hospital kept me in an incubator while my weight was slowly brought to a normal level. They were on the point of releasing me when my *aita* charged the emergency waiting room, armed with a Kalashnikov, demanding my immediate release, as though I were a political prisoner, not just a sickly baby.

It was at that point that the Spanish Social Services intervened.

This sounds farfetched, I know. I have a hard time picturing the scene myself, a mad man with a stocking over his head and a black beret over top of it storming a hospital with a Russian semi-automatic to demand a baby. But the truth of my life is why I gave up on becoming a novelist — there is no story I could invent that would sound more fictional than the story of my own life.

I was too young to be placed in foster care, so I lived the first ten months of my life at the *Hospital Civil de Basurto*. I was just shy of my first birthday when I was adopted by a couple from a border town in south-western France.

They were Ghislaine and Vincent Cassou, the couple I called *maman* and *papa* when we first met. They had a four-year-old son, Luc, and seven miscarriages after him. *Docteur* Lafitte, the local physician, had told Ghislaine in no uncertain terms that she would die if she tried to conceive again. I came home to Saint-Antoine just before Christmas in 1987.

I will never know if *maman* and *papa* planned to tell me I was adopted. The point was rendered moot when my biological *aita*, and his legal counsel, descended on Saint-Antoine the following year. After all was said and done, we rarely discussed my unusually chaotic entrance into the world. If anything, *maman* and *papa* went out of their way to avoid the subject.

Maybe you're old enough to remember the court case, I don't know. Maybe you were sheltered from it, living on the west side of town. I was too young to know what was happening, but my earliest memories are of flashbulbs and being carried above crowds. It went on for more than two years. The media set up a camp, made their own shanty town of new trucks just outside of the town limits. A few of them- you might remember Julien Durand, the little man with the notepad? — never left, even after the judgement was handed down.

  The verdict shocked Saint-Antoine, and the rest of France as well. The judge found in favour of neither family. There were errors of procedure rampant throughout the case, although when I read through the documents a few years ago, I couldn't make logical sense of any of it. All I could tell for certain was that the Spanish Social Services had assigned a professionally derelict old man to handle my adoption, and his ability to complete required paperwork was only slightly superior to that of a houseplant charged with the same task. There was exactly one sheet of paper that could prove my adoption by the Cassou family was legitimate. And it was a photocopy. I was allowed to stay with them in Saint-Antoine because in spite of that, there was ample proof that I had thrived under their care.

  But my biological family was not cut out, either. The judge decreed that although I was to be raised and educated in Saint-Antoine as a French citizen, I would spend the summers in Basque Country, learning the language and culture of my birth family.

§

  Lauran puts his coffee cup down on the table. A brown, foamy residue covers the inner edges, but the cup is empty. I feel my stomach knot. Until this second I had managed not to think of how happy I was just to sit across the table from him again. I'm terrified that he will stand up and leave the café without another word to me. Part of me knows that I probably deserve as much.

  My heart bangs against my rib cage. I light another cigarette, desperate not to show that my hands tremble and fumble when I strike the match. As I inhale, Lauran raises his hand to signal our waiter- two more *cafés noisette*. My sigh of relief is nearly audible. I think Lauran almost smiles before he nods for me to continue, but

I tell myself I must have imagined it; the higher my hopes fly, the further they have to fall.

§

My biological parents refused to call me Sophie; to them I was and always would be Amaia. I spent my first summer with them when I was four-years-old. The experience perturbed me from the moment that I was dropped off in Bilbao. An impartial civil servant was charged with my safe transit over the border; he talked to me quietly while our car rolled through the bucolic French countryside and I felt quite safe until we stopped in the parking lot at the Bilbao airport, where a large man with twisted lips waited, his arms crossed, in front of a rundown van. "That's your *papa*," my guardian said. My *aita*. The strange man smelled like gasoline and the stubble on his unshaven face scratched like sandpaper. He was rough when he carried me, and insisted on carrying me even though I could walk. He packed me into the back of a windowless van where two more strange men held me still because there were no seatbelts, or even chairs. They talked to each other in a language I couldn't understand; the words sounded as though they were spoken under water.

I had no idea where we were going, and could see nothing along the way. If I cried, I don't remember- I suspect I was too shocked to react at all. When the van finally stopped, the two men carried me out of the van by my arms and put me down on a dusty, unpaved road. There were small houses on either side of it, once white, their faded paint chipped and floating away in the breeze like snow falling backward. Some had broken windows; others were missing front doors, or their concrete steps had crumbled. "*Mais, ç'est affreux*," I murmured, but neither man gave any indication that they had heard me.

I let the strange men take me into one of the houses and leave me with a skinny, shaky woman they called *ama*. She bathed me under an icy hose in the back yard, fastened my hair in plaits so tight that it felt like my scalp would rip in half and then left me alone in the kitchen while she wandered the tiny house, silent and listless.

After that traumatic afternoon, I remember only a few scattered fragments of my first summer in Euskal Herria. I learned to speak Euskara- I had no choice. I discovered that I had a brother. He turned six that August, and *aita* presented him with a Browning 9mm pistol. We rarely played together. The children in the small town were dirty-faced and shoeless, but it was they who gave me a wide berth. Ilari, my *anaia*, was one of them, and followed their lead.

Apart from daily hosing in the yard, I was left largely to my own devices. I rarely saw my *aita*, and *ama* was, to put it gently, a little unhinged. She awoke early in the morning to go to mass, then bathed and clothed me when she came back. The rest of her mornings were devoted to her Spanish bible, a tattered leather bound volume that she could not read. After I was dressed, she acted as though I wasn't there; sometimes, I wondered if maybe she really didn't realise that I was. In the afternoons, she wandered the house in a pair of mismatched pumps, only pausing her pointless routine to prepare meals. If I needed to be taken care of, like when I cut my hand on a throwing knife left on the living room floor – I still have the scar, see? – the two strange men from the van would appear as if by magic. There was no telephone to call them on - they just came to the door and whisked me away. Balere and Remiri. I thought they must be my uncles.

Two bewildering months later, I was driven back to the airport in the back of the windowless van and grudgingly handed over to a civil servant, who accompanied me across the border to Saint-Antoine.

It took time for me to adjust to life in France - not just the first time, but every year after. I didn't answer when people called me Sophie. I spoke Euskara instead of French. It seemed when I finally got back into the routine of being Sophie Cassou, summer was just around the corner and I had to become Amaia Sagastizabal again.

My childhood in Saint-Antoine is the only one I knew, but even if the experience was the closest thing to normalcy I had, it was no picnic in the park.

When I started school, the children I had always played with began to act differently around me. They were all very, very kind - too kind; I was treated like a near-invalid until I was about ten. It was years before I found out that Father Philippe, the so-called priest, had told the Sunday school children that I went away every summer because I was sick, so they should keep me in their prayers.

As far as Father Philippe is concerned, anyone who is not purely French is diseased.

I don't suppose I ever thought of being Euskadi as something that was wrong with me, but I never felt comfortable with it. In truth, by the time I was twelve, I never felt quite right anywhere. My classmates in Saint-Antoine had lost interest in my alleged disease; they thought I was odd at best and offensive at worst, mostly thanks to my brother Luc, who waged a personal and public assault on me during his years at *lycée*, calling me Spic and worse. Aside from Margaux, a girl whose great crime was having an American mother, I was alone.

Margaux and I stuck together. For two social pariahs, our teen years were quite charmed. We gained a reputation as bad girls for smoking at lunch hour and took advantage of it, lipping off to teachers and enjoying the company of boys in rebellious phases. Well, mostly Margaux. I only ever had one admirer, the decidedly dull Patrice Carbodel- the grocer's son. And the extent of his efforts to win me over was to slide things down the back of my dress in church. He had the nerve to put a frog in there once! Naturally, Father Philippe attributed my screaming in the middle of mass to my, "cultural affliction," as he described it.

When I think back on the girl I was then, and the things I did - I hardly feel like it was me. Once, in our French class, we had to choose a series of adjectives to describe ourselves. My classmates chose *nice, kind, generous, fun* and *smart* almost exclusively. I wrote *ambiguous, extraordinary, lovely, nervous* and *wild*. When I read my list aloud, as happened every time I spoke in class, a stunned, judgmental silence followed.

I've gotten off the subject. What I meant to say was that in spite of that, I had Margaux. But every summer, I had to leave her. And every summer was...

§

Lauran clears his throat. "It's getting late, Sophie."

I turn my head and look out into the street. I'm almost surprised to see that darkness has settled over Paris. It feels like we just sat down. "Oh?"

"I have to go." Lauran stands up and begins to button his coat, leaving me no chance to protest. "My girlfriend will be waiting."

*My girlfriend.* For one agonising second, my heart stops. A girlfriend. I don't know why that possibility had never crossed my mind. Lauran is smart and handsome and charming to a fault, never at a loss for words unless he chooses to be. It's only natural that another woman would have seen that. Devastating, but natural. I reach for a cigarette. It's a nervous tick, the same way that my *anaia* absently stabs thing when he is alone with his thoughts. I feel calmer when I have something to hold onto; something to stop my hands from trembling and my lips from spilling out endless babbled sentences.

"Of course." I have planned this too carefully to let a few words derail everything. I never expected Lauran to open his arms to me after a few hours of one-sided conversation over coffee; hoped he would, maybe, but never expected it. This will take time. Weeks, maybe even months. But I am not the sort of girl who shrinks away from a challenge. Lauran has a girlfriend now. That doesn't mean he will forever. "But," I light my *Gauloise*, filled with false bravado, "I haven't finished my story. Will I see you again next week?"

"Maybe," Lauran shrugs. He drops a few coins carelessly on the table and walks off down the sidewalk.

## Chapter 2

The apartment I share with Luc has a blue lacquered door with a gold knob in the centre. When I turn my key in the lock and pull on the knob to let myself in, the scent of tomato and basil overwhelms me. My brother loves to cook. He doesn't always do it well, but he enjoys it. "*Bon soir!*" I call as I step inside, kicking my pumps off haphazardly.

Luc appears in the kitchen doorway, wooden spoon in hand. He played rugby growing up, and his shoulders are so broad that he could scarcely fit through a conventional doorframe. The rest of his body matched them, at one time; standing in front of him was like facing a wall. It's been three years since his last scrum. He's so tall and slight now; sometimes I don't recognise him from behind. "You're late."

"Hello to you, too," I roll my eyes. My brother has changed so much, but when he is worried, the impatience that I always thought of as his defining trait still comes out. "I did tell you I would be late, you know."

"Where were you?"

I raise an eyebrow. Luc never asks questions. In fact, when it comes to my life outside of the apartment, he makes a very deliberate point of not asking questions - when I pack my bags to go to Bordeaux for an undetermined period of time, all he ever says is, "Have fun." Part of me is almost certain that he has an idea of what I do while I'm there, or at least why I go — but I can never be sure, and although I sometimes worry about what it might mean, his silence on the subject is one of the things I appreciate most about his personal transformation. It perturbs me that he suddenly wants to know intimate details, especially when I was doing something so harmless. If I come home visibly upset, that's one thing... But I'm happy. I haven't been able to wipe the smile off my face since I watched Lauran walk out of the *Café des Éditeurs*.

I have a momentary flashback to our school days in Saint-Antoine, when Luc would come barreling down the corridor, catch me by the arm in a grip so tight it left bruises, and demand, "Where are you going, Sophie? Did you find another little Spic to play with?"

The memory makes me shudder a little.

But I stare my brother down. "Out."

"Out where?" Luc insists on pressing the issue.

The urge to scream at him to mind his own business overcomes me in a flash. I clench my fists and square my stance. But then I remember that this isn't the *lycée* in Saint-Antoine and the rage subsides a little. Luc and I are roommates, I tell myself. Adults. I relax my hands as I repeat *Docteur* Andre's mantra in my head — *I control my emotions, they don't control me.*

With a sigh, I push my way into the kitchen, ducking under Luc's arm. A tall silver pot bubbles on the stove; I have to stand on tiptoe to see inside. The smell of stewing tomatoes is overpowering. "What's for dinner?"

My brother turns in the doorframe to face me; I can feel his paternal gaze on my back. "Don't change the subject."

"Why do you care so much, anyway?" I stick my finger in the soup for a taste... It burns a little, but it's necessary. "Needs pepper."

"Thank-you, chef Sophie," Luc rolls his eyes. "Madeleine told me you were meeting someone from home. Is Margaux visiting?"

Madeleine. I should have known this was her fault. When I arrived in Paris two years ago, I was a nervous girl with visible scars and one ratty sweater that was so sentimental, you couldn't have torn it off me. To make matters worse, I was assigned the most beautiful, stylish and aloof project partner in a first-year economic theory course. She was Madeleine Muller, a born and bred *Parisienne*. After a few false starts and one particularly shameful incident wherein we both purposely spilled coffee on another, we developed what might be called a friendship. Well, maybe a partnership. At the very least, we combine forces in our school work whenever we can manage it – we still rarely see eye-to-eye, and at times our bickering even aggravates me, but in spite of that, we work as an exceptionally good research team.

Luc has had a mad – and maddening – crush on her since the first day she came through our front door. At first, she thought he was hopelessly provincial. Actually, she still does. But she seems to find it more and more endearing every time she visits... which she has done once or twice while I've been away.

I smile at my brother, teasing, "Has *la Madeleine* deigned to let you through her gates yet?"

"We were just talking, Sophie!" Luc's pale face turns almost purple, he's so embarrassed.

"All right, all right..." I know when to back off. "Why do you automatically assume Margaux is my only friend from Saint-Antoine?"

"I don't," Luc crosses the small kitchen and begins absently stirring his soup. He can't look me in the eye. "I just wanted to know if you would lie to me."

Like a flash, it comes on again - I am livid. "What?"

"I – Madeleine -" My brother is flustered, and he takes it out on the soup, stirring it so vigorously that it sloshes over the sides of the pot; small red drops dot the white stovetop. "She told me you were meeting an old boyfriend."

Damn it. I knew I should have kept it to myself. But every day for the first three weeks of our linguistic theory lecture, Madeleine would poke me in the arm with the end of her pen and ask, "Why do you keep staring at that argumentative boy in the front row?"

At first I ignored her, or shrugged it off as daydreaming. But it went on, week in and week out, and she stopped believing me. "What's the big secret, anyway?" For an aloof Parisian, Madeleine can be surprisingly abrupt when the mood strikes her.

"He's my ex-boyfriend."

Madeleine raised one fine blonde eyebrow. "And...?"

"And..." I hesitated, "... sometimes I still think he might be the love of my life."

Madeleine clamped her hand over her mouth to keep from laughing out loud in the middle of the lecture. She is not a believer in great loves. Or so she claims. For a non-believer, she displayed startling interest in my plans with Lauran... So much so that she apparently reported them to my brother!

"What if I did?" I demand of Luc, my arms crossed and my tone petulant. My emotions have taken over. I was happy about today – the earth didn't move, Lauran didn't fall back in love with me but it was a start, and my brother is spoiling it. The longer this conversation goes on, the more I start to wonder who I think I'm kidding. I lost Lauran just like this – because I can't answer questions that should be simple; because I was – I am – too ashamed to admit my feelings in the face of judgement.

Luc shrugs. "I guess it just occurred to me that I didn't know you had an ex-boyfriend."

"Well, it occurred to me that I didn't know Madeleine slept over that last time I was in Bordeaux." My brother flushes red and stares hard into the soup pot, as if he hopes it might open up and swallow him. "I guess we both have secrets. Now can we eat? I'm starving."

§

Some evenings, Luc and I eat at our wooden kitchen table. We talk about our days, between mouthfuls; his work and my study. Tonight, my brother fills two soup bowls, and serves them unceremoniously on the living room coffee table with a bottle of *Chinon*. The sound of reality television replaces our conversation.

I sit with my knees tucked in to my chest, and my soup bowl balanced on them. The nonsense on TV is of no interest to me, so I watch my brother out the corner of my eye while I eat. We look surprisingly alike for two people who are biologically unrelated; both dark-haired and skinny, with a few pale freckles across our noses that darken in the summer.

You wouldn't think it to see him, but Luc was a bully when we were kids. Not just to me, although I was often his victim of choice — he was the town bully. By the time he was eight, he was bigger and smarter and faster than everyone around him... and he took ruthless advantage of it. He had a cigarette racketeering scheme to support his own nicotine habit, abused the non-athletic mercilessly and taunted me for being a Spic every day from the moment I opened my eyes in the morning. When my birthday came, *maman* would beg him to be kind to me for the day, as if that would be a gift.

When he finished at *lycée*, Luc moved to Paris to study economics. I think I may have been the first fourteen-year-old ever to be relieved to have her parents to herself. (Of course, Luc always made up for lost time and tormented me twice as much at every school holiday. He once replaced all of my Christmas gifts with bricks - *maman* and *papa* took two days to find where he had hidden the real presents, although by then it was really too little, too late.) He blazed through his *licence* at record speed and got a highly coveted job on the trading floor at *la bourse*, which he worked while doing his *maîtrise* at night. All while playing league rugby.

And then I got hurt.

I spent a month in the hospital in Bilbao, recovering. When I was ready to start rehabilitation — I had to completely relearn to reuse my left arm, which was particularly inconvenient since I was born left-handed — I was sent back to my home country. But the closest thing to a rehabilitation facility in Saint-Antoine, with its population of less than three hundred, is *Docteur* Lafitte, the local GP, so I rode all the way from Bilbao to Bordeaux in the back of an ambulance. My *anaia* and his girlfriend, Ilari and Gen, were there when I arrived, like they had promised; they rented an apartment near the train station and have been there ever since, working with Thierry.

Luc was there, too. He had quit his job, left his rugby team and abandoned his *maîtrise* mid-stream. For me. I don't know if he intended to stay. He was unbearably uncomfortable. Ilari's black clothes and piercings perturbed him; they rarely did more than nod hello to one another, and then only if by some terrible accident their visits overlapped. But what perturbed him especially was seeing Ilari with me — the way we laughed and joked like friends. Whenever Luc walked in on us mid-conversation, he would jam his hands into his pockets and stalk out into the hall, waiting conspicuously for us to finish.

I didn't want him there. I had no happy memories of him. But I was confined to the hospital, so if he persisted in visiting, I had no choice but to see him. At first, I would only speak to him if he asked me a direct question, so we sat in silence most of the time. I thought if I kept it up long enough, he would leave. I underestimated him.

"Why are you here?" I finally demanded one afternoon — my physical therapy had stalled. I was frustrated and angry. My brother was an easy target.

Luc shrugged, as if the answer was either unclear or so obvious that it went without saying. "You're my sister," was the best he could come up with.

"And who was I when you were calling me a Spic in front of the entire school?" I snapped.

"You were my sister then, too." Luc's sheepish reply was barely audible. "I guess it took me a while to really understand what that meant."

"You're the smartest person I know, you asshole. How did that elementary concept escape you?"

"Look," my brother sighed, raking his fingers through his hair, "...I'm sorry, okay? I'm here now."

I didn't really believe him, but time told the tale. He was there on the devastating day when the psychiatrist deferred my university entrance for a year because he deemed me psychologically unfit for the strains of higher education. He was there when the neurologist and orthopedist got together to conclude that the nerve damage to my arm was too deep to allow me to properly hold a pen – and I had to relearn to write with my right hand like a six-year-old at school. He was there every time *maman* demanded that I turn my back on Ilari and Gen, calling them, "Those terrorists who did this to you."

He was still there after *maman* gave me the "it's them or me" ultimatum – I chose them. *Maman* never darkened the door of my hospital room again. But Luc stayed. He gave up every single plan he had for his own life. When I was released from the hospital, he invited me to live in the apartment he had rented in Bordeaux. When I was cleared to start school in Paris, he left Bordeaux behind to come with me. He finished his *maîtrise* two years late. He got a job vastly beneath his qualifications, managing a small branch office of *BNP Paribas*.

I eye my brother over the edge of my soup bowl. We have lived together for a little more than three years now. Every day, he has breakfast waiting when I wake up, and dinner on the stove when I get home. I know better than to ask why. I just accept my brother for the blessing he grew up to be.

But sometimes – I tilt my bowl back to slurp the end of my soup – I have to say it. "Thank-you."

Luc looks up at me for a second, raises an eyebrow, and then turns back to the TV.

§

From my bedroom window, I can see *Notre-Dame de Paris* rising up above the gray green roofs of Paris like a beacon. Most nights after dinner, I sit on my window ledge – even in the rain – and watch the sun set over the cathedral while I talk to Gab.

Every morning and every night since he died, I have talked to Gab. I wear his old sweater sometimes when we talk, still, even though *Docteur* André has strictly forbidden me to wear it, even though there are small blood stains on the collar and holes along the wrist cuffs, because it makes me feel closer to him. He was wearing it when he died; it was the only sweater he owned, a threadbare black knit he'd had since he stopped growing when he was sixteen. Even though he had never worn a suit in his life, his *ama* insisted that he be buried in one. Alaine gave away the rest of his things immediately after the funeral — it upset me when I found out, but as the years pass, I have begun to understand how she must have felt, finding out that her husband was in love with someone else at the same time she found out he had killed himself. It would have been too much for anyone to bear, and anything that belonged to him would only have served as a reminder. Ilari took the sweater, claiming that he would wear it; instead, he gave it to me. Just touching the thin fabric was like touching Gab again — for the first year after he died, I never took it off.

The talks, and the sweater, were part of the reason that my psychiatrist kept me out of university for a year — he thought I believed that Gab was still alive, and talking back to me. I never did. But it's hard to articulate, given that I don't believe firmly in any particular god, where I think he is. "He isn't really gone," is all I can ever bring myself to say out loud. I know now why my psychiatrist thought I was unstable.

Gab isn't really gone because he is part of me. He left me with a disfiguring scar just above my heart — it is deep reddish purple and mottled looking, but I still can't help being fond of it, in a strange and conflicting way, because Gab made it. And he believed that he was giving me a gift. Sometimes, I stand in front of my bedroom mirror with nothing but my jeans on, just looking at myself, the way I am now; running my fingers over the dark, craggy flesh where the bullet penetrated my chest and shoulder. When I put my fingers on my scar, time rushes backward — I can actually hear the wind in my ears — and I am transported to Basque Country; to those last days that we spent together. I never feel closer to Gab than in those moments.

It is fair to say that I am still a little unstable.

Lately, my talks with Gab have grown quieter. Some mornings, I have trouble picturing his face clearly. When I first noticed Lauran in my linguistics lecture, I felt guilty — because the instant I saw him, all of the feelings I've always had for him came back in a rush. I told Gab. In life he was madly jealous — I remember once I helped Jess Larrea carry a bag of concrete. I just happened to be passing on the road while he struggled with the heavy bag; he asked if I could give him a hand and I obliged, although my skinny arms likely didn't relieve much of the burden. That night when I met Gab in the *despachos*, he was waiting for me, arms crossed over his chest, mouth drawn in a tight line. "What were you doing with Jess?" he demanded.

"I was helping him carry a bag of concrete...?"

A series of twenty questions about my relationship with Jess followed; the answer to every single one being, "I was just helping him carry a bag of concrete." The more I repeated the truth, the more infuriated he became. "Look, Gab," I tried to start, but he cut me off.

"No, listen to me!" He slammed his fist on the old wooden desk with so much force that we both heard a crack — and then his face contorted with the pain of fracture.

"Oh Gab..." I shook my head and reached for his injured limb, holding his open palm in both of my hands. It was red and swelling; there was nothing to be done except for him to live with the pain. Our town had no doctor and there wasn't one nearby to send for. If he had been anyone else, I would have been angry with his stupidity, but because he was Gab, my heart broke for him. "What on earth were you thinking?"

He was so out of his depth, he could not have begun to explain himself. Loving me was the most difficult thing he had ever done. Without a word, he grabbed me and pulled me, hard, into his chest. "You're my princess," he whispered into my hair as he held onto me, repeating it over and over. "You're *my* princess."

But that was a long time ago. And in death he has proven to be patient and reasonable, which I suspect has mainly to do with the fact that his answers are really just part of my inner monologue and only occasionally sound like anything he might have said when he was in control of his own voice. He reminds me of what I sometimes allow myself to forget — that he isn't really here. I can go on loving him forever, but it will terribly lonely for me to go on being in love with him.

I open my window and look out over Paris. Luc and I live on Ile Saint-Louis, a tiny island in the Seine. It reminds us both of home, a quaint town where everyone knows everyone — it just happens to be in the middle of the capital. But instead of stepping out on the ledge to tell Gab about my day, I turn away from the moonlit city and lay down on my single bed, closing my eyes. I have Saint-Antoine on my mind, the little *commune* on the Spanish border where *maman* and *papa* raised me. It's a pretty enough place, as very small towns go, but it is a divided place, home to French and Euskadi people who never mix. The French, my family among them, are led by a slightly mad, genetic purity obsessed priest. Father Philippe is a short man who bears a striking resemblance to a toad wearing a hairpiece. If you ask him, Saint-Antoine has been a purely French town since 1974, two years after his arrival. The Euskadi have their own church, and their own priest, a fact that allows Father Philippe's selective blindness to persist. If he cannot see the Euskadi, they must not be there.

The French in Saint-Antoine outnumber the Euskadi by about three to one. Churches, shops and businesses are all separate. All but the school. There was a girl in my class growing up named Ana Mutuberria. She was the only Euskadi my age in town. No one ever spoke to her apart from our teachers. I thought about befriending her more than once — inconspicuously sitting next to her in class, then passing her a note in Euskara. But whenever the thought crossed my mind, the sound of Luc's inevitable taunting, "Look, Sophie found another little Spic to play with!" drowned it out instantly.

I lived in Saint-Antoine for eighteen years and I never spoke to her.

Whenever I think of home, I find myself thinking of Lauran. I never would have spoken to him, either. But I ran into him, quite literally, on my first day back at school after a summer in Basque Country. I was fifteen. My day had been miserable — the first day always was. I spoke the wrong language accidentally and forgot to answer to my French name. The joke never seemed to get old; my classmates had sniggered at my expense from eight a.m. until the final bell. I was in a rush to escape their whispers and jokes – such a rush that I didn't see Lauran coming down the hall until I smashed into his shoulder, dropping the geography textbook I had been clutching like a life preserver. It hit the ground with a perceptible thud. "*Barkatu*," I mumbled, embarrassed, as I bent to pick it up. I didn't recognise Lauran as Euskadi. The word just slipped out.

Lauran crouched down and grabbed the textbook before I could reach it. "What did you say?"

"*Barkatu*," I blushed as I repeated myself. I couldn't understand why this boy wanted to embarrass me even more. "*Barkatu*." As I reached to take my textbook from him, I realised my mistake. "I'm sorry, I -"

Lauran pulled the textbook further out of my grasp and stared at me so hard it made me squirm. He had the bluest eyes I'd ever seen. "Who *are* you?"

"Sophie Cassou."

"I'm Lauran." He stood up, and reached out his hand to help me. "I want to know you."

It's hard to pinpoint, but I think that was the moment when I fell in love with him.

I sigh, put my memories aside and sit up. I've always told myself that was the moment that Lauran fell in love with me, too. The fact that he agreed to go to the *Café des Éditeurs* this afternoon gave me hope that he might not have forgotten, but as every hours goes by, I'm less sure.

Paris is dark outside my window. I step out onto the moonlit ledge and look up at the stars.

## Chapter 3

When I walk into our linguistics lecture the following week, Lauran has already arrived. Instead of his usual place at the front of the room, where the professor can clearly hear his argumentative questions, he has taken a seat at the back of the hall, next to the door. It's warm in the room, but he has his coat on – planning a quick escape.

Two can play at that game.

I take the end seat in the front row, next to the other door. "What are you doing sitting here?" Madeleine hisses at me when she marches into the lecture hall on a pair of sky high vintage platforms, her long blonde waves trailing behind her. "You know I hate to sit so close to the professor!"

I nod toward the back of the room, pointing out Lauran's new seat as subtlety as possible.

"Again with this love nonsense?" Madeleine rolls her dark eyes heavenward. "Very well, I will sacrifice my comfort for your impossible love…" she sits down huffily in the chair next to me, "…but don't ever let me hear you say that I've never done anything for you."

"Melodramatic primadonna," I snap.

"Naïve romantic," Madeleine snarls back.

We are about to start slapping each other when the professor walks through the door and takes his place at the front of the room. Believe it or not, most of the lectures we attend together start this way.

The lecture hour passes predictably, with a number of arguments between Lauran and the professor (and a number of collective yawns from the rest of the class.) When we are dismissed, I dart out into the corridor in enough time to wait for Lauran. "Did you really think it would be that easy to avoid me?" I ask when he appears, my eyebrows raised incredulously.

Lauran's blue eyes narrow. "If I really wanted to avoid you, I wouldn't have come to the lecture."

"So you don't despise me enough to sacrifice your education. That's comforting." My biting words float over us like a lead balloon. I am acutely aware that I've gone too far. For a moment we're both silent. I look down at the tile floor, feeling distinctly like the shy, awkward teenager who bumped into a handsome older boy in the school hallway so many years ago. "I'm sorry," I mumble, barely able to make eye contact. "I shouldn't have said that."

Lauran accepts my apology, but his tone is icy when he says, "And I suppose even after that, you're still going to ask…"

I am so surprised, so thrilled that he hasn't simply walked away that words fly out of my mouth in a rush, interrupting him, "…Do you have time for a cup of…"

"I can only spare an hour."

"Well," I grit my teeth, reigning in my temper, "In that case, we have no time to waste. Shall we?"

§

Darkness has descended on the streets of Paris, and the air is bitingly cold. Lauran and I take refuge inside the *Café des Éditeurs*, exhaling puffs of white breath as we step indoors. We choose a small round table in the middle of the room — my chair faces the front window, its white lettering illuminated by street lamps.

"*Deux cafés noisette*," Lauran orders for us, while I sit down to light a cigarette. He takes his seat after me, his penetrating gaze focussed on my hands as I strike the match.

I take my first drag and say, "Yes?" as I exhale, blowing smoke out the side of my mouth.

Lauran cocks his head to the side slightly, and his short blonde hair casts a shadow across his forehead. I remember reaching out to put my hand on his cheek countless times when he made this inquisitive face — it takes all of my strength to hold back now. "I'm loathe to ask, but... I thought you were left-handed."

He noticed. I lick my lips nervously, privately thrilled but painfully desperate to play this cool. The prescription pill bottles that line the bottom of my purse, the handgun in the shoebox at the top of my bedroom closet... my stories are not the kind that friends can have a laugh at over coffee. "I used to be."

Lauran has no idea how to respond to that statement. I've tried it three times before — no one ever has. He just stares at me, waiting for an explanation. "It's all part of the story, I promise. If we can stop talking about my hands, I'll get on with it. Where did I leave off...?"

"I didn't exactly commit it to memory."

"Excuse me?"

"This is your story. The least you could do is keep track of what you've told. I don't have all night, you know."

This time, my attempts to control my temper prove futile. "Absence obviously makes the heart grow fonder. Thank-you for reminding me what a jerk you can be. I think I was going to say was that every summer was worse..."

§

The town where my family lived had no formal name; it was more like a lost suburb of Bilbao, high on the side of the Sakana Mountains. It sprang up in the late 1930s around a roller skate factory which, after the German attack on Guernica, began mass producing arms for the French resistance.

I have often thought that I would like to find a pair of *Bandido* roller-skates in a second hand store, because it seems to me they must be very rare – the factory was almost never used for its intended purpose, and, in addition to manufacturing illegal weapons, served as a meeting place for political subversives. After the war, a group of communists who would later become some of the founding members of The Organisation infiltrated the assembly line. One of them, Zorion Sagastizabal Sr., or *Suge* – the snake, as he was called – stayed in town with his family to oversee the operations of a small terrorist cell while the others moved on to find new recruits.

By the time I was a little girl, *Suge* was long dead, along with his brilliant youngest son, Toribio, and his stable elder son, Zanpier. The town with no name was a destitute enclave of career terrorists and their illiterate families, led by the last Sagastizabal standing; my *aita*.

In the summer, the town could grow a vegetable garden and trap small animals in the woods nearby, so we had enough to eat. I spent hours in the vegetable patch, weeding and watering. The boys in town played with real guns to pass the time, the same way normal boys play war with plastic rifles, practising for the days when they would become freedom fighters like their *aita*s and *anaia*s. Occasionally, a little boy would discharge his weapon accidentally, and we would have a funeral. The girls used the main floor of the abandoned factory as their clubhouse. While they didn't actually hang a sign that said *No Amaias Allowed*, the implication was clear. There were no toys to play with. The only books I ever found were used to hold up the end of my parents' kitchen table. So I played at gardening.

I met Iasmina in the garden. Everyone in town had a job to do to keep things running, in the communist tradition. Iasmina was in charge of the tomato plants. We sat side-by-side in the dirt, day after hot summer day. After two seasons of silence, she turned to me and said, "You're not so bad, you know. All the other girls call you *printzesa*."

"They call me *printzesa*?" I dropped the weed in my hand, horrified as only a little girl can be that other children could be so mean.

Iasmina nodded, yes. "But I've never heard of any princess who pulled weeds. I think you're all right."

What I had with Mina wasn't much of a friendship, in retrospect, but I was grateful just to have someone answer when I spoke to them.

Apart from you, I never told a soul in France what I saw during my summers in Euskal Herria. I kept the guns and the bombs and the late night meetings in the roller-skate factory as my own terrible secret. For many years I didn't know — didn't realise — that when *aita* referred to himself as a freedom fighter, it was just a euphemism for terrorist. Life as I knew it in Basque Country seemed so strange and terrifying when I stepped outside of it, I was sure that no one would believe me if I did tell. And I was never completely sure that I wanted to. After all, these people *were* my family. *Maman* and *papa* had taught me that being family meant being loyal and protective — although I doubt, when they were imparting that lesson, that they intended for me to be loyal to anyone but them.

I can't betray them — they're my family. That's what I used to say to myself. I could use those few words to justify keeping any secret. But the truth is, I protected them to protect myself. When I was eleven, The Organisation carried out the assassination of the young Spanish politician, Miguel Angel Blanco. I was in Euskal Herria when it happened. In the week that I arrived that summer, the town was buzzing. I heard the name Angel over and over. Eight men, including *aita* and Ilari, left town for two days in mid-July. They came back with blood on their clothes, fierce and jubilant.

Four years later, two low-ranking members of The Organisation were captured on a routine cross-border excursion in France and arrested for Blanco's murder. But Father Philippe was on the case long before that. In September 1997, he gave a fiery sermon about what he called the Basque devils, citing Miguel Angel Blanco's murder as further proof that French communities needed to be cleansed of dangerous ethnic elements. When I heard his thundering voice crush out the words,

"Miguel Angel Blanco," all of the pieces of the puzzle connected in my mind, as if the name had magnetised them. I sat rigid in my pew and prayed to God that no one in that church would ever find out the truth about my birth family. I felt no shame for being Euskadi, but I was deeply, grievously ashamed to be the daughter of a murderer – and terrified that I might someday turn out to be like him. I wanted, more than anything, to be normal somewhere, for some amount of time, no matter how short. And the ship of normalcy had sailed from Euskal Herria long before I was born – my only chance was in Saint-Antoine.

§

Lauran covers his mouth with his hand, I expect more out of habit than politeness, but I can see that he is laughing at me. Irritated, I snap my fingers at our waiter, rudely demanding more coffee. Lauran always knew exactly what to do to set me off. I had forgotten that. "What's so funny?" I demand.

"I forgot, that's all," my ex-boyfriend chuckles, still hiding his smile behind his hand.

"Forgot what?" I shove my hand into my purse in search of my cigarettes. If I'm going to get through this afternoon without slapping Lauran, I need something to hold onto.

"The way you talk –" Lauran takes his hand away from his face – his lips are twisted into a mocking grin. " - like your life is a great novel that you're reading out loud in front of an adoring audience."

So it was the ship of normalcy remark that made him laugh. I can admit to myself that I had a feeling I was taking that metaphor a bit further than it was actually able to go. But I would die before I let Lauran know it. "I seem to recall there was a time when you found my particular style of storytelling charming."

Our waiter returns with fresh coffee, and his arm obscures Lauran's face as he says, "That was a long time ago."

When the waiter steps away, Lauran has his hands around his white cup, focussed on his drink. But for one fleeting second, I think I can see an old, familiar tenderness in his eyes. "I'll try to keep my metaphors to a minimum," I offer.

And just like that, whatever warmth I thought I saw is gone. "I think that would be for the best. It will save us time."

"Right, of course. Let me tell you about Luc and Ilari..."

§

I have two brothers; one was a bully, the other a terrorist. If I had a *centime* for every time I wished to be an only child, I would be a rich woman.

But I stopped making those wishes when I was thirteen.

After Father Philippe's Basque devil sermon, I spent a miserable winter suffering with stomach cramps and insomnia, worried that my criminal lineage would somehow, no matter how improbably, be discovered.

When I arrived in Euskal Herria the following summer, my *anaia* was waiting for me. And he had a bible with him. I was immediately suspicious. "What do you want?"

"I want to learn to read."

I did feel profoundly sorry that my *anaia* had been completely deprived of the joy of literature. I've always loved to read, as you know; the idea of life without books is unfathomable to me. But my reaction gave none of that away. Remember that I scarcely knew my *anaia*, and what I did know about him only made me trust him less. "Will you be shouting it from the rooftops next?"

Ilari raised an eyebrow so that it snuck up beneath his thick dark hair. "No...?"

"Then why are you telling me?" I snapped.

"Oh." My anaia blushed and looked down at the bible in his hands. "Well... it's just... You're the only one who can teach me."

I resisted. I flatly refused. But my pesky *anaia* followed me around with his bible like a dog with a stick, desperate to play fetch. "How do you pronounce this?" he would demand, pointing to long, antiquated words. And he would wake me up in the morning to ask, "What does *crucify* mean?" as if he really couldn't wait a second longer to know the definition.

One morning, he got to me early enough that I relented — on the condition that all classes would be held in the afternoon. My *anaia*, the tough guy who had been handling a gun since he was six, practically jumped for joy.

I was, by all reports, an abysmal teacher. I shouted daily, threw the bible across the room on more than one occasion, and often stormed off in frustration mid-lesson. But in spite of all my disruptions. Ilari and I became friends. He told me about his life. He had been arrested - more than once. He had been deported to France. He had been shot at, and he had fired shots on innocent strangers. The stories he told of life Euskal Herria illuminated a world, and an existence, that might have been mine, in different circumstances. I fell asleep every night that summer thinking that by only one minute twist of fate, I might have grown up to be an illiterate mountain girl who earnestly believed that her people were at war.

For the first time, I realised that I was blessed.

Ilari had doubts. He had spent time away from the mountains. In jail and in France. The world of the so-called *txakurra* had shocked him at first. "I thought everyone bathed outside under a hose," he admitted sheepishly.

But all of the small wonders that he had been deprived of quickly charmed him. He was fascinated by penguins. His feelings for the cinema could only be called rapturous. Anytime the subject of fresh apples came up — and it came up inordinately often, mainly because my anaia brought it up — he did three paragraphs on the crispness of their outer flesh versus the soft, juicy texture of the white fruit inside. It was bittersweet to listen to him talk about the world outside of town, which he knew was just a few miles away but was powerless to escape to. His simple joy was contagious — and sad. After all, he was fourteen, not five.

"Do you know what The Organisation is fighting for, Amaia?" my *anaia* asked me once. It still breaks my heart to remember. "It can't be because we don't want to live like the *txakurra*. I can't believe that."

We spent very little of our time on reflection, really, but the reflection is what I remember. Ilari's best friend was Gabrié Duarte. And as chance would have it, or perhaps just probability, since our town was so small, he was Iasmina's older brother. We became a ragtag band, wandering around town in the heat, looking for ways to occupy our aimless hours. Sometimes, Iasmina's boyfriend, Jess Larrea, joined us. We wasted most of our time sitting on the old overstuffed sofas in the *despachos*, the abandoned executive offices on the sixth floor of the factory, discussing nothing in particular.

The conversations we had were not memorable. Ilari was quiet and brooding in a group; he rarely contributed much. Iasmina was flighty and odd. She had a habit of interjecting non-sequiturs like, "The sky looks pretty today," in the middle of a discussion about political theory.

I know, I know, but I'm not making it up. When you take away TV, movies, sports and books, teenagers have very little to say for themselves. Gabrié was illiterate, but he had been raised by freedom fighters. He knew Marx and Nietzsche the way I knew *Astérix* and *Obélix*...

§

"You can't be serious," Lauran interrupts, unconvinced. "How old were you then, thirteen?"

"Yes. And Gab was sixteen. What do you know about it, anyway?" I snap. "Have you ever met a terrorist?"

Lauran's Adam's apple bobs as he swallows. "I suppose I haven't. But I've met a lot of sixteen-year-olds. I used to be one. And I know that even among the literate ones, there are very few real experts on Marxism."

"When I told you this story was going to be unbelievable, which part confused you — the *un* or the *believable?*"

"As much fun as I've had bickering with you, Sophie," Lauran rolls his eyes and looks down at his watch, "the hour is up."

I know how to roll my eyes, too. "And how generous of you to have spent all sixty minutes with me."

Lauran looks back toward the front window of the café, where a tall girl in a black coat strands, tapping her heel impatiently on the sidewalk, and determines that he has time to get in one more shot at me. "You may not be left-handed anymore, but I see your temper is still in working order." He stands up and begins to put his coat on. "I have to go. My girlfriend is waiting outside."

The impatient girl. It can't exactly be said that Lauran and I have fallen back into our old, comfortable friendship but still, those words sting. Could it honestly be that he has so little interest in seeing me that he made contingency plans for an easy escape? Am I just delusional, thinking he might actually forgive me, if I say the words right? I hide my injured feelings behind another insult. "You're so desperate to escape me that you had your girlfriend come to the rescue?"

"No," Lauran's words lose a bit of the special acid he has reserved for me over the past two weeks. "She offered, actually."

I raise an eyebrow. "She wanted to know what she was up against, didn't she?" I've had Lauran's phantom girlfriend in my mind all week, and every day she has become smarter and more beautiful. It's a relief to know she's human — and as insecure about me as I am about her.

"She's a good person. She doesn't deserve to be kept waiting while we sort out some imaginary unresolved issues from ten years ago."

"Don't worry," I reassure him cruelly, "you can just tell her I'm disfigured and she'll feel better."

"You are not disfigure-" Lauran begins to protest. I cut him off, yanking down the collar of my sweater to offer him proof. He winces, as if when he sees the scar, he can actually feel the bullet penetrating my flesh. "I cannot believe you're making me say this," he snaps, "but you are as beautiful as you ever were, Sophie." Then he turns on his heel and leaves the café.

Stunned, I watch him walk away. Outside, he wraps his arm protectively around the impatient girl. They turn right, and take *rue de Condé* toward the *Théâtre de l'Odéon*, two lovers arm-in-arm.

Maybe it's seeing them together. Maybe it's the fact that after unleashing all of his venom on me, he called me beautiful. Or maybe it's just the memory of Gab, who didn't know what teddy bears were and couldn't fathom their existence, lecturing on Marx like an academic without ever having read a word the philosopher wrote down. A lump forms in my throat. Tears pool in my eyes. I toss a few coins on the table and rush outside into the night.

## Chapter 4

I can smell duck breast roasting when I step into our apartment. The sound of a pot hissing and bubbling on the stove nearly drowns Luc out when he calls, "*Bon soir*, Sophie!"

I sniffle, and wipe one last tear from my cheek with my fingers as I close the front door behind me. I try never to let my brother see me cry. I know he means well, but he's so uncomfortable with tears that he goes to absurd, painful lengths to cheer me up. He once came home with a puppy! We returned the poor little thing the same evening, after reading the capitalised, bold script into our tenancy agreement, strictly prohibiting pets of any kind. "*Bon soir*, Luc."

But I'm too late. My brother is standing in the kitchen doorway with a dripping serving spoon in hand, a look of concern on his thin face. "What happened today?"

I can see his pot begin to boil over behind him, scalding broth and rice spewing onto the floor. "Luc!" I cry, "The soup!"

"You're changing the subject," he chides, oblivious.

In the kitchen, the soup pot hisses and clangs. "No, I'm trying to save our dinner!"

Luc suddenly turns pale and hurries back into the kitchen, but it's too late; mounds of starchy, overcooked rice wait for him on the stove. He turns the heat off in a rush, takes the lid off the soup pot gingerly and peers inside. I slip my shoes off and follow him; looking over the edge of the pot, all I can see is an inch of tepid broth with a few dejected grains of rice floating in it.

"Why don't I put some pasta on while you clean that up?" I offer. Luc just nods and starts scrubbing the stove top.

We work in silence for a while, side by side. When the remnants of the ruined soup have been washed away, my brother takes the roast duck out of the oven and starts to dish out our dinner. I pour two glasses of wine. I can't help but feel a bit relieved that the soup boiled over and disrupted the evening inquisition.

I know my brother has the best intentions. I honestly do. But the school yard bully in him can't understand that sadness is an internal force, constantly balanced precariously opposite happiness. Sometimes, one overtakes the other, and I laugh. Or cry. Whenever I'm upset, he's convinced that someone has done something to me. And usually, he wants to do something worse to them in return. He's all talk, mind you — but even his talk brings back memories of the person I wish he had never been.

My relief is short-lived. "So," Luc starts as he puts dinner on the table, "what happened this afternoon?"

This obviously isn't going to be a dinner with a side of reality TV night. I pull out my chair at the foot of our small wooden table and seat myself. I sip my wine. I slice myself a bit of meat and chew it carefully. All the while, my brother stares me down from his chair opposite mine. He taps his foot on the floor in a steadily increasing rhythm, rapidly losing patience.

When I'm good and ready, I tell him, "Nothing."

"You saw your ex-boyfriend again, didn't you?" he presses.

I raise an eyebrow, but go on cutting my food, trying to maintain my composure. "You've been talking to Madeleine, haven't you?"

"At least she tells me things."

I try not to overreact. "Did it ever occur to you to ask me?" I shout at my brother. And I fail not to overreact.

Always the calm to my storm, Luc chews quietly, thoughtful, until I've finished raging. "I suppose I could have asked you…" For someone so smart, at times my brother thinks and speaks so slowly that it's unbearable. I have to hold myself back from screaming at him — again — to get on with it. "…but then again, it wouldn't have bothered me if you hadn't come home in tears. Are you ready to tell me what happened yet?"

Talking about how I feel has never come naturally to me. I think I got so used to keeping secrets when I was little, hiding my material wealth from my family in Euskal Herria and my terrorist lineage from my adoptive French parents, that it became normal. The more years passed, the more I held back. I've gotten better at sharing, in the years since Gab died. But I tend to save it for my psychiatrist. When I'm not at *Docteur* André's office, I like to pretend my life is normal. The more I pretend, the more I convince myself that it really is.

But I can't just dodge the question, it isn't fair to Luc. "Nothing happened." My brother raises an eyebrow, skeptical. "Honestly. I was thinking about when I got hurt. Sometimes it makes me sad, that's all."

Luc may have stayed when *maman* left, but that doesn't mean that he is fond of my Euskadi family and friends. The reason he asks so few questions when I go to Bordeaux is that he would prefer to think that the Sagastizabals, with their left-wing political views and strange, isolate language, don't exist. I think it's hard to be Luc, sometimes. He swallows uncomfortably, runs his fingers through his hair and pushes his macaroni in a circle around his plate.

"Do we have any chocolate?" I ask — partly to fill the silence and partly in an attempt to give my brother an easy out. Chocolate was my drug of choice long before I discovered *Gauloises,* and a chocolate-dipped praline has never failed to boost my spirits, even if only temporarily.

"I don't think so."

So much for that stroke of brilliance. "Well then," I suggest, "why don't we talk about something else?"

My brother nods, recovering almost instantly. "What happened to you at school today?"

I take a bite of my dinner and swallow, the normal rhythm of our evening meal restored. "Nothing out of the ordinary. Did anything interesting happen at the bank?"

"People asked for money. Some of them we gave it to, others we didn't... the usual. I got the strangest phone call when I came home, though. A guy called asking for the lady of the forest...? His voice sounded familiar, but he wouldn't leave him name. And the lady of the forest? What does that even mean?"

Ilari.

Oihane, my middle name, the one my biological parents gave me, means forest. We speak in code when we use conventional phone lines. Just in case.

I laugh, because laughter, even when it is forced, is the easiest way I've found to cover up a lie. Luc can never know about speaking in code. Or that it is dangerous for me to use conventional phone lines for certain calls. "That was my *anaia*! The lady of the forest is sort of... an inside joke."

"I don't get it," is Luc's lame reply.

"You aren't supposed to, stupid. That's why it's called an inside joke. I'll call him back later on my *portable*."

I have a particular *portable* that I use to speak to my *anaia*. I not-exactly-accidentally break that *portable* and have to get a new number almost weekly. The salespeople at Bouygues Telecom have come to know me as preternaturally clumsy.

"Make sure you do your school work-" Luc starts. I just roll my eyes and stand up, leaving him alone at the table with his dinner and his delusions of paternity.

§

I sit cross-legged on my bed and dial the most recent Bordeaux phone number I have for my *anaia*. Ilari breaks a lot of *portables*, too. There is never a guarantee that I'll be able to reach him, but we never fail to connect. I talk to him every week, at times even every day.

My *portable* rings. No out of service warning comes on. After six rings, a generic voicemail notice asks me to leave a message. "Lady of the Forest," I speak carefully into the receiver, then hang-up.

The whole procedure still feels awkward and choreographed after years of repetition, but I know the perils of leaving a breadcrumb trail; little birds are liable to follow you, snacking as they go, until they finally catch up and bite you.

Ten minutes later, my *portable* rings back on schedule. "Hello, Ilari."

"How are you, Mai?" Ilari's voice is low and gentle. He lisps slightly from the piercings in his lip and tongue. I can hear the sound of his footsteps faintly — he paces when he talk on the phone. I don't think I've ever seen him sit still for more than a minute, and when he does sit down, he can't stay still; he finds a pen and taps it on an available surface, until the tapping begins to look more like stabbing and turns into the obsessive drawing of dots... Anything to avoid stasis. "Are you all right?"

My *anaia* rarely asks that question. He never thought I was crazy, even when all of the evidence pointed to the contrary. Reckless, certainly. Suicidal, maybe. But not crazy. Even though he did ask a nurse to sedate me once or twice, but that was because I wanted to see the commandant, and totally unrelated to any psychiatric diagnosis. Gab was his best friend. I think he still talks to him sometimes, too. "Why do you ask?"

"In Paris, I mean. And with Luc. He's so... French."

I laugh out loud. "Of course he's French — he was born and raised in France, stupid. You know, in the same house, with the same parents as me? I'm pretty sure that my official passport says I'm French, too. And to me, Luc is just my brother."

Ilari has no choice but to concede that I have a point. "I still think you'd be better off with us, though. Why don't you come to Bordeaux?"

We have this discussion over and over. "I'm in school. At La Sorbonne. Which is in Paris. I have to stay here."

My *anaia* sighs. I can picture the anxious steps he takes back and forth across the parquet. When I was in Bordeaux, we saw each other every day. We met for coffee and stayed up late watching all of the old movies he had never seen. After so many years of alternating prolonged separation and uncomfortable togetherness, we were like normal siblings. It was heartrending to let that go when I came to Paris. I love it here, but I miss Ilari. I know that he misses me – he wouldn't keep asking me to move back to Bordeaux if he didn't. But he's hopeless at verbalising his emotions. Instead, he paces in his kitchen – his footsteps play a steady melody on the tile – waiting for the right words to come.

They never do. I sit silent on my end of the line, fighting a lump that is forming in my throat. Every day since Gab died I have woken up hoping that this will be the day that my tears will dry up for good.

"It's just... you would be able to immerse yourself in your work so much more if you were here, surrounded by people who really understand you..."

"I'll be there in the first week of November," I remind my *anaia* – and myself. "What would we be doing if I were in Bordeaux?" This is my way of asking Ilari about himself; to get him to stop thinking of me. To get me to stop thinking of me, too.

"I'm working on a new construction site, wiring apartments." Ilari is an apprentice electrician. He learned most of what he knows in the basement of the roller-skate factory, but in spite of his... informal... training, he has excelled in construction since he moved to France. Until a few years ago, I don't think he ever thought he would have a traditional job – I don't think anyone did – and he always talks about his work in a tone of mild surprise, like he can't quite believe he's talking about himself. "You probably wouldn't be much use there, with your hand. You could go to the school with Gen; she keeps saying she needs someone tough to help her keep her unruly *seconde* class in line."

I laugh. "Teenagers? I'll pass. We deal with enough of them in our work to satisfy me for a lifetime."

"Of course there's always work to do with Thierry. But I think he wants you to stay in Paris until you have a full *doctorat*."

Every time I hear about one of Thierry's grand plans, I can't help but smile. He's such an unassuming man, small and thin with wire framed glasses. No one would ever suspect a thing of him. "It sounds like I'll be here for a few years, then...!"

"I'd like to come and visit, maybe, one day. What would we do if I was in Paris?" Ilari turns my question around on me.

"Well, I study most of the time," I admit. "Sometimes after class I go to the *Café des Éditeurs* with Madeleine. Or..." The image of Lauran and his girlfriend leaving the café, his arm around her shoulders, suddenly flashes before my eyes. He told me that I am as beautiful as I ever was – and then he walked away with *her*.

"Or...?" Ilari waits for me to finish my sentence.

"Or sometimes I see Lauran Etcheverria." There is a tremor in my voice now. "My ex-boyfriend."

"The one you...?"

"Yes, him."

"I feel like this is something you should talk to Gen about." My *anaia* is no more comfortable with other people's feelings than he is with his own. "Gen! Gen, Amaia is ready to talk to you!" he shouts, practically throwing the phone away to avoid hearing me break down. "Talk to you soon, Mai."

"Hi!"

Gen is my *anaia*'s girlfriend. They met in Bordeaux when they were young teenagers, during Ilari's brief deportation, by such a coincidental chance that anyone unfamiliar with the law of large numbers might call it fate. She was a privileged young socialite, already carrying a Chanel purse, but also the daughter of an Euskadi mother. My *anaia* was so in awe of everything in France, he might never have noticed her but for the fact that she was assigned to help him at school — much to her initial dismay — because she spoke Euskara.

Ilari was only in Bordeaux for two weeks before Balere and Remiri tracked him down. That was enough time for him to fall for Gen. She, on the other hand, will only admit that, although she was not indifferent, she forgot him as soon as he left. Just like Madeleine, she pretends not to believe in great loves, and laughs at any suggestion of it with a careless giggle that goes something like, "I was only thirteen!" But when her parents divorced three years later, her *maman* packed their bags for Basque Country. And Gen found herself the newest resident of the town with no name. The realities of life in the mountains shocked her — and when she speaks Euskara, she still has a slight tone of breathless surprise in her voice.

"How are you, *chérie*?"

The biggest surprise of all, of course, was that she found Ilari in the mountains. And she will admit that as soon as they met for the second time, she forgot all about missing the comforts of France.

"I'm f-" I start to lie, but then the truth spills out in a rush. I first met Gen when I was fourteen, and we were instant friends. The fact that I tweezed my eyebrows sealed the deal, which sounds silly, but shaped eyebrows are extremely conspicuous in a community where indoor plumbing is a luxury. Apart from Lauran, she is the only person I've ever been completely open with — and has the unique privilege of being the only person from whom I can't hold anything back.

I tell her how I noticed Lauran immediately when our lecture began in the fall... About all of my planning and preparation to talk to him... about how he has been so cold to me... about how he told me I was beautiful... and then about how he left with his girlfriend.

By the end of it, my voice shakes and my hands tremble. "I don't know what to do," I admit, a bit desperately. "He clearly doesn't want anything to do with me. Maybe I should just give up."

"Give up?" Gen is aghast. "But, you can't! If you give up you'll never know what might have been. What if I had given up on your *anaia*?"

"But you did."

Four years ago, Gen left Ilari. She was pregnant at the time. She thought she was only going for a few days, to teach him a lesson; the pregnancy was an accident and my terrified *anaia* had been less than supportive. But then Gen miscarried. The heartbreak drove them further apart, and they stayed separate for nearly a year, even took other lovers. It was only when I was in the hospital, when the only thing they still shared hung in a precarious balance, that they found there were more arguments for being together than being apart.

"No, *chérie*, I never gave up on Ilari. For a while I gave up on me, which was much worse. Promise me, *ma poulette* – promise me," Gen emphasises the words, "that you will never do that."

I make the promise, but it's an empty one.

§

The night air is cold and damp. I wrap a quilt around my shoulders before I step out onto the window ledge. Just like every night, I sit cross-legged and stare up at the sky. "What do you think, Gab?" I ask aloud. Tonight I can see him as clearly as if he were really here, sitting on the railing and looking down at me; his dark eyes, and lashes that skimmed his cheeks when he blinked, black hair long in his face, with a shock of red dyed into it... Cheekbones. Lips, always cracked and bitten, with a silver ring threaded through the lower one. I shiver, "What would you do, in his place?"

Gab shrugs, half-smiling. "I would have coffee with you every day if you'd let me."

I'm surprised by that answer – but I also suspect he thinks he's being funny. "Be serious, please. Even after what I did to him?"

"You did worse to me."

"I never-" I start to protest.

But Gab cuts me off. "You once punched me in the face in front of about ten people. Almost broke my nose."

I remember the moment distinctly. We were arguing. We were always arguing. He had the audacity to call Stalin a visionary, and Gorbachev a quitter. I couldn't let a lie like that go unanswered, but I was too furious to think of a clever response. So I hit him. I stand by my decision. "You deserved it."

"I know," Gab laughs. "But no one else dared give it to me. It was when I touched my face and saw the blood on my hand that I knew I was in love with you. I would have canonised Stalin just to get you to look at me."

For a second I miss Gab so much that I feel like my chest will break open. I know he isn't here. I know that *Docteur* André is right when he says that I let Gab hold me back from living in the real world because I'm afraid to let myself be hurt again. And still I hear myself making an excuse to explain why I should give up on making amends with Lauran. "But he has a girlfriend. It isn't fair-"

"I was married," Gab counters. "You never let that stop you. You were going to run away with me."

"And then you..."

"I know. I'm sorry about that. I loved you so much. I thought that was the only way."

"I loved you, too." It's been years, but those weeks are still fresh in my mind. Ilari came to me in Saint-Antoine, begging for my help. Gab had been jailed and tortured by the *Ertzaintza*. Apart from some small cigarette burns, he was outwardly unscathed. But the person he had once been, the arrogant smartass with an answer for everything, the vulnerable boy who felt more for me than he could properly express, was already dead. "I should have told you that when you were still alive. I should have told everyone."

"I never doubted you."

A sob tears at my throat. I don't know if I'm willing to let this go. Not yet. I want one more chance. One more day. I want to be talking to someone more than just myself.

But it's too late for that. "You were never the one, though. I always loved you, but I had someone else in my heart all along."

Gab stares out into the night. Even now he can't look at me when he admits, "I know. I think that's why I aimed to the left."

Suddenly, I hear my bedroom door creak open. Luc pokes his head inside and calls, "Sophie? Who are you talking to?"

"Just someone I used to know"

"And is that person... um... talking back?"

On the iron railing, Gab is slowly fading away. "Good-bye, my princess."

"Good-bye, my angel," I whisper into the dark. And then I call, firmly, "*Bon soir,* Luc."

## Chapter 5

The following week, I sit through our linguistic theory lecture, dutifully taking notes as the professor drones on about possible explanations for the unusual geographic distribution of Finno-Ugric language speakers. When Lauran interrupts, I concentrate on drawing small circles in the margins of my notebook. I have no intention of chasing after him when the class ends. After all of my weeks of planning, it occurred to me this morning that I don't need anyone's forgiveness that badly. I am practising what *Docteur* André so often preaches — accepting that the past has passed. I can accept that what we once had cannot be recaptured. But I can't turn my feelings off like a faucet, and this has always been about more than forgiveness, so it still isn't easy to be in the same room with him, acutely aware that we are so close, but so very far apart.

Madeleine pokes me in the arm with her pen during one of the professor's tangents about Hungary — he studied in Budapest, apparently, and can't lecture about Finno-Ugric without mentioning *langos*, which I am given to understand is some kind of bread. "Ow!" I protest in a hushed whisper. "Was that really necessary?"

"You seem unusually studious today. Naturally, I'm suspicious."

"We have to write our mid-term dissertations soon."

"I know you, Sophie – you could do that the night before the due date. In your sleep. But because I know you well, I know that you've already finished." I flush red – she caught me. "So why all this fuss about taking notes when you could be swooning over that irritating boy in the front row?"

I shrug, "I'm over it."

"What, one bad coffee date and suddenly he's no longer the love of your life?"

"It looks that way."

Madeleine rolls her eyes heavenward. "You are the worst liar."

§

I wasn't lying to Madeleine, when I said I was over it. Two weeks of snide remarks from my ex-boyfriend was more than enough for me. When the lecture ends, I gather my things and make my way to the door without looking up to see where Lauran has gone. I am understandably surprised when I find myself standing next to him at the back door of the lecture hall. "Sophie," he starts, and for a second, my heart forgets to beat. It just lays in my chest, motionless.

And then it starts again with a bang. "Fancy meeting you here."

"Look, I've been thinking..."

"Oh?" I file out the door ahead of Lauran, taking advantage of the fact that he can't see my face as I roll my eyes. "Do tell."

"I first read Marx when I was fourteen. I'm still not an expert, but that doesn't mean that someone else couldn't have been." I hear Lauran's footfalls stop in the middle of the hall, as if walking and making this speech at the same time are too much for him. He sighs. "Will you at least look at me?"

I stop walking and turn on my heel to face my ex-boyfriend. "This had better be good."

"Goddamn it," Lauran's face reddens, "I'm trying! Jesus. I don't know what it is about you..."

"You obviously aren't interested in talking to me. I understand why – you don't need to strain yourself trying to explain it. I hurt you. Now that you've hurt me, too, we can both move on with our lives. Deal?"

"No deal."

My eyes widen with surprise until the skin around them feels tight enough to tear. "Excuse me?"

"This is not a quid pro quo. You have a scar on your shoulder the size of Jupiter and for some reason you have yet to explain, you are no longer left-handed. You promised me a story, Sophie Cassou," Lauran stares me down, "and I want to hear it."

"Well…" I am at a loss for words. My hands tremble. One syllable is the best I can manage without a cigarette. "Well."

Lauran rubs the back of his neck, embarrassed by his outburst. "And we should really try to stop arguing."

I exhale hard out of my mouth, trying to calm my nerves. I hear the tremor in my voice when I say, "I can agree to that," but my ex-boyfriend doesn't seem to notice. "Let's go and get a cup of coffee."

§

The *Café des Éditeurs* is quiet tonight; most of the round tables are empty, but Lauran and I still gravitate to the same one we sat a last week, choosing the same chairs. I face the window; he faces me. Our waiter brings coffee almost without prompting and places the small white cups gently in front of us. "I'm still skeptical about this alleged sixteen-year-old Marxism expert," Lauran admits as I light my cigarette. "I'm willing to accept the possibility that he did exist, but I'm going to need more context."

I wonder if the fact that the sixteen-year-old Marx expert gave me the scar on my shoulder would be sufficient context to satisfy my ex-boyfriend. But I keep this sarcastic retort to myself and offer, "Cigarette?" extending my box of *Gauloises* to Lauran.

For the first time he takes one, and lights it with his own match. "Go ahead, dazzle me with tales of the boy genius."

I can't believe it. I can't believe him. Anger wells in the pit of my stomach. "Is this funny to you? Which part of my life sounds like a joke?"

"The part-" Lauran stops himself. He sighs and rubs the back of his neck. "We're doing it again."

"I'm just going to start. Suffice it to say that once upon a time, I wasn't as good at arguing as I obviously am now..."

§

Gabrié could argue circles around me. He knew volumes about concepts I could scarcely pronounce. Apart from feeling shame at the means my biological family used — the threats and the guns and the indoctrination — to meet their political ends, I had never come to any conclusions about how I felt about my Euskadi heritage. After all, I had no reason to; I lived most of my life freely and well as a French girl. I went to school. There was always food on the table. The closest I came to being oppressed was suffering through my brother's teasing and taunting at holidays.

But I had the luxury of an outside perspective. My *anaia* had briefly had the same. He rarely spoke up in the *despachos*, but during our reading lessons he confided his doubts — about communism, about The Organisation's methods and most of all, about our *aita*'s leadership. On the mountain, there were no Spanish government officials to forbid us from speaking our own language or observing our customs. I watched carefully, and the more I took in, the more I began to feel that the oppression that Gab and the freedom fighters felt didn't come from Spain. It came from The Organisation, and, more directly, from their local representative — our *aita*, the same man who stormed the *Hospital Civil de Basurto* with a Kalashnikov to demand my release... from an incubator.

And so I argued back. I became a mouthpiece for Ilari, who was being groomed as the next leader of our local Organisation and couldn't speak freely; expressing his opinions as if they were my own. It wasn't long before I stopped being able to distinguish between my own thoughts and the secrets my *anaia* had confided to me.

When I went home to Saint-Antoine at the end of the summer, I couldn't leave it behind. I took out so many books from the library about communism and terrorism that the local librarian, *Madame* Moustirats, denounced me to Father Philippe. I found a way to turn every one of my school projects into personal research; I wrote essays on political ethics in guerilla warfare and studied the dynamics of an entrance wound for my science project. (That stunt got me reported to Father Philippe yet again. I left a lot of atonement rosaries unsaid that year.) While all of my classmates were in love with Damien Sargue, pasting posters of him in their lockers, I developed a mad crush on Mikhail Gorbachev. My behaviour was obsessive, but the more that I read and learned, the more I felt like someone who had lived her life in darkness, only to discover that light had existed all along. There were so many obscure facts to be read, just hiding in dusty old books – I wanted to uncover them all.

The next summer, I travelled to Basque Country armed with everything I had learned. I knew that there was a fight waiting for me, and I had my proverbial gloves on.

For two months, Gabrié and I argued from dawn until late into the night. At times we were alone in the *despachos*; other times we argued in public. When I suggested that Castro was the exception that proved the rule that communism cannot work, Gabrié was so furious that he put his fist through the paper thin wall of his parents' living room. Once, when he dared to call Stalin a visionary and Gorbachev a quitter, I punched him – I nearly broke his nose.

That our arguments were conspicuous would surprise no one. There were about ten people present when I hit Gabrié for a start. We called each other, loudly and publicly, by cruel, profane nicknames; *sasikume* and *potxa*. But my *ama*, still more quiet and listless with every passing year, never said a word, and I rarely saw my *aita*. I expected, at worst, a slap on the wrist for my dissent.

I knew something was wrong when I was packing my bags to return to France. *Ama* sat in my bedroom and watched me, her tiny frame perched stiffly on the edge of my flat bed, silent, as I folded my shirts and stacked my books. Before I left the house, she grabbed me and held me violently against her for a moment, then shoved me bitterly out the door. I looked for Ilari, but he was nowhere nearby. When I turned to look back at the house, someone grabbed me from behind and dragged me to the van. Time stopped. I knew the world was moving around me but I wasn't in it. I didn't breath. I couldn't feel my heartbeat.

Balere and Remiri, my occasional uncles and *aita*'s henchmen, who normally rode in the back of the van with me while *aita* drove, sat waiting on the driver's bench with the engine running. I was forced to my knees on the metal floor of the cargo hold. *Aita* – it could only be *aita*, I knew – slapped duct tape over my mouth and zap-strapped my wrists together. It was only when I felt the cold metal tip of his Browning 90mm on my temple that I came back to life in a rush. But I never tried to scream. I knelt, silent, tears streaming down my cheeks, for the hour long ride to the airport while *aita* raked his stubble across my face, breathed his day-old tobacco and coffee into my nostrils, imposed the weight of his oily, sweating body against me and whispered, word after agonising word, exactly how many pieces he would leave me in if I ever spoke out against communism, The Organisation, and especially against him, ever again.

When we stopped in the airport parking lot, Balere and Remiri leapt into the back of the van and took me from *aita*. They removed the tape from my mouth, washed my face to hide the tears and smoothed my wrinkled clothes. When they finished, I looked exactly the way I had when *ama* shoved me out of the house. They handed me my bags and drove away without a word.

I threw up painfully on the concrete, and then met my social services guardian at the check-in as if nothing had happened.

Two days later, I met you.

§

I deliberately left out the most important sentence in that narrative; *that was the afternoon when I started planning to have my aita killed.* I've never told this story before, but common sense dictates that there will never be a good time to tell anyone about my part in *aita*'s disappearance. I did what needed to be done, and I know that — but no one else ever needs to know it.

I look up at Lauran shyly. I've been staring down at the wooden table for the past four paragraphs of my monologue, unable to make eye contact, because this is not a joke. This is my ugly, messy life and even I wasn't really ready to hear these truths about myself aloud.

Lauran's gaze is fixed on my face, his blue eyes wide with a mix of astonishment and shame, "When I first met you, and my *alaba* asked me what you were like, the only adjective I could think of was skittish. You were always on your guard, looking over your shoulder. Sophie — your *aita* threatened to kill you. Why didn't you ever tell me? I would have taken care of you."

The palpable sincerity in my ex-boyfriend's voice makes my hands shake. I remember a conversation much like this one, one dark summer night in Euskal Herria. I was sitting outside in the warm air with Gab, watching the stars; we had our backs against the brick wall of factory and our knees pulled in to our chests. Gab had his arm around me and I leaned in, resting my head on his shoulder. We talked in a whisper, pointing out the constellations we could see. And then my stomach rumbled. It wasn't unusual — we never had much to eat in Euskal Herria, even in the summer months when we grew a vegetable garden; on a good night, our evening meal was rice, a few boiled vegetables and a mouthful of meat. Good nights were few and far between. That night, we had eaten plain rice.

"Are you hungry?" Gab asked.

"I'm hungry a lot when I'm here." It should have occurred to me that after a lifetime of going without, Gab no longer knew what hunger was; he was simply grateful when there was food and accepted that there often wasn't.

"Why didn't you say something?"

"No one has anything to eat. It didn't really seem worth mentioning."

"Next time you're hungry, tell me — please. I hate the thought of you going without. I'll always take care of you."

It was such a sweet sentiment, I could feel a small smile stretching my lips in the dark and I leaned in closer to Gab, closing any space between us. We didn't say much after that, but the truth was there in the dark with us; no matter how much he wanted to take care of me, there was nothing he could do.

Back in my wooden café chair, I swallow hard. It is painful to drag these words out of myself. My voice is barely audible when I explain, "Because, Lauran, there was nothing you could have done. And because I thought I was taking care of you. I thought I was protecting you. I had told you so many things that already put you in danger. I was stupid." I clench my fists so hard that my nails make crescent shaped cuts over old scars. I let go just before I draw blood.

With a sigh, I slip a cigarette from my box of *Gauloises* and stubbornly light it left-handed, just to prove that I still can. I inhale slowly. "I'm sorry."

Lauran looks down at his hands. I suck the life from my cigarette, drag after tense drag, afraid to say anything else in case it turns out to be the wrong thing, and signal to the waiter for more coffee.

After an excruciating moment, my ex-boyfriend looks up at me again. His expression is distinctly composed — all along, I've been remembering him and thinking of him as the seventeen-year-old I left. In this moment of clarity, I see for the first time that he has grown-up. "How much danger, Sophie?"

And I see that he has moved on. "My *aita* died a long time ago. He was disgraced. There is no danger anymore."

Lauran opens his mouth to reply, but the sound of his *portable* pinging interrupts him. He takes his phone from the pocket of his jeans. For a brief second I can see the screen; the first sentence of the message is typed in angry capital letters. *ARE YOU WITH HER?!*

The impatient girl.

Lauren's *portable* pings again. He frowns and shoves it back into his pocket as he stands up. "I have to run. I'll see you around."

My ex-boyfriend stands and buttons his coat. As he turns to walk away, his right hand brushes against my left hand for a few seconds longer than an accident. The feeling of his skin against mine is the most distinct sensation my numb fingers have felt for years.

"I'll see you," I manage to mumble. But when he is out of sight, I realise I'm not sure if, outside of our linguistic theory class, I ever will.

**Chapter 6**

Back home, I hesitate outside our apartment door. I don't know exactly why. Every day I come home, climb the stairs to our fourth floor apartment and lean into the blue door with my right shoulder to let myself in. But today I stop and contemplate the doorknob, questioning if I really don't have anywhere else I could be.

In the end, my exhaustion wins out. Having coffee with Lauran — all of those memories, all of those truths finally spoken aloud, all of the uncertainty — has done me in. All I want to do is collapse in bed, pull a pillow over my head and shut the world out for a while. Heaving a sigh, I lean in and open the door.

The apartment is eerily quiet. Normally, my brother is in the kitchen at this time, stirring something on the stove. I turn to the right and notice the lights in the kitchen are out. "Luc?" I call out down the hall, slipping my heels off on the mat by the door. "I'm home!"

My brother appears at the living room door, still in his workday suit. His tie is loose around his neck. "We're in the *salon*, Sophie."

There is something suspect in the gentle tone of Luc's voice — but he disappears back into the living room too quickly for me to discern exactly what it is. I march down the hall after him, demanding, "Who's *we*?"

I take the ten steps to the living room faster than I ask the question, and before Luc can answer, I see the answer through the open door; the blonde hair, graying at the temples, neatly pulled back; the slim shoulders covered by a pale pink sweater. I stop dead for an instant. *Maman*. She is exactly as I left her — or rather, as she left me — unchanged by the passage of time. I haven't seen her for almost four years.

She abandoned me in the hospital, my bullet wound still so severe that I couldn't move my left arm, because I refused to give up, "those terrorists." That was her name for the family whose blood I share. I haven't heard a word from her since that day. If she has felt even one ounce of remorse for her callousness, she has never communicated it.

And she does not show it when she turns to face me. "*Bonjour*, Sophie," she says coolly, a glacial look in her eyes that tells me she thinks she has more right to be here than I do.

Fury rises inside of me. I have not seen her for almost four years and I am not about to start now. I turn on my heel and flee across the hall to my bedroom, locking the door behind me.

Safely inside, I lean back against the door, breathless — not from running two metres but from absolute panic and horror. This is the ultimate betrayal. How could Luc bring her here? How dare he?

Raging, I rip my *portable* from the pocket of my jeans and stare at it, desperate to unload my anger on anyone who will listen but unsure of who to call. I realise, bitterly, how few people I have in my life that I can share this particular pain with. Madeleine loves her *maman*. They go for tea at *Maison Ladurée* together every Sunday. So does Gen — she runs up colossal phone bills, telephoning her *ama* in Bilbao almost every single day. I could call Ilari, but that will only make it worse. I have rarely spoken to him about *maman*, but when I have, his reaction is always the same — a shudder. He was old enough during the court case to remember words spoken and measures taken. He saw a side of *maman*, a quiet person who I always believed to be tolerant to a fault, in those years that she never showed during my childhood. "That woman has claws," is all he has ever said about her. It wasn't until I was in the hospital that I fully understood what his words meant.

I'm still staring at my *portable*, rage surging through me, when I hear a knock at my door. I freeze. Could it be her? It can't be. Luc wouldn't do that to me. I — my mind races.

"Sophie?" my brother calls softly from outside.

"Go away!" I shove myself away from the door and fall heavily, suddenly more sad and defeated than angry, on my bed.

"Sophie? I just want to talk to you."

Luc sounds sincere, but I'm still not fully convinced that this isn't a set-up. "I said, go away!" I throw my *portable* across the room for emphasis — it hits the wall with a resounding thud, chipping the white paint.

"What was that?" Luc demands, banging on the door. "Come on, Sophie, please."

"All right, all right... I'll let you in, but I'm not coming out."

There is a long silence before my brother sighs and mutters, "Fine." I start to stand up, but he has already tried to turn the doorknob. "You locked yourself in?"

"Just a minute, just a minute." I unlock the door and open it just enough for Luc to slip inside, then lock it again behind him. I confront him on the parquet, demanding in a harsh whisper, "What is *she* doing here?"

"I asked her to come," my brother sounds genuinely surprised by my question, and a bit embarrassed. "I — I thought you might be, you know," he looks down at the floor, "slipping."

"Slipping?" I don't like where this is going.

"You came home crying last week. You've been sitting on the window ledge at night, having full conversations with someone who is not there. It looks like you just broke your *portable* and cracked the wall! I-"

"And you thought she could help me with that?" I explode. "You thought maybe the solution was having her tell me again that I should disown my family?"

"No, I-" Luc begins a feeble protest that he doesn't know how to finish.

"What do you want me to do, see my psychiatrist more often? You could have just said so! Look!" I pick my *portable* up off the parquet and brandish it as proof. "I'll call and make an appointment right now!"

"Sophie, you don't have to-"

"Then why, Luc? Why would you bring her here?"

Luc throws up his hands in exasperation. "She's still my *maman*, you know!"

"Well, she hasn't been mine for a long time. But," I concede, lowering my voice to an acceptable indoor register as my suspicions are proven false and I begin to calm down, "I see your point. You have the right to see your mother in your own home. I'll just go next door to Stéfane and Martine's until your guest leaves."

Rather than heading for the door, I take a step towards the window. There is only a foot between our window ledges — I've climbed in between them countless times.

"Sophie, please," Luc follows me, pleading.

But I'm already outside on the stone platform, knocking on the neighbours' window. "Stéfane! Martine, are you home?"

"Please," my brother begs, reaching for my arm, "just come and say hello."

My left leg is already over the wrought iron railing. "Stéfane!" I call, still knocking. "Martine, I'm letting myself in!"

Luc finally catches my wrist. "Sophie, she raised you!"

And then she dropped me from the nest when my wings were broken.

Luckily, Stéfane appears at his window before I spit out that venomous retort. I wrench my wrist free of my brother's grasp, but not before our taller, stronger neighbour takes me by the shoulders to help me over the railing. "I think you had best let your sister come over here if she wants to," he warns Luc.

The two men face off for a minute, Luc with his arms crossed and his jaw set; Stéfane glaring over the rims of his plastic-framed glasses. And then Stéfane lifts me gently onto his window ledge. I hear my bedroom window close behind me, but I don't look back.

§

Stéfane is an artist; Martine, his wife, is a mathematician. Their apartment, built in an identical style with all of the others in our building, has been completely remodelled to suit their abstract tastes. Apart from around the bathroom, there are no walls; the whole space is open and bright, bathed in light from the curtainless windows. In one corner, Stéfane has his studio, a mess of scattered paints and brushes; half-finished canvases and discarded sketches litter the floor. The other three corners of the apartment are furnished as a bedroom, living room and kitchen, but there are no lines to distinguish where one room ends and another begins.

I sit with Stéfane at the long, unvarnished table in the corner that serves as the kitchen, chin in my hand. Behind us, Martine boils a pot of water to make tea. "It's been a long day."

Stéfane considers me for a long second. He is a tall man, built like an oak tree, with a hooked nose and wide-set gray eyes. "Stay just like that. I want draw your portrait." He has his wire-bound sketch pad open to a fresh page before I can protest, his calloused fingers making balletic strokes with a half-used pencil.

My over-familiarity with our next-door neighbours has never aroused Luc's suspicion. They moved in just days after we did; I bumped into Martine in the hall and offered to help her with a particularly heavy box. The fact that that simple act of politeness led to my eating dinner with the neighbours almost weekly, and buying them gifts at Christmas, apparently seems like a natural progression to my brother.

Stéfane and Martine are regular people; their jobs and hobbies are real, as are their names. But they are also finds of Thierry and sympathetic to the cause of our people. Although he now has plans for my *maîtrise* and *doctorat*, at the outset Thierry was not overly pleased with my insistence on studying in Paris, given that there are excellent schools in Bordeaux. "There is no future for our cause that does not include you," he stated categorically when I told him my plans. When I stood firm in my decision, he made arrangements to have people close to me, people who would protect me. People who would, as he carefully put it, "serve as a constant reminder of who you are, what you believe, and what your purpose is."

Most of the time, I just think of my neighbours as friends.

"Tell me about it," Martine hands me a red mug of jasmine tea and sits down at the head of the table. She is still dressed in the back pantsuit she wore to work, her dark hair tied back in a severe chignon, but she has changed out of her pumps into a pair of absurd pink bunny slippers. "You've lost Stéfane," she smiles, "but I'm listening."

I open my mouth to speak, but find I don't know where to start. When I think back on my life, it still feels a bit like the world turned on its axis the day I was shot. My *maman*, who I had always believed loved me unconditionally, revealed herself to be spiteful, prejudiced and cruel. My *ama*, a quiet, nervous person who had never seemed to have much interest in me, showed her true colours in a way that no one, least of all me, could ever have predicted. It was painful. When I remember the things I loved and lost – hot cassoulet fresh from the oven; trips to the seaside at Biarritz on holiday; borrowed lipsticks that I never had to return – it's all that I can do not to cry.

No matter how much I miss having a *maman*, I would never – could never – trade away all of the people I love, and the things I believe in, to have her back.

And then there is the small matter of Lauran. I cannot even begin to think about tone of finality in his voice when he left me at the *Café des Éditeurs*... the last, accidental brush of his hand... without the crushing weight of sadness pressing down on my chest until it feels like all of my ribs will crack.

"If you don't want to talk," Martine offers, "we can always have a Rubik's cube race."

There are Rubik's cubes all over Stéfane and Martine's apartment. Martine can solve them in about thirty seconds – she claims she does them to clear her head when she's working on a big problem. The first time she suggested a race, I laughed out loud – but the cube seemed to be taunting me, and I spent three intolerable days lugging it around in my purse, trying to solve it when I had breaks between lectures.

When I finally conquered it, I felt like Hannibal at the base of the Alps — victorious. Martine and I have been racing ever since; once, I even beat her. We took a photo of the occasion; I had it developed and put it in a frame on my dresser. "Why not?" I agree half-heartedly.

Martine retrieves two Rubik's cubes from the refrigerator — she always keeps some in there, in case she has a problem on her mind when she gets up in the middle of the night for a glass of water. She puts one in front of me. Stéfane flips the page on his sketch pad begins to sketch the shape of a cube.

"Ready..." Martine begins to countdown.

"..., set," I fill in.

"Go!" we both shout at the top of our lungs.

Even though they're cold, the rotating sides of my cube move in a smooth, fluid rhythm. In seven manoeuvres, I'm convinced that I have the geometric riddle solved. But when I turn it over, hoping to see nine pristine white blocks stacked three-by-three, there is one telltale red square in the bottom right corner.

## Chapter 7

"Have you ever seen anything like this?" I hold up the Rubik's cube to show Madeleine before our linguistics lecture. "I've been trying to solve it for a week. All I need to do is make the red squares change places. But I just can't."

Madeleine eyes my Rubik's cube, which I have now been carrying around in my purse for seven full days, with trademark skepticism. "I think," she says, tucking a lock of hair behind her ear, "that what you have done here is mathematically impossible. Oh, and a colossal waste of time, *bien sûr*."

I glare at my alleged friend and bend down to shove the Rubik's cube back into the bottom of my black satchel. I hear Madeleine gasp quietly while I'm facing the floor. I sit up in a rush to see what has happened, but it turns out that my research partner just fell in love with a "divine" photo spread in the new issue of *Vogue Paris*, which she has tucked inside her copy of *Réflexions sur le langage*.

"Typical," I mutter, and open my own copy of our heavy textbook to the chapter we are scheduled to cover during the lecture.

The professor arrives, dressed in his Wednesday suit, a three-piece brown tweed that matches the seven remaining strands of hair on his head. He takes a look around the room, pausing for a moment longer than usual to survey the attendance before announcing, "We will begin today on page one hundred and fifty-eight."

Forty students turn the pages of their books at once. Satisfied, the professor begins, "As you will have read…" He makes it through his first sentence without any raised hands. And then his second. He complete a full, unprecedented paragraph before it occurs to me what — or rather, who — is missing.

"Mado!" I elbow my research partner to get her attention.

"I hope, after a jab like that, you are going to say that you have suddenly had an epiphany and recognise Carine Roitfeld's genius."

"Of course not! Haven't you noticed?"

"Noticed what? That I can't hear anything over your talking?"

"As if you care. Lauran isn't here today!"

"Who?"

Madeleine is being deliberately obtuse and we both know it. "The one who always argues with the professor!"

"You mean the one you're in love with? This is a pleasant change of pace — I get a reprieve from his tiresome posturing and your love nonsense at the same time! And on the day that the new issue of *Vogue* came out. I must be lucky!"

"Have I told you lately that you're infuriating?"

"He's just a boy, you know," Madeleine rolls her eyes heavenward. "They miss classes sometimes."

I think of Lauran — the way he writes notes furiously in a small black Moleskine notebook, his blue eyes darting between the chalkboard and his textbook. The way he grinds his teeth every time someone says the words Proto-Indo-European. The way his eyelashes brush against his cheekbones when he blinks… He has never been *just* anything to me. And now that I know for sure that I am just his ex-girlfriend, just an unwelcome disruption to the life he has made for himself far away from Saint-Antoine, I am relieved that at least for a week I don't have to face him.

§

When the interminable two hour lecture finally ends, I have yawned myself into a bored stupor. Madeleine, who still has another class and can't abide my dawdling even when she doesn't have somewhere else to be, rushes off the second the professor says his last word, uttering a hasty *à bientôt* when she is already halfway out the door. Left alone to move at my own pace, I'm one of the last to leave the lecture hall. I pack my textbooks into my satchel, slowly stacking them on top of each other by size. I am in no rush to get home. Luc sent *maman* to a hotel after my outburst last week, but we've barely spoken since — we eat our meals in front of the TV in tense silence and avoid eye contact when we pass each other in the hall. Part of me feels like I should apologise, but most of me still feels betrayed and hasn't forgiven him yet.

I sigh and pick up my heavy bag before making my way towards the door. I have a ten-page paper to write on economic policy in eastern Poland; it isn't due for two weeks but I've already half-finished and spending the evening poring over the rest of it to get the words right doesn't seem like the worst way to pass the time. I have a soft spot for economic policy in former Eastern Bloc countries — it never ceases to amaze me what an indelible mark my dear Gorbachev left on the provinces of the empire that he held so briefly.

The hallway is empty when I step out into it, all of my classmates having rushed off to their next lecture or to the nearest café for a much needed *verre*. Empty, that is, except for a girl leaning against the wall across from the door. She wears a black coat with a leather collar, and something about the unique combination of impatience and aloofness that she projects is vaguely familiar. She taps one foot against the tile floor, as if she were waiting for someone.

"Sophie?"

I jump, startled — and then it comes to me. I've seen that foot tap before, although only from behind, through the front window of the *Café des Éditeurs*. Lauran's girlfriend is standing in the hall and, improbable as it seems, she is apparently waiting for me. I realise that I have no idea what her name is and my hands shake a little. "Yes?"

"My name is Valentine Hervé," the impatient girl extends her skinny hand toward me — she wears a small pearl ring on her middle finger and I catch myself wondering if Lauran gave it to her. "We've never been formally introduced."

Against my better judgement, I reach one trembling hand out to shake. "I'm almost positive that was intentional."

Valentine's grip is firm. She is all business, but in spite of her bluster, she's pretty, even elegant; her dark hair is cut into a smooth bob and her liquid eyes are lined with kohl. It's no wonder Lauran fell for her. "I'm sure you're curious to know why I'm here."

I resist the urge to quip; *actually, I'm just hoping that you'll go away.* "It did strike me as odd."

"I expect that I will strike you as odd — I often give people that impression. But I think we need to have a conversation. I'd like to buy you a cup of coffee."

"I don't know..." I hesitate. "I have a paper to write."

Valentine sighs, already exasperated with me. "Would if help if I tell you that the conversation doesn't end with *Stay away from my boyfriend*? I can assure you, that's not my style." Lauran's girlfriend shows me her teeth — two neat rows of immaculate white. I think she is making an effort to smile, but she has it all wrong. "I just want to talk."

"You don't smoke, do you?"

"No," Valentine raises an eyebrow so that it disappears under her bangs. "Why?"

Those teeth gave her away. "Do you mind if I do?"

"As long as the health risks have been explained to you and you've simply chosen to disregard them, I suppose not."

It takes me a minute. But then I realise that Lauran's girlfriend is completely serious. There have been moments, since Gab died, when I have felt so unbearably alone, so unable to connect with anyone... and then I meet someone like Valentine and I wonder if the problem might not be with me, but with the rest of the world. "Did you have a particular café in mind?"

§

Valentine Hervé and I are fundamentally different people. For one thing, the café she has in mind is the Starbucks at *carrefour Odéon*. For another, she orders green tea. We sit at an outdoor table — partly so that I can smoke, but mostly so that I can escape quickly. I light a cigarette and let it dangle between my fingers as I sip my thick, dark coffee. I understand now why Lauran hesitated to smoke in front of me at first — with his beautiful, healthy girlfriend who is obviously acutely aware of her superiority sitting across from me, all of my imperfections feel magnified. "So..." I clamp my hand over my elbow to keep my cigarette from trembling in my hand, "what did you want to talk about?"

"You seem anxious, Sophie," Valentine observes in a tone that suggests that she wants to psychoanalyse me, not that she is genuinely concerned.

"I have post-traumatic stress disorder," I reply, with candour that surprises me. I have never begun a conversation with someone by naming my medical condition, but Valentine's demeanour is so to the point that, in this bizarre context, I almost sound reasonable saying it. "I'm always anxious."

"That's unfortunate." Valentine sips her tea delicately before she continues, "I thought you should know that I've left Lauran. And no matter what he may tell you, it has everything to do with you."

An icy knot forms in my stomach, expanding outward until the cold tension fills my limbs. "I thought you said..."

"I wasn't finished. I was about to say that I don't think you are at all to blame."

"I don't understand..." I can't find the words to finish my sentence. My cigarette trembles like a falling leaf in my shaking hand.

"I'm not accusing you of anything because, to be frank, you haven't done anything. At least, not recently. Until this afternoon, I lived with Lauran for two years. I left another man to move in with him. We were so intellectually compatible, I was positive that in time, we would warm up to each other more. Don't look at me like that; I know what I'm like. I make a good chess opponent — I'm not easy to live with. But I warmed up, as much as I can. It was Lauran who never did. At a certain point, I began to suspect that he had someone else on his mind. When he had coffee with you for the first time, my suspicions were confirmed."

"But-"

"Stop protesting," Valentine cuts me off. "I repeat, I am not accusing you of anything. I know what happened between you and Lauran all those years ago. You left him with no way to find closure. It's perfectly reasonable that his feelings for you should have remained unresolved."

"They seemed pretty resolved to me," I mumble.

Valentine goes on as if she didn't hear me. "I could respect and accept that. I could live with it. But I cannot live with the fact that those unresolved feelings for you are love. I'm studying psychiatry, Sophie. I understand that the line between love and hate is a fine one. But hate retains an element of rationality and Lauran... Lauran is not rational about you."

If the girl across the table from me were as much of a psychiatric expert as she seems to believe, she would know that people who suffer from post-traumatic stress disorder are prone to anger. I clutch my paper coffee cup so tightly that it crumples in my grip. Sudden, uncontrollable anger. "Did it ever occur to you that maybe he just didn't want you?" I spit the words out, spit out all of my hurt feelings and heartbreak in a vitriolic rush. "Because he isn't in love with me. He's made it perfectly clear that he doesn't want anything to do with me."

I clamp my hand over my mouth, but it's too late. The words have already escaped. Valentine's dark eyes are red rimmed with the salt of restrained tears. "I'm sorry, I shouldn't have said that. I have to go."

## Chapter 8

I rush down *boulevard Saint-Germain*, my satchel slung haphazardly over my shoulder, textbooks stabbing me in the ribs. Tears of rage blind me. It doesn't matter. All I want to do is get away – my mind is so full of tangled thoughts of escape, I can't even remember what I'm running from.

I don't see the man coming towards me until I've walked straight into his chest. I recoil, dizzy from the impact. I shake my head to bring my wet eyes into focus – I know I shouldn't be surprised by what just happened. But then I look up and find myself face-to-face with Lauran. I smile – for the first time I don't think about it, it just happens. This is exactly how we first met. "We have to stop running into each other like this."

"Sophie?" Lauran's face is the stark colour of blank paper. He has left home without a coat. His blue eyes dart up and down the street, frantically searching for someone. "This isn't a good time. Valentine... she's gone. When I got home, all of her things were packed. She didn't even leave a note!"

I sigh and shift my satchel on my shoulder. The idea of Lauran being with anyone but me makes my chest ache. And the idea of him being with someone as cold as Valentine makes me sad for him. But it still feels awful to say, "I know."

"You — what?" my ex-boyfriend just stares at me, his eyes pleading for me to make some sense of his personal chaos. I wonder how many times I have looked at someone this way, and if those people have felt as powerless as I do now.

"Valentine — she came to see me after the lecture. She told me she had left and that it was all because of me but it wasn't my fault."

Lauran sighs and rubs the back of his neck. "That sounds like her."

"Look, do you want to go get a drink?" The words just fall out of my mouth, unplanned, but it's too late to stop them. "It's freezing out and well, you obviously need one — or several."

"I'd like that."

As we walk down the street side by side, I feel myself start to inhale again. I hadn't realised I was holding my breath.

§

We go to *Le Procope*. It's the oldest café in Paris, where they still serve boiled calf's head like in 1680 — it's mainly a tourist trap now, but it has the distinct advantage of being just across the boulevard. The old place as been a haven for writers for centuries and as an aspiring young novelist growing up in Saint-Antoine, I dreamed of one day sitting at one of its wooden tables, sipping wine and absorbing all of the history concealed within its gilded walls. But in the two years I've lived in Paris, I've never been inside — I don't read much literature anymore. My dreams have changed.

The maître d' seats us in the front room, Lauran on the red leather bench and me in the chair opposite him. Out the window next to us, cars rush by down *rue de l'Ancienne comédie*. I order two glasses of wine while Lauran gazes around the room, still a little stunned. "This is the kind of place I always imagined you would spend your time," he observes, "wiling away hours with the ghosts of great writers."

"Do you want to talk about it?"

"About the kind of place I always imagined you would spend your time...?"

"No, about Valentine — why she left."

Lauran takes a long drink from the glass of wine that has just been placed in front of him and shakes his head, muttering, "*Putain*!"

"She told me that you had unresolved feelings for me — which I know is ridiculous, because you haven't exactly been shy about how resolved you are to escape me every week. I probably should have phrased it differently, though," I admit, blushing.

"Your temper?"

"She made some serious accusations. It was all I could do not to slap her!"

Lauran laughs, maybe a little sadly, and downs the rest of his wine. "Valentine has that effect on people."

"Do you love her?" I clamp my hand over my mouth, muffling my apology. "I'm sorry, that's absolutely none of my business."

"No."

"No?"

"No," Lauran signals our waiter to bring him another glass of wine, "it's none of your business. And no," he adds, his gaze fixed on the table, "I don't love her."

"I'm sorry. That must have been..." I trail off; the adjective escapes me.

"Hard. She made it hard to love her. Honestly, after two years, I'm really not sure that I believe in love."

I raise an eyebrow. "No?"

The waiter brings Lauran another glass of Syrah. He drinks most of it in one gulp then looks me in the eye, his gaze unfocused and half-drunk but utterly sincere: "Do you believe in love, Sophie?"

"I don't know," I have to admit. "I've heard compelling arguments for and against it, but it seems that in the end, I always end up getting hurt."

"Your scar," Lauran's eyes widen with the clarity of this realisation. "I should have known."

It's my turn to take a long drink from my wine glass. "I would love to talk about... just about anything else. We have seven years to catch up on. Why don't you tell me what you've been doing all this time?"

"I can sum that up in one sentence."

"I have more than one sentence worth of wine left," I roll my eyes. "Keep me interested."

§

For the next two hours, Lauran tells me the story of his life since the day that I left. After he passed his *baccalauréat*, he took a year out to spend time in the Basque territories in Spain. This is the tradition in his family, he explains; the Etcheverrias are from the Baztan Valley, their home is in a town called Ziga. They have historically been farmers and pacifists and academics, focussed on retaining culture so that it can be passed on through generations, rather than taking up arms to fight for autonomy. "I don't know which is the right way," he reflects. "I considered joining The Organisation more than once, but the gang-like aspect of it made me nervous. I was never quite convinced that I would be allowed to leave if I wanted to... In the end, I followed the path that my *aita* and *aitaita* had laid for me."

He talks about staying with distant cousins who were essentially strangers with a kind of baffled fondness; they made merciless fun of his French accent and played pranks on him constantly. But they also took him to Guernica, where he experienced the horrifying shadow that the Spanish Euskadi have lived under for nearly seventy years; they taught him to play *jai alai*, our national sport, until he could best them with the *xistera*. For the first time, he lived a life where being Basque was not equal to being different. And he learned — recipes, songs, expressions, his own history.

"Did you want to stay?" I ask.

"Honestly? Never. I saw wonders, but I also saw horrors. Towns like the one where you grew up, where little kids carried weapons. I went ostensibly to learn the culture, but the first thing my *aita* asked when I came back was if I saw the full picture. He's a philosophy professor at the university in Bordeaux, and his questions can be a bit nebulous, but that one made perfect sense. My relatives in Ziga are farmers; they are so isolated that they can't fathom a life unlike their own, never mind any threat to their way of life. My *aitaita* left Ziga because he knew that he could be better, and do more, from outside than in. I'm as Basque in Paris as I am in Saint-Antoine, or in Ziga."

There is no doubt in my mind as I listen to Lauran speak that if such a thing as a soul mate exists, he is mine.

He still plays *jai alai*, when he can find a game; there is a small league of devotees in Paris, it seems, but few places to play. Still, he prefers quieter activities — he has a chess game going on in his apartment, he tells me, with both sides played by himself, but it's stalled because he can't decide which side he wants to win.

I can't help but laugh at that. "I have Rubik's cube."

"A Rubik's cube?"

"My neighbour is a mathematician; she does them constantly. She's been teaching me tricks for years, and I've gotten quite good at solving them, but the one I'm doing right now has me stumped. I have just two squares out of place, but they refused to move where I want them to." I blush, "It's a bit silly."

"It's a riddle," Lauran counters, a twinkle of mischief in his eye that sets my heart racing. "You'll find the answer."

Our waiter appears abruptly at the table, looking nonplussed. "Will *monsieur* and *mademoiselle* be partaking in the dinner service this evening? Or will you be sustaining yourselves solely on your unfinished wine?"

Much to my surprise, my watch tells me that it's after eight o'clock. All around the dining room, American couples, dressed in their best khaki pants — the ones that cannot be zipped off to reveal their knees — are struggling with the menu, beginning an evening meal that they expect to be magical but that will ultimately prove disappointing by mispronouncing *escargots*, putting heavy emphasis on the quiet *t* at the end.

"*L'addition, s'il vous plait,*" Lauran requests, more politely than I would have. While our waiter stomps off to retrieve it like a petulant child, we count our *centimes* to pay. Lauran is looking at his wallet, and his words are so quiet that I scarcely hear him over the sound of my own rattling coins when he says, "Thank-you for this, Sophie. You make it so easy."

## Chapter 9

The blue door to the apartment I share with Luc is ajar when I get home. I let myself in quietly, hoping to avoid my brother. I was practically floating above the sidewalk all the way home – Lauran said he would like to have a drink with me! He was polite and charming and earnest and only a little bit drunk. My heart jumps just remembering – and I don't want anything to spoil the feeling of dizzy happiness that is warming me from the inside. I slip my shoes off quietly and tiptoe down the hall, avoiding the floorboards that I know will creak under my weight.

I am two measly steps away from my bedroom door when Luc pokes his head out of the salon. I'm so startled; it feels like I suffer a mild heart attack. "Sophie," my brother starts, "we can't keep living like this."

"No," I snap. "You need to learn to tread a lot louder!"

"Did I scare you?"

"No, I just thought I would jump three feet in the air because it seemed like a fun and quirky way to say hello."

My brother sighs – it is obvious he has had a long day and lacks the energy to formulate a witty retort. "Would you just come in here please? I bought chocolates from *Hugo et Victor*."

He knows my weakness. "Fine."

A book-shaped box of semi-circle chocolates sits open and inviting on the coffee table. I sit down in the middle of the couch and reach for one. Luc sits in the hair next to me, hunched forward so that his elbows rest on his knees. "We have to talk."

"What about?" I ask through a mouthful of dark chocolate and caramel.

"Just in general. We can't keep avoiding each other – this apartment isn't big enough for us to live separately." My brother sighs and runs his fingers through his hair. "I should have said it sooner, but I'm sorry that I asked *maman* to come. I promise my intentions were good. I worry about you. But I realise how that could have felt like a betrayal."

"To be clear, Luc, if there were a scale of betrayals, bringing *maman* here would fall at the ultimate end of the spectrum."

"If it helps," Luc offers half-heartedly, "I think she was even angrier than you were."

"It doesn't." I reach for another chocolate – on some days, when I try hard enough, I can actually bury my feelings under bonbons. I know that Luc isn't exaggerating in his misguided attempt to console me. And I know that if *maman* found out what I do now, she would want to reunite just so she could relish disowning me all over again.

"I shouldn't have said that. Do you ever miss her?"

My feelings about *maman* are hard to put into words. I've worked through so much anger and bitterness that all I have left is a shell of what I used to feel for her. "*Maman*? Not specifically, no. It turns out that, as people go, I don't like her very much. But it's lonely, not having a *maman*. My birth mother is dead – I don't have anyone left. Sometimes," I am surprised to hear myself admit, "I'm not sure if I feel alone because of my condition, or because I really am."

"Sophie… that is the saddest thing I've ever heard." I half expect Luc to suggest that we go down to the pet stores on *quai de la Mégisserie* and look at kittens, but for once he just says the obvious thing: "You'll always have me. What can I do to cheer you up?"

"Let me eat the rest of these chocolates for dinner?" I suggest.

"It's a deal — as long as you promise that tomorrow night we'll have a normal meal with normal conversation. No more avoiding each other."

"I promise," I agree, my mouth full of vanilla ganache.

§

A rush of cold hair hits me when I open the door to the window ledge. Winter has come to the city, sneaking it at night when it thinks it will go unnoticed. Faced with an empty box of chocolates and crashing blood sugar, it strikes me that my earlier happiness was probably an overreaction. Lauran was just being civil this afternoon. And he was drunk. Nothing has really changed. I sigh, grab the quilt from my bed and wrap it around my shoulders before I step outside. *Notre-Dame de Paris* is bathed in iridescent white light and Gab is sitting on the railing, waiting. "I thought you had forgotten about me."

I sit down on the stone ledge, shaking my head. "You said that to me once before — do you remember?"

Gab looks out to the east, too ashamed to face me. "I wish you would just agree to pretend that had never happened."

"I was ten minutes late to meet you and you took a swing at me! It's a good thing I ducked, too — I seem to remember that the wall didn't recover very well."

"I was jealous."

"Of my *ama*!"

"Yes! Of your *ama*, of stray cats you stopped to pet in the street, of the sun that shone in your window in the morning… of anyone who got a moment of your time, because it was a moment that I lost. Jesus…" Gab sighs and shakes his head sadly, "I was so bad at loving you."

"I don't blame you," I forgive him without hesitation. "Your life didn't prepare you to love anything."

"And I suppose his did..."

"Whose?"

"Your ex-boyfriend. I saw you with him today."

"What? Gab, you were watching us?"

"I have eternity and I don't know how to read," Gab shrugs. "What would you suggest?"

"That you find someone to teach you!"

"He's in love with you, princess."

I roll my eyes. "He tolerates me. When it suits him, which is rare."

"Were you in a different café than I was? He said that you make it easy."

"He meant to talk."

"He meant to love you." Those five words fall over me like a sudden burst of cold rain. Lauran said that Valentine made it hard to love her. My heart beats double time. And then, before we left, he said that I make it easy. "The bastard has a point. I hate that he's the one who gets to do it while I'm stuck out here, but I know you always loved him more than me, anyway."

"Shut up," I blush.

"Don't act like you haven't admitted it. I want you to be happy. Honestly, I do."

"Then you should get out of here, because right now I feel like strangling you."

"If you let him get away again, you're going to spend the rest of your life sitting out in the cold with me, which wouldn't be such a terrible thing when you consider my obvious charm, but... I know you would regret it."

I cross my arms and frown at my dead boyfriend. "Promise you're not going to watch."

"I'll get a good picture book," Gab winks. "Good night, my princess."

§

There are so many things I never had a chance to say to Gab; so many memories that we never got to make together. I lie awake in bed after our talk, the realisation that he never said good night to me while he was alive slowly sinking in. We never spent a night together. We were never even in a bed together – the only place we could be alone was in the factory. I never got to lay next to him in the dark and feel his cool skin against mine as we both drifted off; never got to hear him whisper, "*Gau on*, my princess."

Maybe that's why I hold on – because there are so many moments I still want to live with him. Maybe I would have grown to love him more than I ever loved Lauran. I didn't have the time to find out, and now I'll never know. Our two months of happiness passed like a runaway train. We had the whole summer to spend together, and then it was just... gone. "I leave tomorrow," I remember telling him. We were together in the *despachos* – he sat in the executive chair and I was in his lap, running my fingers through the fading red streak in his hair.

"What?" He was blindsided. "Since when?"

"Since always. Summer is over. School starts on Tuesday in Saint-Antoine."

Gab wasted no words. He closed his arms around me tightly and said, "Spend the night with me."

"You know I can't – I still have to pack. Besides, *ama* will notice if I don't come home tonight. The whole town will notice."

"That means this is good-bye."

I closed my eyes and pressed my lips against his for a long moment. "It's not good-bye – it's seen you soon." But the truth was that my eighteenth birthday was five months away and with it, the end of the custody agreement. Never again would I be compelled to cross the border into Spain accompanied by a representative of Social Services, and I had absolutely no plans to make the trip on my own. At least not until I had spent one long, lazy summer in a faraway place where the toilets were indoors and the cupboards were never empty.

But it turned out that *see you soon* wasn't enough for me. I lay awake all night on my hard little bed thinking about how the next time I went to sleep, it would be in my own bed, with clean sheets and *pain au chocolat* for breakfast the next morning, but I wouldn't be able to enjoy it because when I walked outside, all that would wait for me would be the empty streets of Saint-Antoine. No arguments. No late nights passed in the shadow of the factory, counting the stars. No Gab. I tried to sort out how I could feel so much love for someone who embodied everything that I had always been against – I never found an answer, but the love stubbornly persisted, making my heart swell until it felt like it would burst.

I know now that my love for Gab wasn't as unbelievable as it seemed that night; he was a person just like me, and when you got right down to it, that meant we weren't so different. I learned so much from my darling freedom fighter in the short time we had together – but most of all, he showed me the humanity, fragile and prone to breaking, that exists in even the most hardened people.

My eyes finally closed early the next morning, and I drifted into a thin, restless sleep that was almost immediately disrupted by the sound of pebbles bouncing off my window. I leapt up in a daze, searching the room for the sound. And then I realised - Gab. He was outside. I threw an oversized t-shirt over my head in a rush and darted out the side door, half-naked and barefoot. The sun was just beginning to rise over the mountains, bathing the dried and yellowing yard in pink light. Gab was waiting for me, still wearing the same clothes he'd had on the previous afternoon. There were deep, exhausted circles under his gray eyes. "What are you doing here?" I demanded in a harsh whisper. "You haven't slept."

Gab put a finger to his lips to silence me. He took me by the hand and led me to the back of the house, where there were no windows and no witnesses besides the dying olive tree. "What if someone sees us?" I protested, still whispering. "Freedom fighters show up at all hours, we could get caught!"

"Just give me this last minute with you."

Those were the last words Gab ever spoke to me. He took me with both hands and leaned me gently against the sagging wall of my parents' old house, pressing one fingers to my lips, just in case there were more words I couldn't hold back. I nodded, agreeing to keep quiet. He took me by my shoulders and kissed me, tenderly, on my forehead, my cheeks and my mouth. When he pulled back, we stood together in silence, holding each other at arm's length, for a long moment. And then he pulled me into his rough embrace, holding on like he would never let go. I stood there with my eyes closed, my face pressed into his sweater, breathing in his dark, dusty scent, and wished that he never would.

It was the most perfect moment that we ever had together, unspoiled by words that only sounded true. But as I watched him walk away, the gentle morning sun illuminating his shadow, I wished that I had told him I loved him. Or at least that I had said good-bye.

## Chapter 10

"Sophie?"

I am standing with Madeleine after our linguistics lecture, gathering my books and trying to explain, despite her total lack of interest, that my Rubik's cube still has me stumped, when someone approaches us from behind.

He clears his throat and starts again, "Sophie?"

When I turn around, I find myself looking at Lauran. Behind me, Madeleine gasps quietly. I smile, painfully aware that my cheeks have turned the same shade of red as one third of the national flag that hangs in the front of the lecture hall. "Hello Lauran. How are you?"

"I'm fine. I-" Lauran clears his throat again. "I wanted to ask if I could buy you a cup of coffee?"

"Oh?" I raise an eyebrow, suspicious. Whatever he may have said at *Le Procope* last week, it was mostly the wine talking. "Why the change of heart?"

"Well..." my ex-boyfriend rubs the back of his neck and looks down at the floor, embarrassed, before beginning the longest, most convoluted sentence I have ever heard him utter, "the thing is, I've had some time to think, in the past week, and, well, in spite of everything, I still trust Valentine's opinion and if she says I have unresolved feelings for you, I probably do."

"Are you back together?"

"No. She won't return my calls."

"And... you still want to talk about us?"

"Honestly?" Lauran sighs, "Not at all. But I think we should."

"Well." At least the lines in the sand are clearly drawn again. "Coffee it is, then." I reach for my coat, but it gets caught on the back of the chair and my numb hand is no help in extricating it.

"Let me get that for you," Lauran offers. He frees my coat with ease and holds it out for me to slip into.

And just like that, the lines in the sand are washed away by the surf. I nearly faint when his hands brush against my shoulders. "Thank-you."

When I turn to say good-bye to Madeleine, I find she's already gone. My *portable* starts to vibrate in my pocket- I reach for it and find a text message from my phantom friend. *Call me as soon as you get home. If you don't, I'll be forced to get the details from your brother. He'll just end up asking me out again, and we both know I'll say yes – and then I'll be forced to contemplate the terrible possibility that I might actually be falling for him. I beg you, don't do that to me. Just call.*

I can't help it – I laugh out loud.

Not surprisingly, Lauran asks, "What is it?"

I straighten my beret on my head and sling my satchel over my shoulder as we leave the lecture hall together. "Just Madeleine. She's in love."

My ex-boyfriend chuckles: "No wonder she always seems so miserable."

§

The *Café des Éditeurs* is crowded and bustling, full of passersby looking to temporarily escape the cold with a strong café. But the table where Lauran and I are in the habit of sitting is, by chance, free. We take our usual chairs. We order *café noisette*. I light my habitual cigarette, and offer one to my ex-boyfriend; he declines - and then, to my surprise, he takes his own blue box of *Gauloises* out of his pocket and lights one for himself. I can't help but smile a little as I inhale. Our waiter brings the coffee we ordered and places both cups on the table in front of us.

And all the while we are silent, avoiding direct eye contact. We both know where the story goes next — it's a chapter of my life I have always wished I could rewrite, the reason that my cigarette trembles between my fingers. The reason why Lauran would have preferred to spend our semester in linguistics pretending we were strangers.

We are engaged in an elaborate game and the move is mine to make. I take a fortifying drag on my cigarette, steel my nerves as best I can and ask one last time, "You're sure you want to talk about us?"

Lauran stares down at his hands, fingers interlocked around his coffee cup, the flame of his lit cigarette dangling dangerously close to the wooden table. "I — I think we have to," he says, stumbling over the simple words. "Otherwise, this feeling that we've lost something that can't be found again will never go away."

"Does it feel that way to you, too?"

"I... yes, it does."

I can feel my eyes widen, the weight of all these words momentarily lifted. I stare at my ex-boyfriend across the table, stunned. Until this afternoon, I have never heard him hesitate or stutter. If I had known he was a student at La Sorbonne, I would never have enrolled in a language course. Lauran was practically born a linguist — when they hand him his degree, it will be a mere formality. He spoke four languages fluently when we met, and he was never at a loss for a witty reply in any one of them. When he stammered the first time, in the lecture hall, I didn't really notice. The second time, I just let it go — but that was the third time and I cannot just ignore that, sitting here with me, he is barely able to string two words together. "What happened to you? You were always such a smooth talker."

Lauren meets my eyes and shrugs, "I got hurt."

There it is. I sigh and look back down at my coffee cup on the table top — I did this to him.

Lauran was my first boyfriend. I adored him. I was in awe of him – and in awe of the fact that he wanted to be with me. He was older, and so handsome that I felt light-headed when got close to him. And smart. He always knew exactly what to say. Before we bumped into each other in the hallway, I had only known him as a cute boy I sometimes passed in between classes, but he had quite a reputation with the Euskadi girls at school. There were only about ten Euskadi boys in town, and at least eight of them showed no sign that might ever grow into their noses. Lauran was good looking. He knew it. And he abused it shamelessly until we met, making every single one of the Euskadi girls feel like he just might choose her.

But he chose me. I don't know if I ever really got over being dazzled by that. I felt like a better person just standing near him. He had this way of smiling at me across a room that made me feel like everyone else had disappeared. When it transpired that all we really had in common was our heritage, he taught me to play chess. "So that we'll always have something we can do together," he said. After he saw my abysmal English grades, he tried to tutor me. But even though his lessons were thoughtfully researched, I never improved. I was too distracted by looking at his hands and his lips and his eyelashes to retain anything. He loaned me books and asked my opinion of them. He called me beloved. I always wanted to touch him.

I fell so hard, so fast. I told him things I had never told anyone – things that put my Euskadi family in danger; things that put him in even more danger – without a second thought. He was my first everything.

But I always went to his house. We never ate together in the café. I walked myself home, taking a different route every time.

We had been together for seven months when he asked why I hadn't introduced him to my family. It started as a joke. "You aren't ashamed of me, are you?"

I hesitated. I couldn't bear the thought of Luc's taunting. The idea of the sermons that Father Philippe might give on the subject of Basque devils tainting the French citizenry of our pure town made me sick to my stomach.

So I hesitated.

"Sophie," Lauran reeled, "I embarrass you?"

I couldn't answer. The truth was, no matter how much I loved him, I could only love him when no one else was looking. And so I stood up and left him in stunned silence. Until our linguistic theory course this year, we scarcely saw each other again. But I have never forgotten the look on his face when I walked away.

Across the table, Lauran clears his throat, waiting for me to say something.

"I'm sorry," is all I can muster, my words barely audible. I look down at the tabletop, trying to hide the tears that have pooled in my eyes. I can only shake my head. "I'm so, so sorry."

"I adored you."

Those three simple words, pronounced so frankly and without a hint of bitterness, catch me by surprise. I wipe my eyes with my hand, leaving dark mascara streaks on my palm and look up at my ex-boyfriend. "Excuse me?"

"I adored you. You were the first thing I thought of when I woke up in the morning. And you chose your secrets over me."

"I never-" I start, but my protest is a futile one.

"All of those insane things you told me about your family and your life... at first I thought you made them up but even when I realised they were true, I found a way to make sense of them as facts and accept them for what they were. There was nothing you could have told me that I wouldn't have found a way to understand. There wasn't a single person in your life you could have said that about before we met. But you chose them — you chose your secrets instead. Explain that to me. Tell me why."

"Lauran-" even now, my voice shakes as I form the words, "I was scared."

§

It's that simple. It isn't a good explanation, and I'm sure it's not the one you were hoping to hear, but it's the only one I have. And it's the truth. I have felt guilty every day of my life for walking away from you. Some days I dared to hope that you might forgive me, if only I could find the right words to explain myself. On some level I always knew it was absurd, of course — and when we met in September, when it seemed that all we could do was trade insults, I realised I had been deceiving myself all along. I was so cruel to you. The fact that we are sitting here together now... This is more than I believed could happen ever between us after I walked away from you.

The school year passed, and so did another summer in Euskal Herria. I was in a sort of stasis, waiting for some climatic event that would align me with one of my two lives or allow me to escape them both, without any idea of what that might be. All I wanted was to belong somewhere. I wanted to belong in Saint-Antoine; desperately, painfully — but we had a priest who gave sermons on how my people were devils; I had a brother who called me a Spic and parents who never corrected him because, as it turned out, they didn't really think he was wrong. And I would have cut off my right hand for them if it would have made them stop holding me at arm's length, to stop seeing me as different. Different is a curse in a small town. And you... you only made me more different. That's why I left you.

I had spent my whole life grasping at acceptance in Saint-Antoine; pushing away the terrorists who were my real family, maligning their bombs and guns, rejecting their desire for freedom as idealistic at best. I was ashamed of them, but even more than that, I was afraid of them; afraid that a predilection for violence was written in my genetic code and that I might wake up one morning, the very image of what Father Philippe had always believed me to be. I had only known you for seven months. The choice was still the hardest I've ever had to make, if that makes it any less painful. I doubt it does.

The summer after *primaire*, I packed my bags for Basque Country in a miserable state. I was seventeen. I felt like an adult, but I had no control over anything in my life — I wasn't even allowed to pack my own suitcase; convinced I would forget necessities if left to my own devices, *maman* did my packing for me.

I was equally miserable when I arrived in Euskal Herria. I didn't speak to anyone, just left my suitcase at my parents' house and stomped up to the *despachos* to brood.

I went on like a primadonna for three days before someone came to look for me. When I heard the knock at the door, I expected my *anaia*, so I ignored it and went on spinning in slow, aimless circles in the overstuffed executive chair. Ilari would let himself in when he lost patience, I knew.

After two more knocks, he did exactly that. I was in mid-spin when the door creaked open, facing away from the voice that asked, "Amaia?"

It wasn't my *anaia*. It was Gabrié.

"What do you want?" I demanded, glaring as I spun around to meet him.

"I didn't come here for that." He was quiet and contrite, nothing like the fiery, vocal communist who lived in my memory during the winter months while I was at home, buried under a stack of books that would help me prepare new arguments to volley at him.

There is something I should explain before I go on. The community of Basques from whom I descend practises betrothal and arranged marriages. I have long suspected that it is just one more way that my *aitaita* devised to control the population and force the young men, who might otherwise have left for the promise of the city, to stay close to him; to the cause. I was promised to Matei Zabala, a quiet older boy with a sad smile, when I was only four; he was eight at the time. Four years later, he was diagnosed with leukemia. *Ama* took me to visit him in the hospital a few times; once, I picked a bunch of bedraggled wild flowers and gave them to him as gift.

Matei died quietly just after his fourteenth birthday. I was, for all intents and purposes, widowed when I was ten and a half; there were no other boys my age left unspoken for. To be very honest, as sad as I was, I was also relieved; the idea that I might be compelled to stay in Euskal Herria forever by a husband someone else had chosen for me had always frightened me. And I was relieved for Matei, too – he escaped a long, cold, wasted life, staring down the barrel of a gun without ever truly knowing who his enemies were. He was at peace.

It was fascinating to observe how different couples related to each other as years passed. Iasmina and her betrothed, Jess Larrea, were in love from the time they were children. Their affection for each other was always sweet and tender and unquestioning. Ilari was promised to a girl named Mariaenea, who was twice his size. She adored him — he was terrified of her. Gabrié had been paired with Alaine Remeteria, a snotty religious girl with an improbably long nose, virtually at birth. As far as I know, they never spoke before their wedding day...

§

The hands on my watch show that it's after seven. The café is quiet — just a few early diners, tourists with bedraggled maps and tired feet, trickle in the door. "I'm sorry," I interrupt my own monologue, "I didn't realise it was so late. You could have said something."

"No, no," Lauran shakes his head, "it's fine. There's no one waiting for me anymore."

"Of course, I'm sorry. I'm just so used to you grabbing your coat and leaving in a rush..."

"Listen," my ex-boyfriend quietly changes the uncomfortable subject, "I'm sorry if I was hard on you earlier. I've been holding onto those feelings for a long time."

"It's all right." The fact that he is still sitting here with me, still speaking to me after all these years and all that has passed between us, is enough. Even if he wanted to call me names and berate me like he did those first few times we came here together, I don't think I would mind — as long as he stayed. I always felt warm, when I was with him. I remember that because that inexplicable warmth is filling me now. Madeleine might not be entirely wrong when she says that love makes a doormat of every woman in the end – although I do not intend to ever admit that to her. "I owed it to you to hear what you had to say. You always listened to me."

"Can I walk you home?" Lauran asks as we stand to leave. I'm so shocked that I have to steady myself on my chair. My face gives me away, and my ex-boyfriend is embarrassed by my reaction to what was really a simple question. "I mean," he stammers again, flustered, "because it's late, and dark outside."

"Please," I interrupt, to save his pride, "forgive my manners. I've obviously picked up a few bad habits from my terrorist relatives. I would love to have the company."

Lauran has nothing more to say; he just smiles and reaches out to help me with my coat.

§

Paris is quiet tonight; the damp streets are deserted except for the pale glow of the street lights, casting shadows on the concrete. Only the familiar rushing clang of the metro trains rolling by beneath the grates disrupts the peaceful silence. Lauran and I walk side-by-side in the dark down *rue de Condé*, towards *boulevard Saint-Germain*.

"I just live on Ile Saint-Louis," I tell Lauran. I can't think of anything else to say for myself. The space between us is so insignificant, I can barely breathe, never mind string my thoughts together in a coherent sentence. "It's not far."

"I wouldn't mind if it were," my ex-boyfriend replies quietly. He doesn't seem to know quite how to act outside the secure confines of *Café des Éditeurs*, either.

We follow *boulevard Saint-Germain*, mostly in silence, past *Alexandra Sofja*, the frilly little shop that specialises in absurd Victorian-style umbrellas; past the *Bon Bons* candy stand at the *carrefour de l'Odéon* where I buy licorice before Luc and I go to the movies, and past the imposing medieval *Musée Cluny*. We take a left turn on *rue du Cardinal Lemoine*, which leads us over the *pont de la Tournelle*, onto the little island in the Seine. The river is illuminated in shades of emerald, amber and amethyst from the glittering lights on *Notre-Dame de Paris*. "It's this way," I lead Lauran left along *quai d'Orléans*, down the cobbled sidewalk. I can hear the nervous click of my high heels on the ground as we pass the blue and white marked addresses one by one — eight, twelve, fourteen until we finally reach number twenty-six.

I stop in front of the heavy green-lacquered double doors and turn to face Lauran. "Well, this is it."

My ex-boyfriend is wide-eyed, gazing out at vast and brilliantly lit cathedral on Ile de la Cité. "What an incredible view."

"You should see it from my bedroom." As soon as the words escape, I clamp my hand over my mouth, shocked and mortified. "I can't believe I just said that!" I mumbled through my fingers. "I didn't mean it that way!"

"You're something else, Sophie," Lauran laughs so hard that he has to wipe tears from the corners of his eyes. "I'm glad we did this," he adds earnestly. "I feel like I've found something I've been missing for a long time."

I take my hand away from my mouth. "So do I."

"We've always had fun together — I don't know how I let myself forget that. I've been a jerk. Will you let me make it up to you?"

"I'm feeling forgiving," I smile, coy. "What do you have in mind?"

"Dinner tomorrow night," my ex-boyfriend offers. "I can pick you up at 7:30?"

"I'd like that. Good night, Lauran."

"Good night, Sophie." Lauran starts to walk away, then turns back. "I'd like to see the view from your bedroom one day, too."

I can only shake my head and laugh as I reach for the dial pad at our front door, pressing the metal buttons, five-seven-five-nine, in sequence to let myself in. Lauran's footfalls echo on the cobblestones behind me. And then, abruptly, they stop.

"Oh, and Sophie?" he calls out to me in the darkness.

"Yes?"

"I forgive you."

# Chapter 11

My high heels clack against the wooden stairs as I climb the four flights to our apartment, a ridiculous grin on my face. I can't see it, but I know it's ridiculous because I can feel it, pulling on the skin of my face, stretching and contorting it into a familiar but long forgotten position. I am smiling. Uncontrollably. Every time I shake my head at my own silliness and try to relax the muscles in my face, the corners of my mouth pull themselves up further.

Lauran always did this to me. The day we met, I smiled so hard on my walk home from school that the strain cracked my lower lip — I didn't realise it until I saw the drops of blood dotting the top of my math textbook.

I retrieve my *portable* from my purse as I walk up the dimly lit stairs — there are an appalling fifteen text messages and three missed calls waiting for me. I start to navigate to read the messages, but before I can make two clicks, the *portable* starts to ring in my hand. It's Madeleine. "*Allo?*"

"I agreed to go on a date with your brother," my research partner deadpans. "He's taking me to *Septime* on Saturday night."

"Good for you," I reply absent-mindedly, distracted by the winding stairs and thoughts of my own dinner date with Lauran.

"You have completely missed the point!" Madeleine snaps, apparently dissatisfied with my answer.

Coming to the conclusion that I cannot climb two more flights of stairs in heels and pay adequate attention to my research partner's mini-tantrum, I sit down on the second-floor landing. "I'm sorry, Mado, I just can't understand why you going to dinner with Luc is a bad thing. You like each other."

"You didn't call me!" Madeleine is in a rage. I can practically hear the vein in her normally smooth and aggravatingly clear forehead pulsing.

"When?"

"When you got home from your stupid coffee date! I waited for two hours, then I called you, but you didn't answer, so I called Luc and he... he..."

"Mado?" Madeleine's shouted response is so out of proportion with the situation that I almost find myself laughing.

"What?"

"Didn't Luc tell you? I'm not home yet."

"You're not...?"

"Lauran and I were at the *Café des Éditeurs* for almost three hours. I was on my way up the stairs to my apartment when you called, but I had to stop walking – I can't walk and listen at the same time, at least not when you're hysterical."

"I hope he solved your Rubik's cube. You certainly gave him enough time."

I can't help rolling my eyes, even though Madeleine isn't there to see it. "I didn't think to ask. We were just talking."

Madeleine snorts with derision. "More of your great love nonsense, *n'est-ce pas*?"

"Just a dinner date tomorrow night," I shrug, trying to sound nonchalant even though my heart flutters at the thought of it. "I doubt that's what you would call great love."

"*Putain*!" Madeleine curses, just before hanging up on me. "For this, I have to find something to wear to *Septime*!"

§

Fourteen of the fifteen text messages on my *portable* are from a frantic Luc, demanding to know where I am, why I'm not home for dinner and who has kidnapped me. (The fifteenth is from Martine, inquiring about my still unsolved Rubik's cube. Frustrated by my inability to accomplish in weeks what would normally take me hours, I delete it.) They end abruptly at 7:30pm, around the time that Lauran and I were walking down *boulevard Saint-Germain* – that would be when Madeleine called.

I sit on the landing while I clear away all of the messages, then stand up, straighten my too-tight jeans around my calves and climb the last two flights of stairs to the fourth floor.

Standing in the hall, outside the blue door to our apartment, I can hear my brother pacing on the parquet. For a second I hesitate, keys in hand, wondering if I could possibly find anywhere else to disappear for a few more hours – just until Luc's panic about the reality of taking Madeleine to dinner has subsided. But the memory of all the times that Luc sat with me at the hospital, building *theraputty* animals with me to help strengthen my left hand; all of the night terrors he has calmed me from; all of the dinners he has misguidedly attempted to cook, compels me to put my key in the lock. Sometimes, guilt makes me a better person – or at least, a better sister.

"Sophie! Thank goodness you're home!" Luc is elated when he sees me come in.

"Sorry I'm so late, I should have-"

But not for the reason I think. Luc cuts me off mid-sentence, skipping right over the *I was worried sick* speech to, "I need your advice. I'm taking Madeleine out to dinner on Saturday and I don't know…" he runs his fingers through his hair, which already stands on end from repeated stress-induced finger combing. "I don't know anything!"

I can't help but laugh a little to myself as I kick off my shoes. My brother is normally so even-tempered, but when he decides to be melodramatic, he can give Marcel Proust a run for his money. "What have you been doing so far?"

"I don't know," Luc wails, loud enough that I'm sure Stéfane and Martine can hear him next door. "Most of the time she barely acknowledges that I'm alive! She only ever calls to talk about you. And when I call, she almost never answers!"

"What about when you're together?" I'm beginning to pity my brother a bit. I know Madeleine's volatile moods and unconventional opinions like a meteorologist knows the weather — I can predict them, but I can't control them. Luc is an unwitting observer, standing in a downpour without an umbrella.

"When we're together, she's wonderful."

That's what I was afraid of — just the thought of being with Madeleine has my brother practically swooning. It's too risky to give him any real advice — he's in too deep, and if I make the wrong suggestion, he'll end up resenting me for it. "Well," I shrug, only half-serious, "figure out what you've been doing all along, and keep doing it. You're obviously wearing her down."

Before Luc can protest, I disappear down the hall to my bedroom — Madeleine isn't the only one who has to find something to wear out to dinner.

**Chapter 12**

When the doorbell rings on Thursday evening, I am standing in my bedroom, still in my bra and panties, contemplating the contents of my closet. I am faced with a line-up of nearly identical black sweaters, slim cut jeans (also mostly black) and black pumps. Two berets — black and red — hang on hooks on the inside of the closet doors. Based on the empirical evidence, I'm astounded that no one has guessed my true chosen vocation.

I dress like a Marxist. A Marxist who doesn't get out much.

"Sophie!" Luc calls from the hallway. "Lauran is here!"

"Just a minute!"

A pair of gray jeans hangs directly in front of me. I yank them off their hanger and shove myself into them in a rush, one-handed, while I rifle through my closet with my left elbow, in search of a sweater that stands out from the rest. I settle for a black off-the-shoulder number with rhinestones, and slip it on backwards to avoid exposing my scar. Two swipes of mascara, one pair of peep-toe pumps and a generous dose of red lipstick later, I'm as ready as I'll ever be. Facing myself in the mirror, I take a final deep breath to steel my nerves.

When I step out into the hall, Luc and Lauran both gape. I can't decide if I should be flattered by their less than subtle admiration, or concerned about how plain

I look in everyday life. "*Bon soir*," I smile at Lauran before turning to my brother. "Have you introduced yourself?"

Luc shakes his head. "I opened the door, but then I had to stir the soup…"

"Which it looks like it's about to boil over." I swear, if we could go one week without Luc letting soup boil over, it would be some kind of achievement. "But before you go clean it up, I want to give you a long overdue introduction to my friend, Lauran Etcheverria."

Both men extend their hands, and they shake, exchanging *Nice to meet you*s. It's such a simple gesture, it seems almost ridiculous to think of the fact that it's taken seven years for it to happen. But seven years ago, I remind myself, the scene would have been much less simple. There would have been name calling. And tears. Probably mine.

"Lauran is from Saint-Antoine," I add. "We were at school together."

My brother turns pale when he realises the implications of my statement. "I should really clean up that soup," he mumbles, before rushing off to the kitchen, calling out a self-conscious, "Have a nice time!" The empty kitchen hears his words more distinctly then we do.

"Was that too little, too late?" I ask Lauran as I reach into the hall closet to retrieve my (also black) coat.

There is a twinkle of mischief in Lauran's eye when he says, "Better late than never."

§

I'm so caught up in the thrill of walking across *pont Marie* next to Lauran; being with him because he asked me to be; hearing our footsteps echo in unison on the concrete, that at first I don't say much. My date is quiet, too – he remarks, barely audibly, on the chill in the early November air, then jams his hands into his coat pockets and picks up his pace.

It isn't until we're walking down the black stairs into the *Pont-Marie* metro station that I think to ask, "Where are we going?"

Lauran is caught off guard. "I'm sorry, I should have told you. I made a reservation at a little restaurant in Montmartre called *Afghani*. I think you'll really enjoy it. Have you ever had Afghan food?"

We stand side-by-side on the platform, waiting for the number seven train to *La Courneuve – 8 mai 1945*. The white tiled walls on both sides of the platform are cluttered with giant advertising posters for cell phones and sales at *BHV*. A *Selecta* vending machine hums behind us, giving off a neon glow. *Maman* and *papa* brought Luc and me to Paris at school holiday once, when we were little. I was impressed by the candy coloured dome at *Galéries Lafayette,* and I marvelled at how far I could see from the top of the Eiffel Tower. But what I remembered most vividly for years after was the metro stations; the tiles, the garbage, the crush of the crowds and the violent rush of wind from an arriving train. The out-of-place fruit stands, the Technicolour movie posters, the smells and the small orchestra that played Mozart against the garish orange backdrop of *Châtelet* station.

Now that I live in Paris, I almost never take the metro – I can walk to everywhere I might need to go; school, *Monoprix* to get groceries, cafés and movie theatres and boutiques, in ten minutes or less. Every time I take the stairs down into a metro station for a longer trip, I feel like I'm starting out on a grand adventure. But tonight I barely turn my head to take in the surroundings. I'm busy staring at my ex-boyfriend, baffled by the simple way that he has always known how to surprise me. "I didn't know they had food," I admit, blushing a little. Lauran is the only person I've ever met who makes me feel like I haven't seen and experienced everything there is in life. "I mean, not the kind of food you can get in restaurants..." Aware that I've begun to babble, I let my voice trail off without finishing my sentence.

Above us, the electric sign for the train to *La Courneuve* begins to flash double zeros, indicating that the train is approaching. A gust of wind rushes along the platform as the rickety old train pulls into the station. Lauran reaches out and flips the silver handle to open the door to a half-empty car. I follow him in. The worn red and blue fabric covered seats are occupied by elderly ladies in fur coats, mothers carrying groceries on one arm and children on the other and tall men who don't quite know where to put their knees. We stand, leaning against the brushed metal poles between the doors.

"You aren't entirely wrong about that," Lauran tells me. The train begins to move under us, the heavy wheels squealing against the tracks, but it isn't the rocking of the cars that makes me dizzy. Lauran looks straight into my eyes as he talks, and the force of his gaze somehow loosens my grip on spatial reality. I know that there are other people in the car with us, but they seem to be moving out of the periphery of my awareness. All I can see is Lauran. And yet, I hesitate to look at him too directly, afraid that if I look at his eyes, and his lips, for too long, I'll give myself away completely.

I don't know what difference it might make if I do give myself away, and yet, I can't let myself do it. Maybe it's the terrorists I grew up with, whose secrecy I learned too well. Or a little bit of my controlling *aita* in me. I'm always afraid that if I give anyone too much of myself, it will give them power over me.

"As far as I know, *Afghani* is the only Afghan restaurant in Paris. I've never really gone looking for Afghan Food anywhere else. They definitely don't have it in Ziga," my ex-boyfriend smiles. "I've really never travelled outside of France aside from that trip," he admits. "I feel a bit pretentious talking about Afghan food, to be completely honest. But it's good, I promise."

The train pulls into *Châtelet* station in a rush and stops with a geriatric groan. A crowd waits on the platform, loaded down with parcels from the shops on *rue de Rivoli*. The crush of bodies nearly obscures the blue and white *Châtelet (Pont au Change)* signs on the tile wall. The door opens, Lauran guides me protectively out into the surging crowd without every laying a hand on me. We move against traffic, through the long, orange-walled corridor that separates line seven from line four. The sign for *Porte de Clignancourt* is barely visible, but Lauran knows the way and directs me gently when I stray from the course.

On the staircase down to the platform, we have to step around a drawn-looking girl in a black headscarf, begging for *centimes* with an empty soup can to catch the rare donations. "What is Afghan food like?" I ask Lauran, just to fill the silence and avoid looking at the teenaged beggar, who has a fresh, glaring black eye.

Lauran stands with his back to the girl, obviously disturbed. I'm grateful when the double zeroes begin to flash above us. "It's not like anything you ever would have eaten in Saint-Antoine. But then again, you can say that about almost anything in Paris..."

§

We take the train to *Château-Rouge* metro station, where we descend, several stories below the dingy *boulevard Barbès* in Montmartre. I secretly love this part of Paris best of all — during the day, the streets are packed with throngs of people looking for the best price on cheap wash cloths and knock-off cell phones. Immigrant men stand on the street corners, hawking bootleg cigarettes with the rhythmic chant, "Marlboro, Marlboro, Marlboro." Just down the street, on *boulevard de la Chapelle*, there is a man who deals three card Monte; a man who sells putrid-looking perfume in Chanel bottles out of his trench coat; a group of men with all of the fake Louis Vuitton merchandise you could possibly hope to buy; a man who roasts chestnuts in gasoline and sells them from a shopping cart, infecting the street with a toxic stench and, on the median, a crepe stand run by gypsies.

Compared to the tranquil Ile-Saint-Louis, Montmartre is a bizarre, slightly macabre wonderland, much like I imagined the capital when I read Victor Hugo's *Notre-Dame de Paris*. I brought Luc up here once, to show him what it was like, and we left within half an hour. Where I see an intriguing cast of characters, he only saw probable thieves and slow-moving tourists.

When I step out into the night with Lauran by my side, the boulevard is deserted and almost eerily quiet. The hum of streetlights is audible. "Montmartre is exactly how I imagined Paris when I was a little provincial *minette* in Saint-Antoine," I tell Lauran. "It seems a little silly now."

"It doesn't seem silly to me — I always imagined that all of Paris was exactly the way Montmartre is." Lauran rubs his hands together to warm them. "If it weren't for the fact that school is on the *rive gauche*, I would probably live up here. I like it better than anywhere else in Paris."

"So do I. I love the way it feels alive."

We follow *rue du Poulet*, an unlit street lined with garishly painted shops — *Ana's Cosmétique* offers cheap skin whiteners for North African women. Two competing shops, *Sonia Cosmétique* and *Mama Cosmétique*, both hideously pink, are across the street and ten metres down the block, respectively. We pass a barely identifiable *École de Conduite* just as a young man roars past us on a precarious motorbike at about a hundred kilometres an hour — the irony is so poignant that we both laugh out loud.

*Rue de Poulet* meets *rue de Clignanourt* at a triangular intersection dotted by brasseries, discount shoe stores and an American-style hamburger shop. Through the front windows, we can see diners cutting their burgers with knives and forks as we pass.

I follow Lauran across the street to *rue Muller* and when I look up, I can see *Basilique Sacré-Coeur* illuminating the skyline above me, a white beacon in the night. The view is breathtaking enough to distract me from the fact that I have to walk uphill, and cross unevenly cobbled streets, in heels.

At the top of the small hill, there is a café with rainbow coloured chairs at the base of a staircase to the basilica. I stop for a moment to catch my breath and just look up, straight up, at the church on the hill. "I don't believe in God," I tell Lauran quietly, "but when I see a sight like this, I know how much it means to believe in something; how faith can inspire people to great, and crazy, things."

"It's funny that you say that," Lauran half-smiles, wistful. "Whenever I come up here, it always makes me wish I believed in something."

For a minute we just stand there, side by side, looking up at the white cathedral. Lauran rubs the back of his neck, then lets his hand fall and says, "Come on, Sophie, let's go to dinner."

§

The store front at *Afghani* is painted a shade of telltale green, with white lettering in the Roman and Arabic alphabets. A small menu is framed at the door, but unlit — I can scarcely make out any words in the dark before Lauran opens the door and holds it out so I can step inside.

We take two steps down into a small, dimly lit dining room. Gauzy curtains cover the windows — no outside light passes through the thick fabric. A young man, who speaks quietly to hide his accent, shows us to a small wooden table — a traditional Afghan dress is proudly displayed on the wall above my chair.

I leave the food choices to Lauran — maybe because of all the summers I spent in Basque Country, eating whatever was available because there was always a lingering doubt about where the next meal would come from, and when it would come, but I've never been fussy about food. I know what I like, but there is little that I could honestly say I dislike. None of the names of the dishes sound remotely familiar, but I'm perfectly happy as soon as a bottle of wine and a basket of flat, moist bread are served.

"What was it like to be betrothed?" Lauran asks. "I've been thinking about it all day and I can't wrap my mind around the concept of knowing who I was going to marry when I was only four. When I was four, my main ambition was to become Tin Tin."

I take a sip of my wine. "For me, it was surreal. I was only betrothed two months every year — the rest of the time, I lived in a world where marriages were optional, and based on love, or at least a feeling mistaken for it. I think for everyone else, it was just a fact of life. Betrothal, even marriage, rarely stopped anyone in my little village from doing exactly what they wanted to, with whomever they wanted to."

I can't help smiling, "My *aita*'s henchmen, Balere and Remiri, are both married, but they've been having an affair with each other since they were about sixteen."

Lauran nearly chokes on a piece of bread. "Gay terrorists? That's a new one."

"I think they were actually more brutal and ruthless than anyone else – as a way to compensate; to prove their masculinity, or maybe just to prove that they could, and would, take out anyone who questioned their choices. But anyone with eyes could see it, if they wanted to. A lot of people didn't, of course. They operate in Argentina now. Whenever I think of them, I imagine them dancing at *Carnaval* with fruit hats and tiny shorts. They were more subtle than that, mind you – rough and ungroomed and bass-voiced – but I can't help myself."

"And what about you?" Lauran raises an eyebrow, teasing. "Did being betrothed ever stop you from anything?"

"You forget," I smile. "My betrothed died before I turned eleven. There were no boys in the community left unspoken for. Widows live outside of the rules."

§

It seems strange to tell you this – I promise not to dwell on the details unnecessarily. I would skip over this part of the story entirely if I could; I'm sure you don't want to hear about my former lovers any more than I would want to hear about yours. But when Gabrié came to find me in the *despachos* that afternoon, he put his hand on my cheek and my story changed.

Gab and I were inseparable that summer. We still argued – we might even have argued more, especially in public. We spent every free moment we had in the privacy of the *despachos*, away from prying eyes. But in town, Gabrié was promised to Alaine Remeteria and I was an unwelcome foreigner. Everything that we did, everything that we felt for each other was best left unsaid – and so it went unsaid, even just between us. We were our own best kept secret.

If I had learned anything from the mistakes I made with you, it should have been to say what I felt... To be willing to share it with anyone who would listen. I wish now that I had shouted from the rooftops just how much I loved Gabrié. It wouldn't have changed anything that happened, but at least he would have heard me.

Instead, I was more afraid than ever. I lived in a state of uncontrollable paranoia, plotting elaborate routes to the *despachos* to avoid detection, constantly panicked about being caught. At the end of the summer, I was devastated and relieved at once. We said our good-byes privately, and when we did, I knew that Gabrié loved me. He didn't say it, and I didn't need to hear it.

I didn't say it, either, and I have lived to regret it.

That was the last time I saw Gabrié completely alive. Two months later, while I was deep in the throes of studying for my *bacc.* and completing university applications, he was arrested by the *Ertzaintza* when he stopped for coffee at *Café Iruña* on a routine trip to Bilbao. He was supposed to be buying construction supplies to repair the rubble that had once been the front steps on my parents' house – just two bags of concrete and some plywood. He never came home.

§

"Who are the *Ertzaintza*?" Lauran asks through a mouthful of something called *bolani*. There is a feast spread out on the table between us, kebabs and eggplant and leek-filled raviolis drizzled with yogurt, but I've been so busy talking about Gab that I've barely had a mouthful.

"The Basque secret police." I can feel my lips twist into a cruel, mocking smile as I say those words. "A brilliant plot on the part of the Spanish government, really." I reach across the table and stab a ravioli with my fork, popping it into my mouth whole. "These really are delicious."

"How are the secret police a Spanish government plot...?" Lauran is skeptical.

"If the Euskadi catch their own terrorists, there is an illusion of Euskadi autonomy. As long as the Spanish government does not officially involve itself with the police force, they cannot be seen to be interfering in the affairs of the independent Euskadi people. But, Basque Country is in Spain — that makes the *Ertzaintza* a public organisation, just like the Guardia Civil. The only difference is that the officers are Basque, and their task is to persecute — excuse me, prosecute — Basque people for their crimes. And a significant portion of their mandate relates specifically to political crimes."

"It sounds abhorrent, the way you tell it."

"It's not the way I tell it," I can feel my blood pressure begin to rise. "Those are the facts."

"Well," Lauran smiles, in a feeble attempt to lighten the mood, and move the subject away from extreme left politics, "you certainly know the material."

"I've been studying it for almost ten years," I joke. Even if I hope that Lauran will one day see the world the way I do, I know better than to try to indoctrinate him over dinner. "But Thursday has always been my day off from lecturing, so I'm sorry, but I can't tell you anymore about Euskadi politics tonight."

§

We linger over cardamom tea and honey-soaked pastries, chatting about nothing in particular — the weather, the perturbing tendency of our linguistics professor has of scratching his nose with a piece of chalk rather than his finger, the strange and yet completely typical small town where we grew up.

When our waiter brings the cheque, Lauran reaches for it without hesitation. He helps me with my coat, under the guise that I genuinely need assistance because my left hand is weak. But even as he follows me up the steps and out the door into the night, he never touches me. The physical distance between us is conspicuous, and seems almost deliberate, like he's restraining himself. I can only speculate about what that might mean, and none of the theories I come up with point to him still wanting me the way that I want him.

Out on the cobbled streets, I strike a match; the flame pops and flares, illuminating the dark street for brief instant before I light my cigarette. Lauran does the same. We walk side by side in silence to the base of the steps that lead to the basilica, inhaling.

I stop at the stairs and look up one more time at the glowing cathedral, then sit down on the concrete steps with my back to it. Lauran sits beside me; together, we block half the staircase. For a long moment we are silent, cigarettes burning bright against the darkness.

"I had a really nice time tonight, Sophie." My ex-boyfriend says the words into the night, rather than turning to face me.

"So did I."

"This is probably premature, but I'd like to take you out again. This weekend, if you're free?"

"I'd love to," I blurt out in a rush, before I realise, "but I can't. I'm going to Bordeaux this weekend, to visit my *anaia*. I leave tomorrow after my classes are over. You're welcome to come along if you'd like. I'm sure there are still tickets." For the second time in two nights, I clamp my hand over my mouth, shocked by my own words. Lauran just laughs, and shakes his head, making no effort to conceal how funny he finds my little bursts of openness. "I just can't keep my mouth shut around you, can I?"

"It's a change, I admit. You used to be so restrained."

"You could come to Bordeaux, if you wanted," I hear myself off. "It won't be an exciting trip, just two days of chatting with my *anaia* and his girlfriend – who is, I should mention, the worst cook in the known universe. They just have a small apartment and-"

"I'd like that."

"Pardon me?" I'm certain that I must be having some kind of episode – my ex-boyfriend can't possibly have said what I just heard.

"I said I'd like to come. If you don't mind walking down to *Gare du Nord* with me, I'll buy a train ticket tonight."

When I hear Lauran say those words, after I realise I haven't imagined them, my heart does something it never has before – it actually sings. Not literally, of course. But for an instant I step outside of my body. I can see myself sitting next to Lauran; a golden glow from the cathedral envelops us and the opening bars of Beethoven's *Ode to Joy* blare.

And then I'm back on the steps. "Of course," I agree. "Shall we?"

As we walk together down the hill, there is a stubborn skip in my step. I'm so happy, I nearly trip over my own feet twice.

## Chapter 13

I can't sleep.

When I came home, Luc was listless. He followed me around while I packed my overnight bag for Bordeaux, often looking like he wanted to say something, then changing his mind at the last second.

After about twenty minutes of listening to him pace around my bedroom behind me, sitting down then standing up then sitting down again, I couldn't take it anymore. Normally I pack for Bordeaux in five minutes, but with Lauran coming along, I face the added pressure of looking pretty while I'm there. Luc's endless movement was distracting me while I tried to scrutinise my collection of black sweaters to find the best, or comparatively, the least boring, ones.

"What do you want?" I demanded, turning to face my brother.

"Nothing, really…"

"If you didn't want something, you wouldn't have followed me in here when I got home."

Luc sighed and sat down on my bed again. Still, he said nothing. Frustrated, I turned back to my closet and went on sorting my sweaters one-by-one. It was only when my back was turned that my brother finally got the words out. "How old were you, when you dated Lauran?"

"Fifteen." In spite of the fact that I could tell our conversation was going in a rather serious direction, I kept my head in the closet, reasoning that direct eye contact might be too much for my brother to handle.

"And... why did you break up?"

"I wouldn't introduce him to our family. He thought I was somehow embarrassed by him. I couldn't find the words to articulate the truth... Or maybe I just didn't think he would believe me."

"Shit. I'm sure I'm at least partially responsible for that."

"You're ninety-nine percent responsible for that," I snapped, my old wounds stinging. I left that one percent for the nagging feeling I always had that *maman* and *papa* never really disciplined Luc for his abusive behaviour because they subconsciously shared his point of view... at the time it was just a feeling, but it turned out in the end that I was right.

"I'm really sorry. I just want you to know that."

I sighed and turn to face my brother, a pile of sweaters under my arm. "Look, Luc, I've forgiven you. There's no way I could live here if I hadn't." I sat down on the bed across from my brother, folding my clothes in my lap, preparing to be more honest and forthright with him than I ever had been. Or likely ever would be again. "I don't know what it was like to be you, growing up. To watch your parents try and try for another child as if you weren't enough. To have someone else's sister come home one day and be told to call her your own... And then to have her captivate the attention of the entire town, not just your parents, for three solid years while you went on quietly achieving things worthy of real recognition... I'm sure that was hard for you. I have no doubt that it made you angry and resentful. I expect that you blamed me for all of it. I think you're starting to appreciate how hard the manner in which you expressed your feelings made my life, and I'm glad. I've forgiven you, but I haven't forgotten, especially where Lauran is concerned. I know you're a very different person now, so I want to say just forget it; it was no big deal, but... I can't lie to you."

Luc ran his fingers through his hair. "Good to know. What time do you leave tomorrow?"

I stood up and turned back to my closet. These conversations always go the same way. My brother asks when I'm leaving. I tell him. He pauses, like he wants to ask something else... Then he tells me to have a good time and leaves the room.

"My train leaves just before 4:30 tomorrow afternoon."

For a second, Luc paused. He opened his mouth, and closed it again. Then he stood up, told me to have a good trip and left the room.

And now I lay on my back in the dark, quilt pulled up to my chin, eyes wide open on a view of the ceiling. The clock says it's after midnight, but I can't sleep for wondering why Luc never asks about Bordeaux. It could be because he suspects what I might tell him, what he doesn't want to know. After all, if he doesn't know for sure, then he doesn't have to lay awake at night, worrying and wondering what he can do to try to stop me. It could simply be that he is afraid to ask, because he already knows the truth and can't bear hearing me lie to his face. But I am terrified that in reality, it's that he still, consciously or subconsciously, loathes the Basque people, the way he was raised to. Which would mean, whether he fully comprehends it or not, that he still hates me.

§

I can't sleep.

The thought of sitting next to Lauran on the train for three hours makes my heart race. I can feel it pounding all the way through my body, even in my left hand.

Talking about Gab over dinner — or trying not to talk about him, really — made me remember what it was like to be with him. And what it was like to be with Lauran. Thinking about the first time we had sex isn't exactly helping me to feel less anxious about taking him along with Bordeaux tomorrow...

I've had other lovers, of course, but all of them briefly and with a certain amount of disinterest. As far as I'm concerned, most of them are not worth remembering. Gab and Lauran are the only two who really count. At times I've even compared them; although I am so ashamed of having done it that I hate to admit it even to myself.

The truth is that there is no comparison. The first time I was with Lauran was the first time I had been with anyone. It was Sunday morning; he made an excuse to miss mass by telling his parents he had a test to study for. I feigned illness and snuck out of mass just before Father Philippe began his sermon. I ran across town as fast as my legs would carry me. Lauran was waiting at the back door of his parents' house. We walked to his bedroom in silence, avoiding direct eye contact. It was Lauran's first time, too, and neither one of us quite knew where we were supposed to look or put our hands.

We undressed together in his small, brown carpeted bedroom. As soon as our clothes lay scattered on the floor and we faced each other, completely exposed, instinct took over. It was a groping, fumbling, nervous instinct — we broke two condoms, and I hit my head on the wall — but we knew more or less what to do, and figured out the finer details together as we went along.

Afterward, we lay together on his single bed, breathless and giddy and just a little surprised that what we had waited our whole lives, and the first three agonising months of our relationship for, was over so quickly. We had time to try it twice more before I slipped my Sunday dress back on and sprinted home to bed. My cheeks were so flushed from that mad dash that *maman* and *papa* were convinced I was feverish, and they kept me home from school for two days. I spent the whole time in bed, dreaming of how Lauran looked — and felt — naked. It was bliss.

Lauran and I had planned every detail of our escapade, practically down to the minutia. We had no choice. Our parents were strict, and privacy in Saint-Antoine was a luxury, not a right. With Gab, I had no idea what was going to happen. I was brooding in the *despachos* when he found me — looking for an argument, I assumed. I called him a bastard, just like I always did, and demanded to know what he wanted.

He walked behind the desk, too close for comfort — I rolled my chair backward until I hit the wall.

He had me trapped. "I didn't come here for that," he told me quietly, placing one calloused hand gently on my cheek.

I tried to push the desk chair back, beyond his reach, but I was pinned against the wall. I stood up and pushed the chair to the side, inching backward until my back pressed against the floral wallpaper. "What, then? Is someone looking for me?"

"Only me."

Gab took my face in his hands and kissed me so hard that I could barely breathe. My mind raced — what was he doing? Was he crazy? I thought he hated me! I hated him... At least, I thought I hated him. With his body leaning into mine, I was much less sure that what I felt for him was loathing. It might, I realised, have been more like love all along.

That was when I started to kiss him back.

Tough talking, gun toting terrorist, Gabrié Duarte was a virgin at twenty. I should have expected it — his marriage to Alaine Remeteria was scheduled for the following spring, after she turned eighteen — but the way he commandeered weapons and missions and even simple conversations, I felt sure he had commandeered a few of the girls in the village, too. But in private he was shy. He hesitated. He had never seen a naked woman before. So I touched him the way I knew would make him feel good, and I guided him, showing him what I wanted.

We cleared the desk in the executive office. I taught him how to make love to me, and only me.

When it was over, we lay together on the lacquered desktop, shoulder to shoulder, Gab's arm wrapped protectively around my neck. "You're perfect," he told me, leaning in to kiss my cheek. It was the one and only time that summer that he told me openly how he felt about me. "Just like I always imagined."

"Oh? Did you imagine often?" I teased.

"Only every night for the past three years."

I smile into the darkness, remembering that moment. It's my favourite memory of Gab, a story I've never told anyone.

The real reason I don't share it is that after a moment of feeling awestruck by Gab's remarkable sincerity, I found myself thinking of Lauran Etcheverria while I kissed him.

§

I can't sleep.

I can't shake the feeling that this trip to Bordeaux is my chance to finally make things right with Lauran... And that somehow, inevitably, I'll get it wrong and lose him forever.

## Chapter 14

The platform at *Gare Montparnasse* is always crowded on Friday afternoon. Commuters with rolling suitcases race anxiously in time with the clack-clack-clack of the *Arrivées et Départs* sign, counting down until their train rolls to the top of the list and the weekend begins. Students, weighed down by textbooks and laundry, hover in tight circles, chattering about overwhelming assignments — and the more enjoyable things they will do over the weekend even though they know they should work be working on them.

I stand alone near the track, tote bag slung over my shoulder, gazing up at the *Arrivées et Départs* notice periodically in an effort to appear relaxed. For most of my trips to Bordeaux, I sprint into the station five minutes before the train leaves, carrying whatever clothes I stuffed into my tote bag before bed the previous night, coat and gloves only halfway on. I only remember my train ticket about half of the time, and usually have to dig out my *portable* to show proof of payment when the ticket collector comes around.

Today, I have planned every detail. In the morning before school, I chose the most stylish travel outfit I could come up with from my limited wardrobe — jeans, pumps, and my only white sweater, topped with my red beret. I added a navy coat and designer handbag, both cast-offs from Gen's closet, expertly remade by her tailor to fit my tiny frame. I carried my luggage to my classes so I could take my time getting to the train station. If I had set out to prove that I am capable of catching a train on time without being a frazzled mess, I would have succeeded. I arrived painfully early, and have wandered aimlessly into the cluttered magazine shop five times, even though I have no need for reading material, just to distract myself. I'm too nervous to sit — Lauran might not see me when he comes in and think that I've been playing a cruel joke on him all these weeks. Or he might think he's off the hook and leave the station as quickly as he came.

My thoughts are frantic. I look up at the *Arrivées et Départs* board yet again; the train to Bordeaux is still five lines away from the top of the list. A red *Thalys* train for Amsterdam pulls away from the station and the board begins it clack-clack rotation, the white letters rolling over to reveal the next departure. I contemplate ducking into the magazine shop again. And then someone walks up behind me and says, "*Bon après-midi*, Sophie."

Startled, I jump. I can't help it. Ever since Gab died, I scare easily — Luc has nearly sent me into cardiac arrest once or twice, coming home late at night when I'm in bed. I clamp my hand over my mouth to stifle my inevitable shriek. I can't seem to get over being jumpy, but I've learned to cope.

"Sophie?" Lauran's voice is low and gentle, filled with concern. "It's only me. I didn't mean to scare you; I thought you would be expecting me."

I turn to face my ex-boyfriend, hand still over my mouth, cheeks burning. "I am," I start, through my fingers. "I mean…" I free my mouth from my own grasp, "I was. I'm sorry, it's not you. I get scared easily… Loud noises, especially."

"I've noticed," Lauran smiles, a bit wistfully. "You always used to be so on your guard. No one could have surprised you if they tried. What happened?"

For a second, I remember when I realised that Gab had a gun. "Someone did surprise me, once. I'm always a bit afraid it might happened again." I pause, trying to laugh off the devastating memory. "Besides, I thought you might change your mind. Very few people are brave enough to face an entire weekend with the Sagastizabals."

Sweet, naïve Lauran just grins, "I think I'm up to it."

Little does he know what kind of surprise is in store for him... not only will he be visiting terrorists, he'll also be travelling with one! He isn't ready to hear that yet, and I know it. This trip was never part of the plan. If I didn't want to be with him so desperately, I would send him home right now.

Above us, the *Arrivées et Departs* board begins to clack-clack-clack again, the letters rolling over to announce the next train. "It looks like we're up," Lauran smiles. "Are you ready?"

As ready as I'll ever be. "Let's go."

§

I look out the window as the train pulls away from the station. Even though I love Paris, I never tire of the feeling of leaving the city for somewhere else; of imagining that I am at the beginning of a wonderful adventure, not just a weekend visit to my *anaia*. When the train is out on the track, and I can see the glass-panelled roof of *Gare Montparnasse* shrinking in the distance, I know we're on our way.

I turn to face Lauran, and I can see that he has been watching me, not the scenery passing outside the window. "You look like you want to ask me something."

Lauran shakes his head and smiles. "Not really. It's just that we left off in the middle of your story last night, and I'm curious what you'll say next."

My heart pounds a wild staccato rhythm against my chest. I have to look back out the window to hide the fact that I'm hyperventilating a little bit. Two weeks ago, we couldn't stop spitting insults at each other. Last week, I had given up on us entirely. I can't get used to this kindness. Every time Lauran says a word that even hints that he might still have feelings for me, I swoon – and panic at the same time. "Well," I tell him, deliberately cryptic, "I suppose I'll start at the beginning of the end; the day that Ilari came to Saint-Antoine."

§

"...It was February, two weeks after my birthday. I was eighteen and on top of the world. My application to La Sorbonne's French literature program had been accepted — even my special petition to include a linguistic component had been approved by the CELTA school. I spent an absurd amount of time researching my perfect Parisian apartment. And when I wasn't contemplating a gray and white colour scheme with turquoise accents, I was planning potential topics for my graduate thesis. Already. I wanted to focus on the portrayal of the political process in Dumas' novels about the three musketeers. It was obsessive, but I couldn't stop myself — I had heard so much about the alleged "real world" from my teachers that it seemed to me that it must be a wonderful, romantic place, nothing at all like judgemental Saint-Antoine or ignorant Basque Country. I was dying to get out into it; to be free of the cloisters of my double life forever. My teenaged misery had lifted the moment I woke up on my eighteenth birthday. I was free of Euskal Herria — and soon I would be free of Saint-Antoine, too.

If I could go back and tell myself what I know now, I know that I wouldn't believe me.

All my life, I had had only one true friend in Saint-Antoine, Margaux Lacabanne, the town... well, slut, for lack of a better word. But I had made a surprising alliance that fall in Patrice Carbodel, the grocer's youngest son. Patrice had always floated on the periphery of my existence, occasionally too close for comfort — he once put a frog down my dress during mass — but I knew very little of him after *quatrième*, when he started dating my nemesis, Caroline Touron.

You might remember Caroline, the self-proclaimed angel of Saint-Antoine. She called me *Sophie l'Orpheline*, a nickname that stuck for years. But my real quarrel with her was that we always got equal grades, even when I scored higher than she did. The nonsensical bonus points teachers gave her, just because she was the mayor's daughter, were infuriating beyond measure.

When I came home from Euskal Herria after what was ostensibly the last summer I was obligated to spend there, Patrice and Caroline had split up. I went into

*Épicerie Carbodel* one September afternoon to buy cigarettes. Patrice was working the cash register and the store was empty. We got to talking about our plans for university — I was stunned to learn that he was almost as ambitious as I was. He had been accepted to a *classe préparatoire aux grandes écoles* in BCPST1 — biology and earth science, essentially, at *Lycée Pierre de Fermat* in Toulouse. He couldn't wait, he said, "to live somewhere where I'm not the grocer's son."

I knew exactly what he meant.

Margaux found Patrice insipid and nerdy. Patrice didn't know what to make of Margaux's habit of stealing from the offertory plate at mass to fund her online shopping habit. (Strangely, he wasn't at all bothered by her nymphomania.) Unless it was unavoidable, I spent time with them separately.

I was out with Patrice that night, strolling down *rue Principale*. It was raining, but only just. I was babbling on about an abstract political theory — meritocracy, I think; still one of my favourites, even though I know I'm idealistic for thinking it's possible that political appointment might be based on anything other than wealth and influence. My friend seemed to be listening politely — until he abruptly picked me up, slung me over his shoulder and ran down the street like a lunatic while I screamed bloody murder.

When he put me down two blocks later, I punched him. Not hard enough, evidently. "What is wrong with you?"

That's when he kissed me.

I pulled back instantly. "Patrice, what are you doing?"

He pulled me in again, as if to offer a demonstration. It was when he put his clammy lips against mine again that I heard it.

"Amaia!"

I tore myself out of Patrice's grasp. "Stop that!"

The voice came closer. It was unmistakable. "Amaia, it's me!"

To be clear, when I turned eighteen, I didn't plan to cut ties with my biological family. I planned to visit. I wanted to see Gab again, and my *anaia*. But I wanted to do it on my own terms, not because I was bound by a court order and held at gun point.

When I turned around, Ilari was right there. In his combat boots and dark coat, he almost blended into the night, but his eyes were bright. "Amaia."

"What are you doing here?" I hissed.

Patrice grabbed my wrist protectively. "Do you two know each other?"

My *anaia* reached for his gun. For a second I saw my two worlds on a collisions course. "Put that away!" I snapped at Ilari in Euskara. He nodded and tucked his Browning 9mm back under his coat. "And you," I wrenched free of Patrice's grasp yet again, "Let go of me, for God's sake! I don't feel that way about you, all right?"

"Who is he?" Patrice demanded, a tremor in his voice. He was visibly upset – his lower lip quivered; his nostrils flared – and obviously convinced that Ilari was my boyfriend.

"He's-"

"I'm her brother," Ilari interrupted, in heavily accented, but otherwise flawless, French. All I could do was gape. My *anaia* had spent two weeks in France once – just long enough to learn to say *Je m'appelle Ilari* and *Où sont les toilettes?* His newfound linguistic ability explained how he had crossed the border... But raised a thousand other questions.

There was an awkward scene in the street. Patrice protested that Luc was my brother. Ilari scoffed. I asked Patrice if he knew where I went in the summers. Father Philippe told him I was sick, and that he should pray for me, he said. I got angry. I accused him of spending time with me out of pity. He swore up and down that it wasn't true. And then he said it.

"I'm in love with you."

"I have to go," I told him, mortified. Then I turned to Ilari and whispered desperately in Euskara, "Please tell me that you parked close by!"

My *anaia* just laughed and motioned for me to follow me. We left Patrice alone in the rain on *rue Principale*. I've never seen him again, but I heard he was accepted to the *École Normale Supérieure de Lyon* two years ago. He's probably close to finishing his *licence* by now...

§

"What a heartbreaker you were," Lauran teases.

"I never meant to be!" I protest. "It was one thing with you... But Patrice blindsided me. In the six months we were friends, he never gave the slightest hint that he had feelings for me!" I realise that I'm yelling. "Sorry. I guess I'm still a bit sensitive about it."

"I can tell."

My ex-boyfriend isn't the only one who can tell — passengers in rows all around us have turned to see who the crazy girl is. I squirm in my seat, trying to duck out of sight. I can hear *Docteur* André repeating his mantra in my head, "I control my emotions, they don't control me." This awkward outburst that has disrupted an entire train car full of people is obviously the sort of thing to which he has so often referred, but following his instructions is always easier said than done.

"Listen," Lauran offers, "I'm going to take a walk and get us some coffee. When I come back, we'll pick up where you left off. And I promise not to tease you. Deal?"

"Deal," I agree. But as Lauran walks away, I can't help but think of how Ilari must have felt that night when he came to get me. I don't know if I'll ever be fully ready to say these words out loud.

§

The coffee on the train is served in paper cups. It is weak and murky, with an oily film floating on top. But Lauran bought it for me, so I drink it, anyway. He watches me as I take my first sips, a bit warily. "Look," I start.

"I'm sorry," Lauran turns away, embarrassed.

"No, it's a reasonable reaction. I can be a bit... intense sometimes. I could have been more open with you about that." My hands are starting to shake – tiny waves roll in my coffee cup. "The things that happened to me, that I'm going to tell you about, they were difficult. They changed me. They are why I jumped out of my skin when you touched my shoulder. I'm not always completely stable, and I'm not always easy to be around."

"Sophie..."

"Just listen, please. This is hard for me." I take a sip of my weak coffee. "Outside of my psychiatrist's office – and yes, to be clear, I have a psychiatrist who I see once a week, not to mention the several bottles of prescription pills in my purse – I've never told anyone the things I'm telling you. Not even my brothers. I don't know how well it will go, honestly. But I'll keep talking as long as you still want to hear."

Lauran doesn't miss a beat. "I'm listening."

§

"I hope you have a really good explanation for this," I told my *anaia* as I climbed into the cab of the dilapidated village truck, parked under a tree a few roads away from *rue Principale*. The truck was older than I was – we called it *mirari*, because it was a miracle that it could still be started after so many years of abuse. I always liked *mirari* – just seeing the van that Balere and Remiri drove made me shudder, but the truck was like an old friend; a constant in the chaos.

Ilari said nothing. He started *mirari* and drove slowly through town, then out onto the highway without a word. I know now, faced with telling you what he had to tell me, how anxious and ashamed he must have felt. But at the time, I was annoyed. He had virtually abducted me and he had nothing to say for himself? Within ten minutes, I was livid. "I guess you'll tell me when you're really ready," I snapped. "And you can start by explaining where the hell you learned French!"

Still, he said nothing.

We crossed the border without incident, just before midnight. Once we were in Spanish territory, Ilari's nerves got the better of him. The clutch in the truck slipped. We swerved. My *anaia* stomped on the clutch but he couldn't get it back — I had to lean over him and yank on the steering wheel to pull us away from a deep ditch.

"Stop the truck, Ilari," I ordered.

My *anaia* is a good soldier. He did as he was told, pulled over to the side of the dark road and cut the engine — *mirari* gave a quiet cough and shuddered down.

I turned in my seat to face Ilari. "You'd better be ready to tell me now."

Nothing could have prepared me for the words that my *anaia* said. "We got kicked out of The Organisation."

What do you say to someone who tells you that they've failed at a vocation that has ostensibly no requirements beyond a willingness to prey on innocent people? I didn't know. I still don't. "What did you- I mean, what did *aita* do?"

"He refused to respect the ceasefire."

The ceasefire. The words fell like a bomb over me. The listless way the men had wandered around town for the past few summers... the tension in the air... the sudden increase in accidental gunshot wounds... All Ilari needed to say was those two words and everything made sense. I closed my eyes hard and opened them again. "How long have I been kept in the dark?"

"*Aita* said it was part of the plan..." was Ilari's lame excuse.

"And you listened to him? *Aita* is a lunatic!"

"Amaia-"

I turned away. "I have a family — a normal family — in Saint-Antoine. Please take me back to them."

Ilari relented and turned *mirari* on. Then he turned it off again. "Amaia, I need you." The words were strained, barely audible. My *anaia* is scarcely capable of declaring strong feelings for a particular brand of firearms. To hear his desperate attempt at emotional expression was excruciating. "Please."

I turned back to face him. "You need to tell me everything, from the beginning."

My *anaia* swallowed hard and nodded in agreement.

We sat at the side of the road until three in the morning. Ilari told me how, shortly after he came back from Bordeaux, he got shot in the leg during a minor skirmish with the police. Instead of risking detection by the *Ertzaintza* by sending his son to the hospital, *aita* had a local woman treat the wound. She left my *anaia* with a limp and an enormous scar. While he was recovering, *aita* had him declared legally dead.

From a bureaucratic perspective, my *anaia* was a ghost. If anyone other than my *aita* had come up with the plan, it could have been brilliant. As a dead man, Ilari was free to move as he pleased, to cross borders and infiltrate organisations. But *aita* kept him at home, allegedly grooming him for leadership. "All I ever learned," he told me, "was how to make a bomb that doesn't work."

In March 2006, The Organisation declared a permanent ceasefire. Permanent can apparently be defined as fourteen months — that's how long it lasted. When the ceasefire was lifted, no one shared the news with our village. It was a deliberate move, and the intent was obvious. But The Organisation underestimated just how removed from the world the village is — they assumed the villagers would get the message.

They didn't. They went on acting as if there was a ceasefire in effect. *Aita* became increasingly obsessive and difficult to control. He went on private missions, targeting children and the elderly. Ilari left the village briefly — he was frustrated and angry and the nagging doubts he had held at bay for so long had blossomed into a desire to leave terrorism behind. He lasted two days in Bilbao.

And then, reading a newspaper while drinking his morning coffee at *Café Iruña*, he found out that the ceasefire was over.

He went home, but he kept the truth to himself. He was afraid to fight again. He was even more afraid of what *aita* would do if he learned the truth. The secret made him nervous and twitchy — he slept less, even less than before, and found himself constantly watching his own back, afraid of being found out. At first, hiding the truth had seemed like the road to self-preservation. But the longer he held onto it, the more he realised he would eventually be found out – and with every passing day, the list of potential consequences grew longer.

"There's something else," he added. It was dark in the truck, but I could hear in his voice that he was afraid.

"What is it?"

"Thierry knows about me."

All my life, I had heard the name Thierry whispered behind closed doors. No one knew exactly who he was or what he did, but Thierry *was* The Organisation. It all began and ended with him.

"How?"

"Balere and Remiri. They're pushing me to take over. They say my time has come. I have an appointment with Thierry in Bordeaux next week."

"But-" My *anaia* was in danger. We were both sure of it. *Isaiah* 65:6 came to me in a flash, even though my days of Bible study were long over. *Behold, it is written before me: I will not keep silence, but will recompense, even recompense unto their bosom, your iniquities, and the iniquities of your fathers together, (saith the Lord, which have burned incense upon the mountains, and blasphemed me upon the hills: "therefore will I measure their former work into their bosom.")* "They can't sacrifice you! Not for this!"

"It could have been worse," Ilari's voice shook. "It – could be worse if I don't go. More people could get hurt."

For a few terrifying moments, my *anaia* and I sat silence in the darkness, holding hands as we came to grips with the reality that he might be a lamb going knowingly to the slaughter.

Ilari broke the silence, "And there's one more thing."

"Please," I begged, "no more."

"Yes."

"What is it?"

"I can't tell you. I have to show you."

We drove the rest of the way to Bilbao without saying much. I smoked compulsively, butting out on the dashboard only to light up again seconds later. I eventually fell asleep, and woke up just as Ilari was pulling *mirari* around the last bend in the mountain road that lead to the dusty village. The sun was rising over the mountain peaks, illuminating our home in a pale orange light. I yawned and stretched. In a small way, it was good to see my home. "Ilari? I never asked about Gab. How is he?"

"He's married to Alaine now, you know." There was an edge in my *anaia*'s voice that I hadn't expected. As far as I knew, my affair with Gab was still my best kept secret.

"I know," I grinned. I feel so stupid now, remembering my callous reaction, but I actually enjoyed being the other woman. I loved knowing that I was wanted. I knew I was vain and narcissistic, but I didn't care. I finally knew, I thought, why Margaux always seemed to have so much fun. "I still want to see him. Let's surprise him! Before you give me any more bad news. It will be fun."

My *anaia* stopped *mirari* in front of the factory. "Will you promise me one thing?"

"Only if you agree," I teased, opening the passenger door to step out.

"Promise that you'll forgive me."

I dropped my box of cigarettes. The lid fell open and they scattered all over the dusty ground. Gab was the bad news.

§

The countryside passes outside of my window in a dusky blur. The sun is going down — soon there will be nothing to see but darkness. But I can't look at Lauran and say these things out loud at the same time; it's too much to bear.

"Sophie?"

When I hear my ex-boyfriend's voice I look up, startled. I know that I am on the train to Bordeaux but I was talking for so long that I started to feel like I was back in Euskal Herria, living my heartbreaking memories all over again. "Yes?"

"Do you want a drink? I thought I might go to get a glass of wine. It might-"

"So much."

"- make this easier."

We both laugh. "I'll come with you. I'd like to stretch my legs."

I follow Lauran down the narrow aisle way, through two train cars to the dining car, which is little more than a bar that sells chocolate bars and crackers. There is a queue winding through the car, right to the door, and we're the last ones in it.

At first we stand quietly, but the line moves at an excruciatingly slow pace and it is soon clear that we may not have our wine before we arrive in Bordeaux.

"This next part," Lauran says, "this is about the *Ertzaintza*, isn't it?"

I smile. "You remembered."

"I thought a drink might make it easier for you to talk about it. Not that you're likely to get one at this rate."

"You thought a drink might make it easier for you to listen to it," I kid.

"That, too."

I tilt my head to the side, pondering. The line for the bar inches forward. "What is it that scares you?"

"I think it's what I don't know," Lauran is thoughtful. "I thought I knew about the world, and our people. I spent a year living in rural Spain, milking sheep and playing *jai alai*. But the more you tell me, the more I realise how sheltered I've been."

"That's funny – I'm the opposite, but the same. It's the things I know that scare me."

§

After twenty minutes in line, we walk back to our seats with small glass bottles of bitter wine and plastic cups to drink it from. Lauran follows me through the cars — I can feel his eyes on me, watching the way I move. I can't help but smile. I still wish he would touch me — my hand, my face, anything, just one slip of the hand to let me know that he wants what I do. But at least if he's looking, I know that he's thinking about it.

It would be so much easier if I just turned around and kissed him now. That would tell me everything. But I'm a Sagastizabal, a schemer at heart — and that isn't part of the plan.

Our chairs are empty when we get back — we're lucky. People change seats on the train like a silent game of musical chairs is in play, and you're never completely guaranteed to get your seat back if you leave it.

I manage to open my tiny wine bottle and pour myself a glass. But I'm not exactly quick — by the time I take my first sip, Lauran's glass is half empty. "Are you ready for this?"

He swallows. "I'm ready."

§

The *despachos* were on the top floor of the factory. I followed my limping *anaia* up seven flights of wooden steps — the climb was excruciating. All the way, I begged Ilari for some clue about what was waiting at the top of the stairs, but he said nothing. With his leg, I doubt if he could have talked and climbed at the same time, but that didn't lessen my anxiety at all.

It felt like days before we reached the top. Ilari put his hand on the brass doorknob, then paused. "Gab was arrested in Bilbao in September. It was the *Ertzaintza*. He came back two and a half months later."

"Ilari! Is he...?" I didn't even know what I was asking. My mind whirled with possibilities, each one more elaborately devastating than the last — electric shocks, water boarding, unnecessary organ removal – none of which I could articulate.

"You'll see."

My mouth opened, but before I could protest, Alaine burst through the door with such force that she shook the frosted glass. "You!" she spat at my *anaia*. "And you!" she hissed at me, before storming past us and down the stairs. Alaine is a small girl, with long, lank hair and a nose like a goose. She could be aggravating, certainly – she had a habit of rolling her disapproving eyes heavenward when anyone talked about anything more interesting than bread-making techniques – but never intimidating. Not until that moment. I closed my mouth and followed Ilari into the *despachos*.

The *despachos* were a train of three adjoining offices. We passed through the first, a waiting room with dusty overstuffed furniture, and the second, a secretary's office, with a small wooden desk and plain chair. At the door to the third, the executive suite, Ilari hesitated. He turned the doorknob gingerly, as if even he didn't know what he might find on the other side. "Gab," he called out. "I've brought someone to see you."

I could see Gab before he could see me, over Ilari's shoulder. He looked exactly the way he had when I left him, except his eyes – they were wide and blank, with tears streaming from them like rainfall.

"Gab? Amaia is here."

I stepped out carefully from behind my *anaia*. I felt like I was approaching a wild animal – I moved quietly and slowly, to avoid startling him. When he stood up suddenly, I was the one who jumped. But I took another step forward. "Gab?"

He didn't say a word. But when I was within arm's reach, he grabbed onto me and wouldn't let go.

## Chapter 15

I dream about that afternoon in the *despachos* with Gab. I dream about the way he clung to me like a life preserver in rough waters, forty minutes ticking by on my watch without a word — almost without a breath. When he finally did move, it was only to sit down. He pulled me into his lap and stroked my hair. All the time, silent tears rolled down his cheeks. It was unsettling, to be with him like that; to be with him and yet not with him. But I stayed for hours because there was nothing else I could do.

I dream of how I whispered that he was safe, that I was there with him, that everything would be fine, painfully aware that the only truth I might be telling was the obvious one. I was there. He looked just the same as when I had left him the summer before — his head had been shaved; his hair was growing in, though, thick and black, and the holes where his lip and eyebrows rings belonged were empty. But he was instantly recognisable; he looked like himself, just as long as I didn't look into his eyes.

Ilari came for me, eventually. "Alaine comes every day at four," he warned. I dream of how hard it was to extricate myself from Gab's grasp. I kissed him. I told him I would come back as soon as I could. And still, when I stepped away, he grabbed my wrist. The force of his grip made me turn back — he didn't say a word; I remember, I wasn't sure if he talked anymore. He just stared at me, his eyes imploring. A lump rose in my throat so that I couldn't breathe and hold back my tears at the same time. "I'll be back soon," I repeated. "I promise."

Gab's grip on me loosened, and I fled.

§

I wake up just as the train pulls into *Gare Saint-Jean*. "Good morning, sunshine," Lauran grins down at me.

As I smile up at him, I realise the only explanation for my vantage point is that I have been sleeping on his shoulder. Mortified, I sit bolt upright and try to subtly pretend that nothing happened. I'm a miserable failure, all shaky hands and darting eyes, which only makes me more embarrassed. "Well," I manage to stammer, "It looks like we made it."

And just like that, the moment is over. What was turns into what might have been.

We take our luggage and walk out onto the platform in silence. Ilari and Gen live close to the station, in an apartment on *rue Malbec* – we walk there in silence, with Lauran following behind me so that he can find his way. With every click of my heels against the pavement, I berate myself for hesitating.

The scolding doesn't last long – we arrive at Ilari and Gen's heavy red front door in less than five minutes. I punch in the building code from memory and with that, we're inside, our suitcases sliding easily across the mahogany tiles on the floor.

My *anaia* and his girlfriend live in the first apartment, behind a white door. I'm about to ring the bell when the door swings open. Gen and my *anaia* are both on the other side with their arms open. A chorus of hellos rings out into the hall and I am scooped up by four arms at once while Lauran stands quietly, waiting for a sign that he hasn't become invisible.

"*Bon soir, bon soir.*" I am thrilled, and relieved, to see my family, but not so much that I want to spend the evening with them on their doorstep. I try to gently nudge Ilari and Gen into their apartment, but when that fails, I announce, "I want to introduce you both to Lauran."

Silence descends instantly. "Lauran, this is Ilari, my *anaia*, and his girlfriend, Gentzane."

My *anaia* can scarcely stop gaping to say hello. Even Gen is uncharacteristically speechless. After two stunned handshakes, I actually have to ask, "Do you think it would be too much trouble if we came in?"

§

Gen tries to cook dinner. This happens every time that I visit, and the sordid story is always the same. Ilari and I — and today Lauran — sit at the small brown kitchen table, chatting quietly and drinking inexpensive wine from the local *Monoprix* while Gen attempts to coax rice, vegetables and meat into something resembling a meal. Occasionally I try to help, but Gen usually doesn't want help — once she has rolled up her sleeves and yanked her long black curls into a ponytail, the kitchen belongs to her; the fact that she has no idea what to do with it becomes temporarily irrelevant.

The last time I visited, we had a small fire in the oven. Once, Gen managed to successfully bake a *tarte au chocolat* — only to drop it on the floor, where it crumbled into a thousand sticky pieces.

"How do you two know each other?" Ilari asks, as any conscientious older brother would.

The question twists my stomach into a series of elaborate knots. Lauran and I exchange hesitant glances before I answer quietly, "We knew each other a little, growing up in Saint-Antoine. We just happened to run into each other again this year at school, in a linguistics class."

Ilari raises an eyebrow. "But aren't you…?" he starts to ask Lauran.

"I am," Lauran answers in his flawless, but obviously French, Euskara.

"And you grew up in that town with the genocidal fucking priest? That must have been a treat."

I can't help but smile. Ilari has changed so much. He wears his hair short now, without his trademark streak of patriotic red dyed into it, and all the piercings but the one through his eyebrow have been removed, one by one. But the one thing he can't seem to get a handle on is his language. He uses the word *fuck* like it's a punctuation mark. The reflex only gets worse when he's anxious or uncomfortable. I reach for the wine bottle to top up his glass – to help him take the edge off.

"It actually wasn't a bad place to grow up Euskadi," Lauran tells Ilari with a chuckle. "For one thing, we had our own priest."

Ilari laughs. "I'm sure Amaia has told you that our childhood was unique. I don't know if I can say all that fucking much about what it's like to grow up Euskadi in Spain, in a global sense, because of that. But I've always been curious about how the culture differs in France…"

"Amaia," Gen calls out from the counter, interrupting, "can you help me for a minute, *ma choupinette*?"

I raise an eyebrow, immediately suspicious. But I'm a guest, so it's only polite to agree. I excuse myself, leaving my *anaia* and Lauran chatting casually about the Euskadi experience.

"What do you need me to do?" I ask Gen. "Do you want an apron, maybe?" She's wearing an obviously new plaid dress straight from the Isabel Marant showroom. I can almost hear it crying out for her to spill on it.

"Is that him, *chérie*?" Gen whispers giddily, her green eyes alive and glittering with girlish glee.

"Is who him?" I take a large, sharp knife out of my sister-in-law's hand before she inattentively slices a wedge off her index finger instead of a carrot.

"Lauran! Is he the one you've been trying to win back for all of these months?" I don't answer – but I let my blush give me away. "Oh, *ma belle*, he's so handsome! And it must be going well, *non*? After all, he came all the way here with you just for the weekend!"

Gen has somehow found another knife – I slip it out of her hand as I shrug, a little embarrassed to admit, "I don't know. He took me out to dinner, he came here with me... But he hasn't touched me." I can't help but sigh. "Not even a brush of the hand."

"And his girlfriend?" Gen raises one Audrey Hepburn eyebrow inquisitively. "I can't imagine she would have allowed him to run away with you for the weekend."

"No, she left him."

"There, you see!" This is Gen's moment of triumph. "I'm not so sure he wasn't the one to do the leaving." My dear sister-in-law is about to go on when she abruptly slices open her finger. "*Putain*!" she exclaims as she bleeds all over the carrots.

The scene plays out the same way every time. "Gen, suck on your finger while I find a Band-Aid," I command. I excel in a crisis. "Ilari, can you call for a takeaway? No one can eat what's left of this."

"I was waiting for the order," my *anaia* laughs.

As I rush out of the kitchen in search of the first aid kit, Lauran catches my eye and gives me a small, secret smile. For an instant, I believe that Gen just might be right about him.

§

Ilari and Gen live in a tiny apartment, barely big enough to fit the two of them. But in spite of the fact that space is at a premium, Gen insists on having her baby grand piano in the middle of the living room. Ilari has tried a hundred times to convince her to trade it in for a smaller model, but she refuses, feigning a sentimental attachment – the piano was a gift from her *papa* for her thirteenth birthday.

Gen hasn't seen her *papa* for almost thirteen years, and has never said more about him than, "the bastard," so her reasoning is less than plausible. The truth is, she can't bear to get rid of the piano because of how beautifully it plays. I know; I took piano lessons from the time I was three, and I've never come across an instrument that comes close to Gen's Serge. (She named her baby after *monsieur* Gainsbourg, naturally.)

After dinner, Gen and I, slightly tipsy, stumble towards Serge. Our career as a living room pop star duet is always most promising after several glasses of grocery store wine. Serge is the only piano I have access to, and I'm powerless to resist the charm of his immaculate ivory keys. My left hand doesn't have enough dexterity to play anymore, so Gen fills in on the lower half of the keyboard. We never play the Mozart and Rachmaninoff we grew-up with, just songs from the radio — which we sing as loudly as we can, for as long as we can before the neighbours upstairs bang on their floor in protest.

We giggle all the way to the piano bench, although it occurs to me halfway there that I don't remember what was funny. Dinner was easier than I expected it to be — the takeaway, from a little restaurant down the road, was so bad that eating it became a bonding experience. We challenged each other to come up with stories of worse meals we'd eaten — I told the story of the time that Ilari convinced me that *txipirones* were just Euskadi gummy worms. The conversation was natural, and as Gen and I trip over each other on the way to our stage, I realise how happy I am.

Ilari and Lauran follow us to the living room, albeit more soberly. "You're in for a treat," I hear my *anaia* say. "They're actually both pretty fucking talented, when they're not drunk. And when they are drunk, they're a comedy act."

"We are taking requests!" Gen announces, banging on Serge's keyboard to make sure that anyone who wasn't paying attention is now.

"Drunk girls' choice," Ilari replies.

Gen and I only have to look at each other to know where to start. We bang out the ten best songs in our repertoire one after another, laughing like mad women whenever there is a break between verses. Ilari and Lauran take in our performance from the couch — I hear occasional laughter coming from their direction, but I'm too caught up in what I'm doing to really pay attention.

That is, until I hear Ilari tell Lauran, "Ask them to play *Lady*."

Lauran hesitates. "Really?"

"Trust me, they excel at reinterpreting house music. *Lady* is their big hit."

"Sophie?" Lauran calls out, skeptical, "your *anaia* tells me that you have a talent for playing house music on the piano…?"

"You call my *alaba* Sophie?" I hear Ilari ask; he sounds genuinely confused, as opposed to upset.

Lauran never gets a chance to answer. "Lady!" Gen shouts with glee, and we launch into an over-enthusiastic version of the very first song we ever played together. We both hate *Modjo*, and their repetitive number one hit, but before we became true living room pop stars, we needed songs that we could easily figure out how to play without any sheet music. The most overplayed song from our adolescence was a natural choice.

"I feel loved for the first time, and I know that it's true, I can tell by the look in your eyes!" we sing our big finish at the top of our lungs, heads through back in the air. Gen leans a bit too far back and tips right off the piano bench, landing in a giggling heap on the carpet.

Ilari sighs and stands up. "Looks like the show is over for tonight," he says as she scoops Gen up off the floor into his arms. "Time to say good night, *maite*."

"*Bonne nuit, mes chères*," Gen yawns dramatically as my *anaia* carries her away.

"Good night, you two," I can't help smiling.

When Ilari and Gen disappear down the hall, I turn back to Serge and play the first bars of my favourite song — Beethoven's haunting *Fur Elise*. Even without the left-handed part, it sounds like a symphony.

## Chapter 16

"It's fine, I'll just sleep on the floor."

"No, no, it's my fault, I didn't even think about it — I can sleep on the floor."

Ilari and Gen live in a one-bedroom apartment. They always have. I know this. When I stay with them, I sleep on their pull-out couch in the living room. And yet, when I impulsively invited Lauran to join me for the weekend, sleeping arrangements never crossed my mind. Even tonight, when Ilari carried drunk Gen to bed and I began my usual routine of folding out the couch, the obvious problem didn't occur to me. Not until Lauran innocently asked, "And where will I be sleeping?"

Now we find ourselves at an awkward impasse, pacing what is left of the living room with the bed pulled out, arguing over who will sleep on the floor.

"Sophie, that's silly," Lauran protests, pacing towards me. "It was an honest mistake; I don't expect you to give up your bed for me. I'll be fine on the floor, it's only two nights."

"But you're a guest!" If my French parents taught me anything, it's that I must, at all times and without exception, be polite, formal and obedient of social convention, no matter how illogical it may be. "I can't possibly let you sleep on the floor!" I throw my hands up in the air in exasperation.

And nearly hit Lauran in the face. We've paced to the same place in the living room, and stand face-to-face at the end of the pull-out bed, only three inches apart. I look up at him. He looks down at me. Time seems to stop moving forward. I can feel his breath on my face. We both start to lean in... and then abruptly turn away, stalking to the other side of the room. "This is ridiculous," I sigh, sitting down on the edge of the bed.

Lauran sits with his back to me. "Juvenile."

"Do you think we could agree," I turn to face him, "to approach this situation like adults?"

"It seems like the only reasonable thing to do."

"All right. I'll sleep on this side of the bed, and you can take that side. Since you are a guest, you are entitled to use the bathroom for changing and washing purposes first."

"Soph-" Lauran starts.

"Like adults," I remind him, and he takes his pajamas to the bathroom without further protest.

§

I take my time getting ready for bed. I have no special routine – I brush my teeth, wash my face and borrow some of Gen's expensive face cream. I crawl through the motions at a painful pace and slowly, so slowly, slip out of my clothes. I trade my jeans for a pair of plain black pants that do a reasonable job of hiding how skinny my legs are, but when it comes time to slip my tight black *Zadig & Voltaire* t-shirt over my head, I pause for a moment and face myself, bare-chested, in the mirror. I reach my stiff left fingers up and gently run them over my scar. Up until a few weeks ago, all I had to do was put one finger against the darkened skin before the wind rushed through my ears and I was back in Basque Country, reliving my last moments with Gab. And every time I remember the moment I realised that Gab was holding a gun, it's like he's pointing it at me all over again. But now, as I trace the contours of my scar with all five fingers, I feel nothing — no pain, no regret. I don't even see an image of Gab in my mind's eye. All I can think of is Lauran, sitting alone in the living room, probably wondering if I planned this whole trip just to get him into bed and wishing he hadn't agreed to come along.

I slip my t-shirt over my head and sit down heavily on the edge of the bathtub, hesitating. This isn't the way I had hoped things might turn out. When Lauran asked me to dinner, I was so sure — even if only for a split second — that he wanted what I do; that he wanted to be with me like when we were teenagers, only better this time because now we could be completely honest with each other. But as the hours and days have passed, my doubts have crept in again — and they were officially confirmed in the living room not five minutes ago; here I am, about to share a bed with him for the first time in almost ten years... and it's only because we couldn't agree on which one of us should spend two nights sleeping on the floor.

I guess, when I get right down to it, it's disappointment. When I walk out of this room, I have to face the reality of lying awake all night with my back to Lauran, so close to him and yet agonisingly far away.

I heave a sigh, stand up and face myself in the bathroom mirror. My eyes are green, like my *anaia*'s. In the summer, the pale freckles on my nose turn brown. My hair is dark, straight and hangs down to my collarbone in thick layers. I'm not a beauty queen, but even with my make-up off, I'm pretty enough. I've never had any trouble with men. Just with Lauran.

But, I reason, I have to sleep. So I turn the bathroom light off and pad back out to the living room in the dark.

§

"Sophie?"

Lauran and I lie on our sides in the dark, back-facing-back, as far apart as the small pull-out bed will allow us to be. I am wide awake. Apparently, so is he.

"What is it?" I whisper.

"I had no idea you played the piano."

"Oh?" I can feel myself turning an embarrassed shade of pink, even though no one can see me. "I'm sorry I subjected you to all of that. It's just that I so rarely have access to a piano anymore, when I come here I can't resist."

"What are you apologising for?" I can hear Lauran roll over in the bed to face me. "I loved watching you. Okay, it was bizarre… But it was good, too. I've never seen you so uninhibited."

I roll over to face my ex-boyfriend. I can just see his silhouette in the dark, his head resting on his elbow. When he is thoughtful, he always rests his head this way, even in school, as if he can think more clearly when his brain is tilted to one side. "That's because this is the only place in the world where I have absolutely nothing to hide."

"There are always so many secrets with you," Lauran shakes his head.

"It's not a choice, honestly. Life gave me secrets… maybe some people would have chosen not to keep them, but I did."

"Oh? Just what are you hiding, Sophie?" my ex-boyfriend teases. "Are you an alien, sent to earth to study human behaviour?"

"No!" I can't help laughing.

"Maybe you're an international spy? A member of the KGB?"

"Of course not! Are you insane? The USSR broke up twenty years ago!" I can't control my giggling anymore – the fact that Ilari and Gen are asleep in the next room and I'm in danger of waking them only makes things worse.

"Then there's only one possible explanation," Lauran concludes.

"What?" I cry, reaching out to jokingly shove him away.

He catches my hands and holds me at arm's length. "You, Sophie Cassou, must be an elephant! I know you're hiding your trunk on you somewhere!"

We both burst out laughing, loud enough to wake the neighbours, never mind Ilari and Gen. We laugh so long and so hard that I can feel the bed shake under the weight of our mirth.

It's only when we start to calm down, our laughter giving way to quiet chuckles, that I realise Lauran is still holding my hands. He realises it at the same moment, and we lie in silence, just looking at our joined hands bridging the gap between us, almost in disbelief, like we aren't sure how they got there, and wondering what exactly to do next.

"I just don't understand," Lauran breaks the silence, his words hardly more than a whisper, "what could possibly be so bad that you think you can't tell me about it."

"Old habits," I admit.

It's dark. We're still holding hands. This isn't part of the plan, but this moment feels like my big chance — maybe my last chance. I decide to throw caution to the wind and do exactly what I feel like doing.

I lean in and kiss Lauran.

I thought it might surprise him, but he doesn't hesitate for an instant. The second my lips touch his, all of the time and distance and bitterness fall away. We are exactly as we always were — it's absolutely natural, as if we've been together all along.

We pull back for a second, breathless and stunned. Lauran looks at me, wide-eyed and grinning, like he can't believe his good luck. I look at him, really look, just to make sure that he's here and I'm here and this isn't just happening in my imagination.

"I wish you had just done that instead of running into me in the hallway," Lauran half-laughs.

"So do I!" I blurt out, too absolutely happy to be anything but honest. And then I kiss him again.

The past rushes forward and the future leaps back at once. We are exactly what we always were and everything that I hope we might be, all at the same time — hands and lips and skin and breath.

But when Lauran reaches for the hem of my t-shirt, I hesitate. "My scar…"

"It doesn't matter."

"You wince every time you see it!"

"No more secrets, Sophie," Lauran whispers, kissing my neck just below my ear.

"No more secrets," I promise.

And he lifts my t-shirt over my head. This time, I let him. Once my bare skin is exposed, Lauran's fingers find the rippled, broken flesh on my shoulder and breast almost immediately. I can't blame him — I'm sure that curiosity would have made me do the same thing in his place. But no one has seen the full extent of my scar since I left the hospital and no one has ever been allowed to touch it. It's bad enough that most of the time, even just putting my own hands on it brings back memories that are so strong it's hard to breathe. I let Lauran explore, but I do my best to divert his attention to more interesting parts of me — it doesn't take much. All I have to do is reach for the waistband of his pants and he moves on, kissing my bare torso all the way down.

§

What we do isn't making love. It's sex. We are just two people who have waited for each other for years, fantasizing all along about what it would be like to be naked together again. When Lauran slides into me, years of tension release and I moan audibly.

Lauran is not a teenager anymore — and we aren't in his bedroom at home, trying to do it as many times as we can before mass ends. The women he has known since we've been apart have taught him to do things that make me sigh and writhe under him.

I am not a little girl anymore, either. When I arch my back and tighten my thighs, there are no lingering doubts that I might be doing the wrong thing or trying too hard. We were always good together, but now that we're older, we're better.

We finish just as we began — abruptly. Lauran, deep inside, discovers a part of me I've never felt before and we crash together, sweaty, dazed and breathless.

After, we lie awake in the dark, pressed against each other, front to back. Lauran holds me close to him, his arm over my chest, fingers tucked tightly between the mattress and me. Neither one of us says a word — none come to mind. But the man in the bed with me kisses me fiercely, covering my hair and cheek and neck with all of the things he doesn't know how to say.

I don't know when but, eventually, we sleep.

## Chapter 17

"Good morning."

There is a split second of sheer panic when I wake-up the next morning. It's early, and pale streams of sunlight are just beginning to filter in under the shades on the living room windows. I know where I am, but I have no idea who is in bed with me or why they might be there. I am concerned that it might be Gab's arm around my shoulders, which would mean I am having a full-blown psychiatric episode. "Good morning," I hesitate, turning my head very slowly towards the person beside me, as if seeing them gradually might lessen the shock.

But then a pair of blue eyes appears above me, a curious smile on the lips below them. "Having a hard time waking up, are you?"

Lauran. The memory of our night together comes back to me in a rush, and I can feel my cheeks flush pink with excitement. "So you weren't just a pleasant dream, after all."

"Definitely not." Lauran flashes me a wicked grin — the same one he used to give me on the rare days that I wore a skirt to school, just before he brazenly flipped it up at the back to get a look at what I was hiding underneath. "And I can assure you that what I am about to do is very real."

"Oh?" I start to ask, but he has already disappeared under the quilt.

§

"Did you ever think we would do this again?" Lauran asks afterwards, as we lay naked on top of the sheets, legs splayed but arms firmly around each other.

"I never thought you would speak to me again!" The idea seems so ridiculous now that I can't help but laugh, but it's also the truth.

Lauran pulls me into him, turning my body so that we press up against each other. He kisses my forehead gently, the way I've seen my *anaia* kiss Gen when he can't believe the words coming out of her mouth but also finds himself unable to be angry with her; the way I have always thought looked like real love.

"I never thought I would, either," he admits.

I know I shouldn't ask — not unless I'm really sure I'm ready to hear an answer that could easily ruin these otherwise perfect moments. But I can't help it. "What changed?"

"I saw you again." Lauran leans in close and whispers, "You're impossible to resist."

"Oh, sure," I push him away, teasing, "that explains exactly why you ignored my existence for almost the entire month of September. And then you barely deigned to give me the time of day, unless it was to insult me, for most of October."

"I didn't know…" Lauran starts, avoiding my eyes.

"I can't believe I've changed that much!"

"No, not that. I didn't know if I could be with you and, well, not with you," the tops of my darling not-exactly-ex-boyfriend's ears redden. "I'm not normally an argumentative student, you know."

"Oh?" Not a single linguistic theory lecture has gone by when Lauran hasn't argued with the professor at length on some subject, no matter how obscure or unimportant.

"It was the only way I could stop myself from staring at you."

"You're just saying that!" I laugh Lauran off — it's easier, somehow, than taking the compliment.

"I'm serious. It was embarrassing. The girl sitting behind me during the first lecture actually called me on it. She tapped me on the shoulder while the professor's back was turned and suggested, none too subtly, that I should keep my eyes to myself."

I clamp my head over my mouth to hold back my laugher. "That's awful!"

"It wasn't my finest moment. And neither was the moment when you accidentally on purpose ran into me in the hallway. I'm sorry about that. Maybe I've already told you, but I wanted to say it again." Lauran pauses his monologue to take a breath, and then goes on. "I'm glad you forced my hand. I know that I can be with you, without all the rest of this, if I have to be. But," he kisses my neck and ear and lips, "this is much more fun."

I kiss him back — I'm inclined to agree.

Down the hall, I hear the alarm begin to ring in Ilari and Gen's room. "Shit," I mumble, without pulling away at first. "They'll be out here in five minutes." I pull away from Lauran as gently as I can — I've wanted to feel his arms around me for so long, it's painful to move away from them. "Shower. Clothes. My *anaia*..."

The last two words light a sudden fire under Lauran — he disappears to the bathroom like a shot, carrying his day-old clothes under his arm.

§

Just as the bathroom door closes behind Lauran, the bedroom door opens and Gen, still in her racy black lace nightgown, steps out into the hall. She is sleep rumpled, her long hair a tangled mess, but still ethereally beautiful.

There is no time for me to find my clothes. Gen has to take only two steps on her long legs to make it halfway down the hall. Desperate, I roll over to face Serge's sunlit keyboard and pretend to be asleep. I hear every step that Gen takes towards me like it's thunder. "Good morning, *chérie*.!" she calls in a quiet singsong voice and my palms begin to sweat. I know exactly what she will do next — the routine is the same on every Saturday morning that I spend in Bordeaux — and the anticipation is about to cause me heart failure.

Even though I can't see her, I know when Gen walks into the living room. I can feel her standing at the edge of the bed and I wait, wait for her to lift the quilt. A cool wash of air hits my back when she does, and I wait, but the squeal I'm expecting doesn't come. She hasn't noticed.

Yet.

Gen slides into the open space between the quilt and the mattress. "Wake up, *ma choupinette*," she whispers, sidling across the bed to lie next to me. I edge slowly away from her, but there are only so many centimetres that I can move without falling onto the floor. For a second I consider doing exactly that, but the physical accuracy required to take all of the sheets with me to hide my nudity is just too complex and risky.

Besides which, by the time I've finished considering it, Gen is right next to me, wrapping her arms around me from behind. I realise that she is touching my breasts an instant before she does. "Um, Gen...?"

"Amaia! Are those your...?" Gen giggles, shocked.

"Yes, and I would appreciate it if you let go of them as soon as possible."

Gen immediately moves her hands and slides back across the mattress, a safe distance away from me. "Can I assume, then, that you've had an enjoyable morning so far?"

I roll over to face her, twisting the sheets around me to hide my bare skin. "You might say that it's been... surprising. In a lot of ways."

Gen throws her head back and laughs with devilish delight. "You see! I knew he was in love with you — I could tell from the moment you came through the front door. I can't imagine why you doubted yourself, *chérie*. Or, for that matter, why you doubted me."

"Gen..." I start.

But my *anaia*'s girlfriend has already launched into a dramatic scene of feigned hurt feelings. "Have I ever steered you wrong? Don't you trust me?"

"Oh, shut up," I roll my eyes. "You know I trust you."

"You're right," Gen immediately snaps out of character. "I went overboard."

"Besides," I go on, resting my head on my arm in contemplation, "since when does sex have anything to do with love?"

"So you did!" Gen gasps, gleeful.

"I wouldn't be naked on your pullout couch otherwise."

"You know, he never took his eyes off you last night — not for a second. Even when he was talking with Ilari, he was always looking at you. There's more to that than just sex, *ma belle*." I shrug Gen off, mostly out of a sense of self-preservation — the less I expect, the less I hope for, the less likely I am to have my heart broken. "Very well," my sister-in-law is resigned, "if I can't convince you, I'm sure that Lauran will find a way. I'm going to go make breakfast."

"Be careful you don't hurt yourself," I tease, only half-kidding.

"Oh, didn't you know? *Make breakfast* is code for getting dressed and going to the *pâtisserie* down the street to buy croissants. Talking of which," Gen has a mischievous twinkle in her eye as she hops out of bed, exposing my bare skin to the air for a second, "you might want to consider getting dressed yourself."

"I do hope you don't mean while you're still standing here watching."

This banter could go back and forth for hours — in public, Gen and I are often mistaken for sisters. Once, when we told a cashier at *Monoprix* that we weren't, she exclaimed, "But you bicker just like twins!"

But it's early, and Gen hasn't had her requisite three cups of coffee, so she can only come back with, "Touché," before she walks back to the bedroom she shares with my *anaia*, closing the wooden door behind her.

I lay back, relieved to be alone, and take a deep breath. Today is a new day — and the world I woke up in only existed in my dreams before this. If experience has taught me anything, it's that fantasizing is not the same as practising. There is no way to prepare for what might happen when your wishes come true.

There is still the clothing problem. No sooner have I rolled over to make a dive for my discarded pajamas than the bedroom door opens again. This time, it's Ilari. "Morning, Mai," he mumbles, rubbing his dark-rimmed eyes.

I throw the blankets back over myself in a rush. "Morning. Did you sleep well?"

"As well as ever."

This means not at all. When he was thirteen, my *anaia* was involved in the assassination of Miguel Angel Blanco — several people fired on the young politician at once, and to this day, Ilari doesn't know if he was the one who killed him. He never will. The suspicion that he might be a murderer hangs over his head like his own personal cloud, following him wherever he goes. He suffers from insomnia. But like all good soldiers, he refuses to recognise the fear and anguish that has plagued him ever since, the heart palpitations and sweating palms that keep him awake at night, as anything more than a matter of course, given his chosen vocation.

I love my *anaia*, but his ability to stubborn and stupid at the same time sometimes amazes me.

"So you know." I look down at the quilt, embarrassed.

Ilari raises an eyebrow. "I didn't think it was a secret."

"I guess it wasn't," from anyone but me, that is, "but..."

"Life goes on, Mai. No one expects you to do anything different." I start to protest, but my *anaia* stops me. "Just be happy. That's all I want. Well, that and a cigarette."

I roll my eyes — trust Ilari to ruin what might have otherwise been a very sweet moment. "Jesus Christ."

"It sounds like you need one, too. Join me outside?"

"I can wait, thanks."

"Suit yourself," Ilari shrugs before slipping on his unlaced Doc Martens and heading for the door.

Alone again, I know I can't waste time. I swing my legs over the edge of the bed, still wrapped in the quilt. But no sooner have I put my feet on the carpet than I hear doors open and close behind me again. Resigned, I accept the inevitable fact that someone is going to walk in on me naked in the living room, and sit at the edge of the bed, facing Serge's ivory keyboard, to suffer my embarrassing fate.

But it's only Lauran who comes around the corner, dressed in the same jeans he wore yesterday, a black sweater pulled carelessly over his taut frame. His blonde hair is still damp and tousled from the shower. This is the first time I have been with him in the morning; we were always sneaking around when we were teenagers, and every moment that we had together was furtive, rushed. The way he looks now, so relaxed and carefree, his guard completely down, makes my hands tremble a little. This is a Lauran I don't know — yet. And I desperately want that to change.

"I thought you would be dressed by the time I came back."

I run my fingers through my sleep-tangled hair. "There were some mitigating factors that got in the way of that..."

Lauran leans down and kisses me on the mouth. "I'm glad you're not, though."

"So am I."

"Where is Ilari?"

"Outside smoking."

"And Gen?"

"Shower."

"We have how long...?"

"Ten minutes, maximum."

"That should be just about all the time I need," Lauran grins — then he kneels down on the carpet and puts his face between my open legs.

## Chapter 18

Breakfast is on the table when I walk into the kitchen, the last one to be dressed and ready for the day. Gen obviously got over-excited on her trip to the *patisserie*. Sweet pastries and croissants are stacked four-high on a decorative plate in the middle of the table. I stand in the doorway for a minute, twisting my still-wet hair into a bun on top of my head.

Ilari sits in his usual place at the head of the table, scowling at the newspaper while he nurses a cup of black coffee. Lauran sits opposite him at the end of the table, both hands wrapped pensively around his chipped white mug.

"Coffee, *chérie*?" Gen stands at the counter with her back to me, already filling my usual mug. She has forsaken her black negligee for an oversized gray sweater and black cigarette pants that look more suited for an afternoon of tea and macarons at *Maison Ladurée* with the Vogue Paris editorial team than a morning trip to the *pâtisserie* down the block. I feel suddenly insecure in my torn jeans and black turtleneck.

"Please."

But the instant he knows I'm there, Lauran reaches one hand back in search of mine and all thoughts that are not *Lauran wants to hold my hand* leave my head in a giddy flutter.

I take Lauran's hand and let it lead me to the chair next to his. We lace our fingers, holding them entwined under the table — it feels like being a teenager again, wanting so badly to touch him, to always be touching him. Only now I have nothing to hide. If we wanted to, we could put our hands on the tabletop. I've never had the freedom to be open about being in love before, and it gives me a quiet thrill.

"Did you get *pain au chocolat*?" I ask Gen, even though the sensation of Lauran's skin against mine has me too exhilarated to eat anything.

"You bloody French people," Ilari shakes his head. "I don't know how you can stomach so much sugar for breakfast."

"Do you even eat breakfast?" I ask my *anaia*, fully aware of the answer. We never had breakfast, growing up in Euskal Herria. A spoonful of cold oatmeal before fried bread at noon was an indulgence. The concept of a morning meal was a complete surprise to him when he was deported to France, and, like the turnstiles in the metro and the fact that most people don't know Alvarez Enparantza from Santa Claus, is something he stubbornly refuses to get used to.

"Not as a rule, no."

"Then *ferme ta gueule, mon chou*," Gen cuts in, kissing my *anaia* sweetly on the forehead to soften her thinly veiled insult. "Of course I have *pain au chocolat*! I also bought *croissant aux amandes, choux à la crème* and two *tartes au citron*."

I help myself to what looks like *pain au chocolat*. "You'll have pastry for days!"

"The *pâtisserie* closes tomorrow — we have to be prepared," Gen says these words gravely, as if she is preparing for wartime food shortages, not a one-day closure of the local bakery. Then she turns to my *anaia*, "On the subject of being prepared, you and I have to make a trip to *Printemps* today. We need to replace our mugs."

"What?" Ilari stares at Gen liked she just suggested they take a day trip to the moon. This is obviously the first he has heard of any trip to *Printemps*. "Are you sure it can't wait?"

"But *chérie*, I'm so embarrassed, serving our guests from these chipped old things. It's just not proper. My *maman* would be so ashamed!"

"Guests? Gen, it's only Amaia here; I don't think she cares if her mug has a miniscule bloody chip in it. Do you, Mai?"

I stare intently down at my *pain au chocolat* and say nothing. I want to live through this meal — if I get in the middle of Ilari and Gen, I won't make it another two minutes.

"Besides, she's only here for two days..." Ilari goes on.

"And we'll see her for dinner when we get back — so everything works out perfectly. Right, Amaia?"

I choke on my coffee.

Rather than checking to see if I'm all right, Gen takes that as a yes. "There, you see!" she exclaims, vindicated. "I'm sure that Amaia would like to show Lauran around the city today, anyway."

Suddenly, my sister-in-law's scheme becomes painfully clear. I can feel my cheeks burn, and I look deep into my mug, mumbling, "I'm sure we could find a few sights to see..."

"Perfect! Oh, but before we go our separate ways, *chérie* ..." Gen gets a twinkle in her green eyes; she's up to something. "I have some things I want to show you. Won't you come with me?" She grabs my free hand before I have a chance to answer. "Excuse us, *les gars*."

I leave my breakfast untouched.

## Chapter 19

I meet Lauran outside – he leans against the front of the apartment building, looking out at the horizon down *rue Malbec*. I have kept him waiting like this for over an hour – entirely against my will, I might add. What Gen had to show me was a two-foot-high pile of her rejected designer clothing, most of the silks and cashmeres virtually unworn.

I try not to be offended by Gen's overwhelming generosity – because that is all it is. It's not that she thinks there is anything wrong with how I dress; she just cannot fathom a social scenario where she wouldn't feel insecure while wearing jeans. She wants to spare me the same sense of awkwardness that she has so often felt since the fall from grace that came with her parents' divorce. She forgets that I've lived my whole life in jeans and feel even more uncomfortable in expensive things than she does in casual ones.

Gen dressed me in a skirt from *Vanessa* and a top from *Isabel* – she says the designers' names like they're her friends. For all I know they may be. I happily traded my department store pumps for Louboutins, but the rest of the ensemble made me cringe when I saw myself in the mirror. "I look like a stranger."

"Nonsense, *chérie*," Gen brushed me off, rifling through her full-to-bursting jewel box. "All you need are a few *bijoux*, you'll see." She went on to pile three necklaces around my neck. I nearly buckled under the weight of the gemstones and pearls.

"I'm sorry I kept you waiting so long," I tell my not-exactly-ex-anymore-boyfriend.

Lauran just shrugs, indicating it doesn't matter. "You look... stunning."

"Really? I feel odd."

Lauran looks down at the sidewalk, bashful, as he admits, "Well, to be fair, I thought you were stunning before."

I am instantly relieved. "Oh, good, because I snuck my jeans into my purse. Do you mind if we stop at a café so I can change?"

"Of course not," Lauran takes my hand and laces his fingers between mine. "We should probably get you some breakfast, too. Your *pain au chocolat* was still sitting in the kitchen, untouched and lonely, when I came out here."

I can't think what to say. Instead, I stand on tiptoe and plant a kiss on Lauran's unsuspecting cheek. Then, both grinning, we set off hand-in-hand down *rue Malbec*.

§

By the time that the yellow stones of *Place de la Victoire* loom ahead of us, my stomach is violently protesting the lack of breakfast. My legs aren't thrilled about being bare, either. We stop at the first place we see, *Café Cassolette*, on *Place de la Victoire*. The café is decorated in an odd, American collegiate style that seems particularly out of place in a square that began as a village in the Middle Ages and served as the home of the guillotine during the revolution. But they've just opened their doors for the day, and I can smell *Nutella*, so I don't hesitate to take a square table by the window with Lauran. "I'm just going to change quickly," I tell him, and sneak away with my jeans tucked under my arm.

I spend far more time in the bathroom than is strictly necessary. Trading Gen's cast-off skirt for my well-worn jeans takes only half a minute, but I dawdle in front of the mirror, fixing my hair and compulsively reapplying lipstick. There is no rhyme or reason to it, except maybe that I'm afraid that when I walk back out into the café, Lauran will be gone and I will wake-up from the beautiful dream that I have been living.

After five neurotic minutes, I steel myself, reasoning that there is nothing more I can possibly do with my hair, and march back to the café to face whatever awaits me.

Lauran is still at the table, absently reading over a menu. He looks up and smiles when I sit down across from him. "They don't have *pain au chocolat*, so I ordered you a *moelleux au chocolat* instead. I figured it was safe as long as there was chocolate. Unless...." he suddenly hesitates, "you don't like chocolate anymore...?"

"Are you kidding?" I can't help but feel a bit relieved that I'm not the only one who is having a hard time adjusting to this new reality. "I would trade my right arm for a good quality chocolate bar!" This is no exaggeration. When I was a teenager, I would spend all of my allowance on chocolate. I hid it in hollowed out books, shoe boxes, even under hats. I don't think the amount of chocolate I ate would really have bothered my parents – but the fact that I never had any money baffled and irritated them. It was a vicious cycle; get allowance, buy chocolate, eat chocolate, need more money to buy more chocolate... I had to hide the evidence.

Lauran reaches across the table and takes my hand. He seems wistful, like he's just realised how much time we wasted being apart, and I can't help feeling the same. "I always wondered, but I never asked – what is it about chocolate? I like it just as much as the next person, but..."

"...I border on obsession," I fill in. "I know." I notice a waitress carrying a *moelleux au chocolat* walking in our direction and my eyes widen with glee, unintentionally proving my point. "I think it's because of my two childhoods." I take a bite of my breakfast before I start to explain. "Oh, this is perfect! But I digress... In Saint-Antoine, we always had more than enough to eat, but in Euskal Herria, my family barely scraped by. You saw Ilari turn his nose up at breakfast this morning. He spent his whole life eating what there was to eat, if there was anything to eat.

He's indifferent to taste, because he never had the luxury of being picky. But every summer, while my stomach sat so empty it felt like it would cave in on itself, I knew exactly what I was missing. I had nightmares about food being just out of my reach. When sugarplums danced in my head, they were taunting me. One summer, *maman* packed me a box of *Petit Lu* chocolate biscuits for my trip. I savoured them, but there just weren't enough to last two months and every day that they were gone was more devastating. I promised myself after that never to go a day without chocolate. And apart from the cruel summers in Euskal Herria, I never have. Life is too short not to enjoy what you love."

"Speaking of enjoying what you love..." Lauran pushes my half eaten cake away and leans across the table to kiss me.

§

"Do you feel more comfortable now?" Lauran asks as we're leaving the café, slipping his hand into the back pocket of my jeans. I've decided to take him to the *Jardin Public*, where we can play chess on the outdoor tables the way we used to do on his bedroom floor after school.

"Much." I can't help smiling as we walk down *cours d'Albret*, his hand in my pocket and my arm around his waist.

"Gen seems..." Lauran hesitates to find a word that will accurately describe his impression of Gen without insulting me, "... a bit-"

"Pushy?" I fill in.

"I was going to say assertive, but yes."

I can't help but laugh. "There is really no way to explain exactly what makes her think that her used clothes are vital to my success in life."

Lauran looks down at me. "Try." When he focuses his blue eyes directly on mine, there is no way I can say no to him – I can hardly speak at all!

"All right," I agree. "I suppose it's fair to say that for Gen, a normal life with public school and holidays by the sea and an after school job was never in the cards..."

§

She was born right here in Bordeaux. Her father, Théodore Sevran de Condorcet, was a parliamentarian, the head of a major bank and even, it was rumoured, a direct descendent of Sevran de Gerbey, the great revolutionary minister of war from the Girondin period, although this was proven unequivocally false about ten times over. Her mother was his second wife, Andresa Arambel, called Ande, a tall Euskadi woman twenty years his junior of virtually inexplicable provenance; she was unknown in Bordeaux society and extremely discreet, never revealing any details about her past... she never so much as said how she had met Théodore. (It should be noted that M. Sevran de Condorcet was never forthcoming about that, either.) Their only daughter, whom the Sevran de Condorcet family, including Thierry's three children from his first marriage, refused to recognise, was christened Geneviève Gentzane Arambel Sevran de Condorcet.

Gen grew up French. Despite the rift in her extended family, she was never excluded from society. She studied at an exclusive private school with the children of other parliamentarians and bankers. She took piano lessons and learned Latin and played tennis. As far as she was concerned, she was French. Her *maman* spoke to her in Euskara, but she stopped responding in Euskara when she was eight and didn't utter another word of the language for five years. She had everything she wanted – all she had to do was ask and anything she dreamed of would appear – and I think she believed that never hearing the word no meant that she was happy.

Her dreams were the same as the dreams of any society girl. She wanted a French bulldog puppy and an invitation to the Crillon ball and an apartment in the seventh arrondissement of Paris and, eventually, a rich husband. Her best friends were society girls who wanted the same things. They never argued – it would have been improper — but they were in constant competition, always trying to be prettier or more popular or better dressed than the others. If you asked her about them now, she would only refer to them as *les salopes*.

When she was in *quatrième*, something happened in her life that seemed insignificant at the time. A boy joined her class in the middle of the year and she was called upon to act as his guide because he was Euskadi. She rebelled against her marching orders — she hadn't spoken Euskara in what felt like a lifetime, for one — but she was saddled with the out-of-sorts boy, who spoke no French and whose behaviour was alternately sullen and awestruck, for two weeks. He didn't come back for a third week of school, and apart from feeling some relief, Gen gave him no more thought. She–"

§

"That was your *anaia*, wasn't it?" Lauran interrupts. "He came to Bordeaux when he was deported."

I can't help but smile. "You've been listening closely!"

"It seems almost unbelievable that they met like that, all those years ago."

"Doesn't it? It's what people unfamiliar with the law of large numbers would call a coincidence…"

"Smart ass," Lauran accuses.

"Some things never change."

Lauran takes his hand out of my back pocket and wraps his arm around my shoulders, kissing me on the top of my head. "I'm glad. Tell me more."

"Well, what I was going to say was that…"

§

She went on with her life as she had before his arrival, shopping and going to parties and smoking clandestine cigarettes with her giggling girlfriends. She had a series of boyfriends who bored her. And she spent more and more time out of the house as her parents' arguments became longer and more frequent.

Andresa Arambel and Théodore Sevran de Condorcet divorced in 2001, when Gen was sixteen. It was quick process. Théodore ceded to all of Ande's demands, including sole custody of their daughter, with the stipulation that she would go quietly and refuse to speak to the press. Gen was in her first month of the second year of her *baccalauréat professionel*, with plans to study law, when Ande dropped the bomb on her. "We're moving home."

For someone who had only ever known Bordeaux as home, this announcement was confusing and, when its ramifications sank in, devastating.

The divorce settlement left Ande and Gen wealthy, but Gen was never able to recapture the life she had in Bordeaux. All of her society girl dreams died on impact. She finished her *bacc.* at a private school in Bilbao where she was an outsider, rejected by Spanish students for being Euskadi, and by Euskadi students for being French. She felt like no matter what she did, she could never say the right thing, so she developed an obsession with always looking the part. I doubt her perfect wardrobe improved her social life at all, but it made her feel like she was in control of something. She's never really let go of that anxious tic, and she projects it onto me when I visit.

The problem was that looking the part only helped for so long. When Gen's first torturous year of Spanish *lycée* came to an end, she looked forward to a holiday at the seaside, maybe in Nice or Saint-Tropez. Instead, her *maman* took her home, to the mountain village where she grew up. Ande had built a house there — a two-storey mammoth among mice — and intended for it to be their new home.

I've described the town with no name to you before — the paint chips wafting in the breeze, the crumbling homes and the communal toilets — so I'm sure you can imagine what a shock it was for a society girl to set foot on the dusty streets for the first time, instantly destroying her favourite Miu Miu sandals. She and Ande were ostracized by the community, as could only be expected. Their proclivity for modern technology — they had a telephone, and running water — and tendency to wear short skirts made the townspeople immediately suspicious. The fact that Ande had left town, and more importantly, abandoned the fight against *txakurra* oppression twenty years earlier made the situation all the more tense. People spat on them in the street. They had only two allies, Balere, who is Ande's brother, and their *aita*, Birjaio. But both always arrived late at night and came in through the back door to avoid having their sympathies discovered.

What happened next was a complete accident. My *aita*, who we probably ought to have known as early as then was losing his grip on reality — or at the very least taken what he did as a sign of it -, in his infinite wisdom, decided that he would welcome the new neighbours. By pounding on their front door every morning for an hour, beginning at five a.m..

Ande had expected worse, and tuned it out. But it made Gen nervous and edgy. She was already upset with her mother for bringing her to such a cruel, decrepit place and the fact that Ande would do nothing about the mad man banging on the door left her livid.

*Aita*'s mission went on for three days before Ilari found out what he was up to. My *anaia*, who had been declared legally dead several years before, was by that time his father's keeper, a responsibility that kept him up most nights...

§

"You know," Lauran interrupts, thoughtful, "when I was seventeen, I just went to school and dated you or wished I was dating you and played soccer and chess. How did you all live this way?"

We've arrived at the *Jardin Public*. Most of the flowers have died in the November frost, but the chess tables are still busy, occupied by old men in parkas contemplating maneuvers with the fierce tenacity of generals at war. We find the one available space and sit opposite each other — but instead of setting out the game pieces, Lauran reaches across the table for my hands and threads his fingers through mine.

I wish that I could stop time, just for a minute, to savour the feeling of Lauran's hands in mine and think of nothing else in that suspended moment. But instead I have to answer, truthfully. "For Ilari and me, that was as normal as life got. It wasn't exactly a chess game in the park," I admit, only half-joking, "but we were used to it. For Gen, it was very, very hard." After a pause, I pick up the white queen and ask, "Shall we play?"

"Only if you can play and talk at the same time," Lauran jokes.

"I can play with one hand tied behind my back; I'm sure an open mouth won't get in my way."

"Big talk from a girl who learned to play chess from me."

I laugh out loud and nearly drop my knight into the grass. "I've had years of practise to help me recover from your lessons, thank-you very much."

"Then you talk, and we'll play."

"Fine," I agree. "As I was saying, Ilari had become his *aita*'s keeper..."

§

It was Goren Urestilla who woke him at sunrise on the third day of *aita*'s alleged mission. I should tell you that a few years later, Goren shot Dunixi Ormaetzea in the back, at his right shoulder. It was utterly accidental, and not a single person in town raised an eyebrow when Goren said, "I thought he was a tree!" by way of explanation. He is built like a brick house, and has the mental acuity of one, too. But he is a dedicated, unquestioning supporter of the cause... mainly because he couldn't form a question if he tried. "Ilari!" he shook my *anaia* awake, holding Ilari's thin bed covers in his meaty hands.

Ilari, stunned, blinked and shook his head. "How did you get in my room?"

"You have to see it!" Goren went on shaking the sheets, his enthusiasm taking control of his hands. "The commandant is welcoming our new neighbours!"

Cursing under his breath, my *anaia* leapt out of bed, grabbed the first clothes he could find and pulled them on as he rushed out of the house, barefoot, to avert what — if he was lucky, - would only be aggravation, and not disaster.

By the third day of the knocking, Gen was at her wit's end. Sleep deprived and raging, she paced her bedroom. Once or twice, she rushed to the top of the stairs, determined to confront the nuisance — then thought better of it and padded back to her room, temporarily defeated. She had no good ideas. She didn't even have any bad ones.

And then *aita* started yelling.

Gen didn't stop to think. She took the stairs two at a time and flew across the living room to the front door, which she flung open with all of her strength...

...at exactly the same second that Ilari grabbed *aita*'s arm and twisted it behind his back.

"Do you have no decency?" Gen shouted at her assailant, at full, hysterical volume. And then she saw Ilari. She recognised him immediately. "You!"

And Ilari recognised her. "You..."

Gen promptly slammed the door in his face and fled to the sanctuary of her bedroom.

§

"Knight to Queen's Bishop three," I flash a cheeky grin at Lauran, interrupting my own story. He left himself wide open in only eleven moves. "Checkmate."

Lauran blushes. "You are a lot better than I remember. But I can use your story as an excuse for being distracted, right?"

"Whatever makes you feel better," I tease him, and lean over our game to kiss him, taking out a few pawns as I go.

"That helped," Lauran admits. We put away the kings and rooks, and leave the chess table arm-in-arm. "Now that you have my undivided attention, why don't you tell me how this story ends?"

"In an apartment on *rue Malbec* in Bordeaux, of course...!"

"You know what I mean."

"All right, all right…"

§

I don't think my *anaia* gave a single thought to what he did next — he just did it. After frogmarching *aita* home and locking him in the house as securely as he could, he turned right back around without even stopping to put shoes on. He was betrothed to Mariaenea, it's true, but he had never stopped thinking about his dark-haired *Bordelaise* guide and her giddy laugh. She was the first girl he ever met who hadn't seen him in diapers, and to say that she had made an impression is an understatement.

For two days, Gen refused to see him. Ande met him at the door each time and turned him away, morning, noon and night. But my normally shy *anaia* persisted. By the second morning, Ande began to feel sorry for him. "You seem like a nice boy, in spite of your parents," she said. Ilari, who was on a mission, chose to take the compliment buried in those unkind words.

On the third morning, Ande was waiting for him when he knocked. "The answer is still no," she told him. "It's a shame. She could really use a friend."

Ilari saw his chance and he leapt at it. "Just let me in. I'll convince her."

Ande shrugged. "If she throws you back down those stairs, I can't help you."

My *anaia* decided those odds were close enough to being in his favour. He climbed the stairs quietly and knocked at Gen's door. Expecting her *maman*, she invited him in.

I've heard this part of the story so many times that I almost feel like I was there to watch it happen — the words and actions play out like a movie in my mind whenever I think about it. Gen lay listless on her bed when Ilari crossed the threshold of her room, but she jumped up as soon as she laid eyes on him. "What do you think you're doing here? How dare you just let yourself in?"

"I — I wanted to apologise for my *aita*. And, maybe — say how surprised I am to see you."

Those two sentences were the most anyone had said to Gen without insulting her since she arrived in Spain. She was disarmed. "Why are you being so nice to me?"

Ilari was quiet. He knew this was the kind of moment that one wrong word could irreparably fuck up. "Once," he said finally, "I introduced myself to a room full of strangers in a language I didn't speak. You were the only one who didn't laugh at me."

"I did laugh. I just covered my mouth."

"I know."

"But…" this is when Gen started to cry. "I was horrible to you!"

"I forgive you."

"Why?!"

"Why not?" Ilari shrugged.

That was all it took. With two words, Ilari's love for the brunette from Bordeaux stopped being unrequited. Apart from one cruel winter, they've been together ever since.

§

We've just half a block away from *rue Malbec* when I finally finish telling my *anaia*'s love story.

"When you tell our story," Lauran asks, looking down at me, "Does it sound like that?"

"I've never really told it."

"Why not? I've always liked it."

"To be honest, I've always thought the end of part one left a little to be desired. And part two is just beginning."

Lauran smiles as we step, hand-in-hand, off the sidewalk to cross onto *rue Malbec*, "Let's make it good, then." And he wraps his arms around my neck, kissing me in the middle of the street.

## Chapter 20

I wake up naked in Lauran's arms on Sunday morning, with Ilari shaking my bare shoulders. "Amaia! Amaia, wake-up!"

"Oh my God!" I sit bolt upright and yank the sheets tightly over my chest. "What on earth is so important?"

"Your meeting with Thierry." My *anaia* tries desperately to look anywhere but at me, his cheeks burning. "You're going to be late."

"Shit!" Little girls who want to help the cause of Euskadi freedom are not late for meetings with Thierry. I am the only little girl who wants to help the cause, and even so, I know this unwritten rule. It's just not done. "I'm up, I'm up!" I leap out of bed with a sheet wrapped around me. Satisfied that he has done his part to help Euskadi nationalism for the day, Ilari darts out to the kitchen as quickly as he can manage with his limp.

I get washed and dressed in a rush, inhale a cup of coffee in one gulp and leave the leftover *pain au chocolat* behind in favour of breakfast on the go – a cigarette. Twenty minutes after my abrupt wake-up call, I stand in the kitchen, poised to leave, while Ilari and Lauran are seated at the table (drinking from the same chipped coffee mugs they had yesterday.) "I'm sorry I have to leave in such a rush," I apologise to my maybe-sort-of-boyfriend, kissing him on the cheek, "but I'll be back in a few hours and then we can catch the train, *d'accord*?"

"Amaia," Ilari scolds, "if you don't leave in the next thirty bleeding seconds, you'll be late."

"Fine, fine, good-bye."

On my way out the door, I hear my *anaia* say, "So, what has Amaia told you about her chosen profession, exactly?" But I'm in such a rush that I don't think anything of it.

§

Thierry is a lawyer by vocation. He has an office in the city centre, just a few blocks from *Place de la Victoire*. I'm late, so I have to take the metro to get there. When I arrive, out of breath, his receptionist, Renée, is at her post, a sour expression on her lined face. Renée has been with Thierry since he opened his practise. She has seen me hundreds of times in the past three years, but she never greets me with anything that remotely resembles familiarity, never mind friendliness. "Bonjour, *mademoiselle*, how may I help you?"

And so I am faced with the arduous task of introducing myself for the hundredth time and trying simultaneously to catch my breath. "Sophie Cassou to see *monsieur* LeGrand."

"He is expecting you. Please, go ahead."

What Renée lacks in social skills, she makes up in discretion. In all of the years that she has worked for Thierry, she has never one suggested that she has any knowledge of his real business, nor made any inference to the effect that she has noticed that all of his clients are Basque. As far as she is concerned, Henri LeGrand represents me in my case against the French and Spanish governments; my files show that I am pursuing damages for hardships suffered due to the state-imposed custody agreement.

It will be twenty years before the case is heard by a jury at the rate we're moving. I turn the brass doorknob and let myself into Thierry's office, closing the door tightly behind me. "*Bonjour*, commandant."

"*Bonjour, mademoiselle* comrade."

The scene in Thierry's office is always the same. The commandant sits behind his desk in his uniform of jeans and a black t-shirt, a wall of legal tomes behind him, meticulously catalogued by the colour of their leather bindings – red, blue, black and green. On his desk sits a box of chocolates – the ones I like best, from Pierre Hermé – open but untouched. An empty wooden chair is directly across from him, waiting for me to fill it.

At times it still seems strange to me, to walk into this room, knowing what I've come for. Until three years ago, my life was leading me down a clear-cut path to study literature at La Sorbonne. I had vague ideas about becoming a novelist, but my only real dream was to get to Paris and let my life begin. The rest, I was sure, would take care of itself.

All of that changed, after the shots.

§

When I was in the hospital, I spent the first two weeks of my stay in a coma. Statistics show that most people with gunshot wounds to the left side of their chest die, even if the bullet doesn't so much as graze their heart. It looked, during those first two weeks, like I just might prove them right.

Gab was with me, for those two weeks. We sat together in my hospital room, watching me sleep; watching tearful visitors come and go; watching the nurses change my bandages and sheets. We had time together like we had never had it before; there was no one to hide from, no dirty secret to keep. All we did was talk. He told me what the *Ertzaintza* did to him – horrible, hideous things that I'll never be able to prove are true, but will never be able to doubt completely. He told me about his funeral; how he watched everyone cry but couldn't understand why they were so sad because now that it was all over, he was happy and free and finally got to be with the girl he loved. He told me that he still believed in The Organisation, but not in its methods. "There has to be," he repeated over and over again, "another way."

And then one day I woke up in bed with Gab sitting cross-legged at my feet. I still hadn't really come to, but I knew that something had changed because I was no longer outside of my body; I was the girl in the hospital bed with a tube in her nostrils and a long IV needle held in her arm by a piece of tape. But I wasn't afraid, because Gab was still with me, so I sat up and faced him, crossing my legs so that we were a mirror image of one another. He took my hands in his. "I just found out."

"What is it?"

"Where I'm going, you're not coming with me. Not yet." I didn't understand. Gab sighed and looked down at his hands before starting again, this time more gently, "Do you remember how we used to argue about the cause of Euskadi freedom, and you would say that even if my bombs and guns accomplished something, I would have nothing meaningful to contribute to the establishment of an independent Euskadi nation?" I nodded, swallowing hard. My words sounded impossibly cruel when they were repeated back to me. "It turns out you were right."

"No, no," I tried to dissuade him. "I was stupid. I didn't know what I was saying."

"But you were right. They told me. They said that my work is done, but there is another way – and you know what it is."

"But I don't!" I started to cry. "I don't know."

"You do. And when you wake up, it will be right in front of you, as clear as day. You can free our people, my princess. You – the skeptic, the Gorbachev admirer – you hold the key."

"I can't do it without you."

"You have to. But I'll watch over you every day. I'll always be there. I'll always listen."

"Really?"

"Really. Ilari will help you — they promised me that. And they're sending someone else, too. Someone you've been missing for a long time. I wanted you to wait for me, but they said you would need someone to help you when I couldn't. He'll be reluctant at first, but if you tell him what you're doing and why you have to do it, he'll understand. And he'll support you."

"But... why do I have to do it, Gab? I don't understand! I just," I choked on a sob, "I want to go with you."

"You can't — you have to free our people first. Every Euskadi people grow up with cages around their hearts. You're going to set them all free. And when you're done, you can come home to me." Gab looked down at our clasped hands, his solid composure suddenly shaken. "Promise you'll always love me."

"I promise, I promise," I sobbed.

"Promise you'll never forget me."

"I promise, I promise."

Gab wrapped his arms around me and held on for a moment that I wished could last forever. "I love you, my princess," he whispered.

"I love you, too."

"I have to go now."

I tried to hold on, but Gab faded slowly out of my grasp until he was gone. That was the last time I saw him — I know, even if I can't explain it properly, that he wasn't in my imagination then, but that he has been every time we've talked since.

The next night, I dreamt of Lauran. It was a real dream — he was out living his life when I lay in the hospital and I knew both of those things. But in my dream we were two busy people in the city, rushing toward each other on a crowded sidewalk. He didn't see me. I didn't see him. Until we ran into each other, just like we had all those years before in the school hallway. "Lauran!" I exclaimed as we collided.

"Sophie!" He was just as shocked to see me.

And then, in the dream, Gab's words came back to me — *And they're sending someone else, too. Someone you've been missing for a long time.* "Are you the one they sent?" I asked.

Lauran raised one blonde eyebrow. "I don't know what you mean."

*He'll be reluctant at first, but if you tell him what you're doing, and why you have to do it, he'll understand.* "There are some things... I have to explain to you. Will you listen?"

"I suppose so."

And we walked off together down the sidewalk.

§

When I woke up in the hospital, the world was blurry at first, but even in the haze, I recognised *ama*'s blue eyes on me. She gasped when she saw my eyelashes flutter. "*Ama?*" I croaked. After weeks without making a sound, my voice was weak and thin.

"Amaia! My Amaia..." *ama* grabbed my hand and held on as if she could keep me from descending back into unconsciousness by the sheer force of her grip, weeping on my crisp white bed sheets. "I told them you were a fighter."

Those three sentences were the most that *ama* had said to me for years — she so rarely spoke at all that the soft, breathy tone of her voice was unfamiliar. In all the years I had summered in Euskal Herria, I had never really gotten to know my *ama*. She took no part in the court battle that awarded her partial custody over me — and when the custody was awarded, she took rudimentary care of me until I was old enough not to need it. Our relationship was based largely on hellos and goodbyes. I learned not to let it hurt. But I had never stopped wondering why.

I don't know what it was about that moment — maybe because I didn't really know if I would live and I didn't want to die without knowing... Maybe simply because it was the first time I'd had the chance to ask. "*Ama?*"

"Don't talk, *maite*. Save your strength."

"Why didn't you fight to get me back?"

My restless young *ama* was quiet for a long moment. She wiped her eyes with a mascara-stained tissue, then leaned forward to kiss me on the forehead. "You were born a fighter. You should have died but instead you grew. You should have died two weeks ago but here I am talking to you. All of the talk about Ilari being the saviour of our people? It's nonsense. You are the one, *maite*. I always knew. But heroes die young. I didn't want that for you. I thought, when they took you away, that you would be spared from this life." I breathed low and slow through my oxygen tube, taking in every word. "But fate came back for you."

"I love you, *ama*," I whispered. It was the first time I could remember saying those words.

"*Maitatu*, Amaia."

That was the last time I saw my *ama* alive. Jess Larrea went to our house two days later to fix the front door and found her, hanging from a rafter in our front hallway, a wooden chair lying upended on the floor behind her. She was thirty-eight. Although she could not read or write, *ama* was an elegant, eloquent woman to the last. Her limited education meant she could leave no note, but instead she meticulously tore a page from her beloved Spanish bible, the one she had memorised from listening at mass, and left it lying on the floor below her feet. It was Mark 13: 32-37 – *"But of that day and that hour knoweth no man, no, not the angels which are in heaven, neither the Son, but the Father, take ye heed, watch and pray: for ye know not when the time is. For the Son of man is as a man taking a far journey, who left his house, and gave authority to his servants, and to every man his work, and commanded the porter to watch. Watch ye therefore: for ye know not when the master of the house cometh, at even, or at midnight, or at the cockcrowing, or in the morning. Lest coming suddenly he find you sleeping. And what I say unto you I say unto all, Watch."*

§

Formalities aside, "Amaia," Thierry greets me in his usual quiet way. He is not the type to express enthusiasm, even by so much as changing the tone of his voice. "Welcome."

"Hello, Thierry." I take the chair across from my lawyer and cross my legs. "I hope you've been well."

"And I you." My lawyer reaches for the box of chocolates and holds it out to me, offering. "Would you like one?"

"Yes, thank-you." I reach delicately for a square of *caramel au beurre salé* wrapped in chocolate and, holding it between my thumb and forefinger, take a bite from the corner. "You spoil me."

"It has been too long since your last visit to Bordeaux. We have much to discuss." I nod in thoughtful agreement, chewing. "Tell me about your studies."

"Very well," I agree, and I begin my report.

§

Those first weeks were hard for Ilari. I was the one with the gunshot wound, it's true. But when I woke from the coma, I had an incredible sense of clarity and purpose. It was just like Gab had said; it was right in front of me. I knew what I had to do.

When Ilari first visited me, after I rejoined the world, he looked near death himself. Gab. *Ama*. And me, almost... all within two short weeks, the world he knew had crumbled all around him and he stood in the middle of the wreckage, bewildered and alone. He shuffled into my hospital room, slowed by the weight of the grief that he dragged behind him. When he saw me sit up to greet him, he collapsed into the chair next to my bed; relieved of its anxiety, his body instantly gave in to exhaustion.

And then I said, "I need to see Thierry."

My *anaia* called the nurse. "What kind of drugs are you giving her?" he demanded of the pink-uniformed woman who came to answer.

"What do you mean, sir?"

"She's delusional!"

Little did he know... My *anaia* never believed I was crazy, but his declaration came just after a particularly unpleasant visit from my psychiatrist, and no one doubted that he was right.

Every day when Ilari came back, I said the same thing. Every day after the first, he just ignored me. After a week of getting nowhere, I changed my strategy. "What if I told you that you didn't have to spend the rest of your life shooting at Spaniards?"

My *anaia* sighed and set down heavily in the brown visitor's chair. "I'm listening."

"There is a way. But you have to let me speak to Thierry."

"Where did this sudden obsession with Euskadi nationalism come from? I thought you got shot, not hit on the head."

"I did."

Ilari sighed. "Explain it to me, then. What the hell would possess you to even consider thinking about the possibility of getting involved with someone so fucking dangerous?"

"It's what I have to do."

"In what bloody universe?"

"This one. Gab told me."

"Gab is dead, Amaia," my *anaia* reminded me gently. "You know that."

"Yes, but..."

"That means you can't talk to him anymore. And he can't talk to you."

I tried to explain myself, but that only made things worse. Ilari called the nurse — she only hesitated for a second before concluding that I was deluded again. The tranquiliser she administered knocked me out right through the night.

But still, I refused to give up. I knew what I had to do and I wasn't about to let my over-protective *anaia* get in my way. Every day when he came to visit, I asked to see Thierry. I listened to Ilari's exasperated, curse-filled response. And then I asked again.

"What makes you think," my *anaia* demanded one quiet Tuesday afternoon, "that you can say anything to him that I haven't?"

I only needed one word to respond. "*Ama*."

It was unkind, but I was running out of options. For one millisecond, Ilari gave himself away and I saw the way his heart was slowly cracking open flicker across his face — then he composed himself and asked, "What does this have to do with *ama*?"

"She was with me when I woke up."

"I know that, Mai."

"She told me I was the one. Not *aitaita*, not *aita*, not even you — me. She told me that she had always known."

"Mai, *ama* wasn't well…"

"Haven't you ever wondered why she didn't fight to keep me? She wanted to save me from my destiny, she said."

It was at this point that Ilari called the nurse. He always visited at the same time of day, so it was always the same nurse who answered — a short, fat woman with a stiff perm and a collection of candy pink uniforms. "*Señora*," my anaia greeted her, "I think my sister is getting a bit excited…"

The nurse sighed and gave my chart a cursory glance. "This again?"

"*Señora*, she has been through a lot in the past few weeks."

"I assure you, *Señor* Sagastizabal, that we are aware of your sister's history. We review her medication and progress with the utmost scrutiny. These constant requests for sedation are, frankly, counterproductive. Amaia is in full possession of her mental faculties and entitled to express herself."

Ilari swallowed and nodded his assent. There was nothing he could say.

As she left the room, the nurse muttered, "Basques — everyone an extremist in his own way."

I turned to my *anaia*. "Do you really want to live the rest of your life like this? A punch line for jokes and a target for insults?"

Ilari looked at the tiled floor and said nothing.

"Do you want to live the rest of your life playing shoot 'em up with *aita*, gunning down ten civilians for every one imagined slight?"

Still, my *anaia* said nothing.

"Or do you plan to work for the commandant, without knowing what that might mean and without the courage to ask, because that seems like the path of least resistance?"

When my *anaia* broke his silence, he did not do it halfway; "You know I don't have a fucking choice!" His shouted words echoed down the hospital corridor.

I answered him quietly. "I'm telling you that you do have a choice. But you have to let me see Thierry."

"I don't want to discuss it anymore."

Just like that, the issue seemed to be closed. But two days later, a small, balding man with wire-framed glasses knocked at the door of my hospital room. He wore a black t-shirt tucked into his jeans and my first thought was that he must have taken a wrong turn on his way to visit someone else. "Can I help you?"

He cleared his throat. "I understand that you've asked to see me."

I squirmed into a sitting position. A small part of me wondered if the man was really there, or if he was visiting me the way that Gab did. "I have...?"

"Allow me to introduce myself." The man extended one small hand to meet mine. "My name is Henri LeGrand, but you would know me better as Thierry."

"My name is Sophie Cassou," I reached out and shook Thierry's hand as well as I could under the circumstances. "But you probably know me as Amaia. Welcome. I'm glad that you've come."

"I must tell you, *mademoiselle* Cassou, that I am not the sort of man who is in the habit of taking impromptu trips across a border whose existence I contest in order to meet with teenaged girls. My work keeps me very busy. I have chosen to visit because of your impressive lineage. I do hope that you are as serious as your family tree would suggest."

Thierry made that speech to intimidate me. He wanted to know, and he wanted to know quickly, if he was wasting his time. Just a few weeks earlier, I would have stumbled and stuttered a response to such firm direction. But that afternoon, I squared my shoulders and looked the commandant straight in the eye. "I understand that you have entered into a sort of contract with my *anaia*, whereby he will work for you in exchange for your willingness to reinstate our village as a member of your organisation. I would like to propose an alternative arrangement, with myself as his replacement."

Thierry raised an eyebrow behind his wire frames. "Ilari is a trained soldier with a lifetime of field and strategic experience. What relevant qualifications do you have that might make you a superior choice?"

"For one thing, I do not have my *anaia*'s nervous disposition. I am Euskadi-born but French-raised and educated, thus capable not only of doing ground work to secure an independent nation but also of providing a meaningful contribution to the development of a new state. The way that I see it, you and I want the same thing."

"I want a great many things, *mademoiselle* Cassou," Thierry warned.

I countered, "As do I, *monsieur* LeGrand. Perhaps you have heard how I found myself in this hospital bed?"

"I have been advised of the unfortunate circumstances, yes."

"Perhaps, then, you can appreciate that beyond the fact that I can take a bullet, I have a truly unique perspective to bring to your organisation. I grew up both sheltered from and surrounded by violence. And what I have learned is that people are only free if they believe in their freedom. I support your ceasefire because I am certain that it is the only way to achieve our ends. The few who act on behalf of the many have had their moment, but genetic succession in terrorism has distorted the purpose and ideals laid out by the founders of The Organisation. It is my belief that our people will be galvanised and will rise up themselves, if we show them that they have the reason to. Terrorists are feared and misunderstood, *monsieur* LeGrand. Rebels are admired. Protesters are emulated. This is what I bring to the table that my *anaia* does not."

"I see." For the first time since his arrival, Thierry's face betrayed his thoughts. He was intrigued.

"We will make strong partners, I'm sure. But before we can begin, there are three small matters to be settled. Firstly, I, like you, want Zorion Sagastizabal permanently removed from anywhere that he might cause damage. I am sure you understand what I mean by this and trust that you are capable of making the necessary arrangements. Secondly, I want Balere and Remiri far away, where they cannot cause trouble. I understand that you have connections in South America. Perhaps they could be of service to you there... without their wives, I might add. Finally, when those two matters have been settled, I expect that our ceasefire will be declared permanent."

The look on Thierry's face had, by the time I finished, turned from intrigue to bafflement. He took a moment to collect himself before speaking. "When I first joined the organisation, I moved through the ranks quickly. I met most of the old guard along the way, but the one I was most in awe of was *Suge*. He was brilliant, ruthless and, once, I witnessed as he had a bullet removed from his arm with nothing but a swig of wine as an anaesthetic. Do not misunderstand me — I was impressed by Ilari and believe that he has much to offer the cause. But you are the living embodiment of your late *aitaita*." Thierry stood and reached out to shake my hand. "Welcome to The Organisation, *mademoiselle* Cassou."

Two days later, *aita* was gunned down in a suburb of Bilbao. His death inspired very little mourning, and a cursory investigation of the murder did not locate his killer. Within the week, Balere and Remiri were on a cargo plane en route to Buenos Aires.

"Thank-you, commandant."

§

Conversation between Thierry and me has never completely shed the formality of our first meeting. I give him a thorough account of my activities at school, without using contractions or personal pronouns. He nods his assent and occasionally adds a comment like, "I see," but generally avoids displaying anything that might be called enthusiasm. The fact is that although we have renounced violence, our work remains extremely dangerous. All of the G20 nations still consider The Organisation a terrorist group. Any time shots are fired in Spain, we are immediately the prime suspects. Even a meeting like this one is technically illegal. And I am a twenty-one-year-old girl. Thierry tries to protect me by keeping his encouragement to a minimum. Equally, I try to prove that I am not a child by acting mature and knowledgeable beyond my years. This has brought us through the first three years of our partnership almost seamlessly.

To be fair, we have had difficulties. Ilari protested my membership in The Organisation vociferously at first. He really only came back into the fold a year ago, when he saw the work that we had done with Euskadi youth – disarming them, educating them, just talking to them and listening to what they have to say about who they feel they are or could be – was nothing like the Organisation activity he had been part of. The fact that he temporarily defected was a source of tension, never mentioned but always present. But, by and large, we are quiet collaborators, working together the only way that we know how.

"Your progress at school encourages me, Amaia," Thierry says when I finish my report.

"Thank-you, commandant." I take a chocolate from the box and bite off the corner.

"There is, however, another matter that we must discuss."

"Oh?"

"I have been advised that you brought a young man along with you to Bordeaux this weekend. Based upon the report I received, I am given to understand that he is one of our people, a fact that pleases me."

My stomach tightens. I know who gave the report and suddenly, I'm uncertain where it might lead our partnership. "Thank-you, commandant."

"Does he have any involvement with our organisation?"

"Not that I am aware of."

"Very well," Thierry nods. "In that case, I feel compelled to remind you that at all times, your primary responsibility is to our cause. I do not wish to call into question your dedication by any means, but love is a powerful and dangerous force. Please, Amaia, I implore you — do not forget who you are and what is truly important to you."

A sour taste fills my mouth and I swallow my chocolate, ashamed without being completely sure what I've done wrong. "Yes, commandant."

## Chapter 21

I look out the window onto the crowded tracks of *Gare Saint-Jean* as we begin to pull away, the train slowly chugging on the start of our journey back to Paris.

Lauran was waiting for me when I returned from my meeting with Thierry. We gathered our things and walked down *rue Malbec* to the *gare* in a quiet rhythm. I commented absently on the blue sky, and my ex-boyfriend politely agreed that it was a nice day. It occurs to me now, as *Gare Saint-Jean* fades into a distant blur on the horizon, that those are the only words Lauran has said to me since I left him this morning.

A nervous chill runs through me. I don't know what has happened since I left the apartment, but I know instinctively that something has changed since our happy, tangled hours in bed this morning. "Lauran?" I start. I can hear the tremor in my voice. "Is everything all right?"

My ex-boyfriend looks straight ahead at the empty seat in front of him as he answers, "On Friday night, you said no more secrets. What did that mean, exactly?"

I can feel myself start to shake. "I meant what I said, Lauran."

"Then how," he turns to face me, his jaw set and his pale eyes cold – I recoil instinctively, leaning further back towards the window, trying to shrink into safety, "exactly how would you define your relationship with the commandant? The one that I had to hear about from your *anaia*!"

"I never intended to keep that from you."

"That's a pretty big fucking secret, Sophie!"

"But," I stammer, "It wasn't a secret! Honestly!"

"If I were the second-in-command of a major terrorist operation," Lauran is livid, "I think I would tell people I wanted to be intimate with. I think I would be upfront about it. I think I would want to know if they really wanted to be involved with all of the parts of my sordid little life."

"No, you wouldn't." My words are calm and measured, a stark contrast to Lauran's emotional monologue. The weight of a flood of tears presses down on my eyes, but I hold it back. I can only hope that the other passengers on the train will think that we are rehearsing a play. I look down at my hands as I explain, "You would tell as few people as you could manage, to avoid putting them in danger and compromising your own position. You would hide the truth from anyone who did not ask direct questions – even, no most of all, the people that you loved. And if you ever considered telling someone, because you felt that you could trust them, that they cared enough about you to accept or, in a dream world, support your work, you would approach the truth slowly and gingerly, as if you were crossing an old wooden bridge to reach it. At every step you would test your footing – give subtle hints of your ideals and gauge the reaction to see if it might be worth moving forward. For what it's worth, you are the first person I've met who made me feel like I might get to the other side of that bridge. But we aren't there yet. You still think that my organisation is a band of terrorists. I have so much to teach you about the work that The Organisation really does before I admit that it's mine."

When I look up, I find Lauran contemplating my face – the coldness in his eyes has given way to reflective sadness. "I'm sorry, Sophie," he places one hand tenderly on my cheek. "I don't know how to handle this."

I can only shake my head. "I knew you weren't ready."

"Would you ever consider... I mean..." my ex-boyfriend struggles to find the right words. "I don't even know how to put this without coming across like a chauvinist. Do you plan to do this for the rest of your life?"

"Yes."

"And if anyone ever asked you to make a choice," Lauran looks into my eyes with such unmistakable earnestness that it's almost painful to meet his gaze, "would you consider giving it up?"

I remember the words that Thierry said to me this afternoon, but there is no need for their reinforcement. I know the answer to the question and offer it without hesitation. "No."

Lauran pulls his hand away from my face, as though my simple answer has burned him. He turns away from me and looks at the empty chair in front of him, searching the mirrored back of his fold-away tray table for some clue about what to do that my eyes can't give him. "I really thought that things were different this time," he says quietly.

"I think," I try, more out of a desperate need to find some way, any way at all, to fix this, than because I believe that these words will fix it, "that they can be."

"This is *lycée* all over again." There is an audible crack in Lauran's voice. "Somehow, no matter what I do, I always come in second with you."

Crushed by the weight of that allegation, I sit back heavily in my chair and gaze out the window at the landscape as it passes in a blur – I don't know if it's the speed of the train or the tears in my eyes, but the fields of the Loire Valley are nothing but a haze of yellow with green spots. There is nothing that I can say that will undo what Lauran feels. And I am so devastated by the fact that, after all the broken trust we have managed to build back up, he still lets a few small words lead him to doubt me, that I cannot find the strength to attempt the impossible. I just sit back and listen to the sound of my heart breaking in time with the rhythm of the train's metal clatter.

"Sophie? Please, say something."

"Is there anything I can say that might make you feel differently?"

"I don't know," Lauran admits.

"I don't either. But I would rather live with that uncertainty than open my mouth and find out there's no hope."

We sit in silence for a long moment, privately contemplating the precipice on which we find ourselves. I can't help but wonder if there is any way we can turn back now, since there is no way to move forward. But I'm afraid that we're going to go over the edge no matter what we do — and I can see from here that we won't survive the fall.

Lauran is more pragmatic. "I'm going to get a drink," he announces, and walks away.

§

I expect that Lauran will be back by the time that I run out of convincing reasons why I shouldn't follow him to the bar — but he isn't. I wait another ten minutes, telling myself that there must be an uncharacteristically long line in the drink car. But still, he does not come back.

I could use a drink myself, I reason. This is all the encouragement I need to stand up and follow my ex-boyfriend's path along the train cars.

There is no line for the bar. This is hardly a surprise. I order a glass of red wine and carry it to the table where Lauran sits alone, chin in hand, staring pensively out the window. "When we met again," I remind him, "I asked you for one cup of coffee. I wanted to tell you a story."

"Sophie," Lauran starts.

"Now, I'm asking you for one glass of wine. I want to finish what I started — even if you don't believe in the things I believe in, I think it will help you to understand why I was so quick to answer you the way I did." My ex-boyfriend says nothing. "After the train arrives at *Gare Montparnasse*, we can go our separate ways

– I'll understand. But do you really want to do that without at least knowing how I got my scar?"

Lauran softens slightly – I can see the corners of his mouth turn up into what just might be called a smile. "Sit down."

"Thank-you." I settle into the plastic chair and take a sip of my wine. "I know you'll spend the rest of your life wondering, so I'm going to relieve the suspense. When I was eighteen, I was shot…"

§

I've gone over the events in my mind a thousand times, but no matter how I recall them, I don't think there was any way I could have known what kind of danger I was in. I made real progress with Gab, in the hours that I was free to spend with him. Alaine, his wife, visited him in the *despachos* twice every day. At ten o'clock every morning, she brought him bread and coffee. And then, every day at four o'clock, she came to take away his dishes and replace them with dinner, if there was any. I knew better than to let her see me coming or going – my vanity had dissipated completely. Even though Gab had never felt anything like love for her, and might not even have known that they were married, he was still Alaine's husband. Whatever the reality of their marriage was, it would have been mean-spirited of me not to hide that I was the other woman.

I went to the *despachos* three times a day – first at sunrise, so that Gab and I could start the day together, then at eleven and again in the evening after dinner. Any time that I was away from the *despachos* was just time that I was waiting to go back to them; I was listless and distracted and hardly noticed what was happening around me.

The things I didn't know could have filled an encyclopedia. Thanks to my *aita*'s erratic behaviour and refusal to respect orders, the village had been expelled from The Organisation. Ilari had told me that much. What he had neglected to mention was that, forever a rebel, *aita* was trying to form a rival terrorist faction –

his grip on reality, I understand, was quite loose. The rest of the village — including the soldiers who had once idolised him, and fought for him — was plotting against him. And Balere and Remiri, who had always been so gentle with me, had shown the other side of their two faces; Ilari's summons from the commandant had not simply fallen out of the sky. They were behind it, and they had let my *anaia* know in no uncertain terms that if he did not come back with news that their membership in The Organisation had been reinstated, it would be best that he not come back at all.

All I thought of was Gab. After my first two days in Euskal Herria, the tears stopped falling from his eyes. After three days, he spoke for the first time and I think my heart almost exploded. I thought I was working some kind of miracles. I thought that I was witnessing the true power of love and that if I just worked hard enough, I could bring Gab back to life.

I was naïve and stupid.

When I told Ilari that Gab had spoken, all he said was, "At least now we know he still can. I was starting to think that the *Ertzaintza* had hit him on the head or something."

But I refused to allow my *anaia*'s pragmatism to get in the way of the idea that I was saving Gab. It crossed my mind, once or twice, that I wasn't entirely certain what I might be saving. The more Gab talked, the less sense he made. There were moments of lucidity, but he most often spoke to people who weren't there on subjects that did not exist. At times I thought he was making reference to his imprisonment, but on reflection, I could never convince myself that I was sure. Still, I wanted to believe, so I believed.

I had been in Euskal Herria for only five days when Ilari had to leave for his meeting with the commandant. Before he set out on the road, we sat down at the kitchen table in our parents' house to have coffee together. We were both terrified but too stubborn to admit it, so we danced around the subject of the danger he faced without every really mentioning it. It might have been the last time we were ever together, and afterward I was ashamed that I hadn't at least told my *anaia* that I would miss him.

When our coffee was gone, we went out into the yard to clean our dishes under the hose. As he washed his empty porcelain cup, Ilari stood with his back to me and said, "I don't want you to go to see Gab while I'm gone."

"What? Why?"

"He's been waving a gun around today, ranting and raving. We don't know what the hell he might do."

"But... why don't you just take his gun away?"

"Are you insane?" Ilari shut off the hose and turned to face me. "What the fuck makes you think that it's any safer for me than it is for you?"

I had to admit that I didn't know. But still, I balked at the idea of staying away from Gab for almost three days.

"Amaia, I'm serious," Ilari emphasized. This was as close as we got to real emotion. "Stay away from the *despachos* while I'm gone. It's not safe. Promise me."

I promised, but my heart wasn't in it.

§

"You went anyway, didn't you?" Lauran demands from across the table, exasperated.

"I'm getting to that," I answer without saying yes or no. We both know the truth, anyway.

"You're the only person I know who can be selfish and unselfish at the same time. It's infuriating."

I decide to take my ex-boyfriend's words as the compliment that they might have been only a few hours ago and move on. I put my plastic wine glass to my lips and find it empty. "Let's have another drink, shall we?"

"Please."

We approach the bar together, but at the same time, far apart. The physical space between us, the space that just a few nights ago was so insignificant that it took my breath away, looks like just a few centimetres but feels like a chasm. I order my drink quietly and let my ex-boyfriend follow me back to our table.

When we find ourselves sitting face-to-face again, I continue...

§

I intended to stay away. I know that seems out of character for me, but it's true. Ilari wasn't in the habit of telling me what to do, so I knew his instructions were serious. And I knew that Gab wasn't himself. I knew that even when he was himself, he was sometimes dangerous.

The problem was that I had nothing else to do. It's not easy to move from a life with TV, *portables* and the internet to one where even books are scarce. I had so much time. And the only thing I had to do with it was think about Gab — so close, but so far away.

On Saturday night, I sat a solitary vigil on the living room couch; looking out my parents' front window I could just see the window of the *despachos* from my spot on the bedraggled cushions. I tried to look anywhere else, but resistance was futile. I watched the shadow of Alaine enter through the door, and I watched as Gab sent her back through it, shame-faced.

I'm sorry; this is probably more than you need to know. But even you must have done something stupid for love once. I sat in the living room and tried to hold myself back, but the scene I had just witnessed was all of the validation I needed — even after months of imprisonment and torture, Gab would always choose me over his wife.

In the end, it was all I could do not to run up the six flights of stairs to the *despachos*. When I arrived, Gab was lucid and happy to see me. We talked like old times — we even had a small disagreement about the feasibility of installing a communist government in Euskal Herria. It felt like a living, breathing miracle.

And then, at a lull in the conversation, Gab said, "Let's run away together."

"What?"

"Let's run away together! I know somewhere that we can go — we'll be safe and free and no one will ever keep us apart again."

Something in me hesitated; maybe it was the idea that there was a safe place we could go. Something about safety in Euskal Herria as I knew it didn't ring quite true no matter who suggested it. "Are you sure?"

"Of course I'm sure. I've been thinking about this for a long time now."

"Is it far?"

"It won't take long to get there, I promise."

I didn't hesitate a second time. "Yes!"

We grabbed hands and raced down the stairs at a run. I was so giddy that I don't remember the first two flights at all. By the third, I had begun to wonder if I was really ready to wake up the next day alone with Gab, not knowing if he would still be himself. When we reached the fifth, I was beginning to think it might be best if I convinced Gab just to spend the weekend at a hotel in Bilbao before we started on the rest of our journey.

By the time we touched ground on the main floor, my plan had changed to spending the weekend at a hotel in Bilbao before we came home.

We ran out of the factory in a rush, still high on the adrenaline of our furtive escape. There is a feeling of indescribable joy that comes over you when you do what is wrong but feels right and that propelled us forward. I reached to squeeze Gab's hand and realised that it had somehow slipped from my grasp. I looked to either side of me — he wasn't there. "Gab?"

I stopped.

I turned back.

"Amaia."

Gab stood ten feet behind me, his feet planted squarely on the dirt road. I will never forget the moment that I realised he had a gun. And that it was aimed at me.

*I know somewhere we can go. Safe. Free. No one will ever try to keep us apart again.* The words reverberated through my mind like echoes in a mountain range. *I've been thinking about this for a long time.*

"I love you more than anything," Gab called out.

I had no time to protest. A shot rang out in the night and my world went dark.

§

I have to pause. Not because Lauran has anything to say — his blue eyes are so wide with shock, his cheeks so ashen that I suspect he won't be able to say anything at all before he has another drink — but because I have never before told that story outside of a psychiatrist's office and the feeling of reliving it, even just in words, is visceral.

I have to check to be sure my left shoulder isn't bleeding.

Across from me, my ex-boyfriend covers his mouth with his fist and swallows. He keeps his eyes on the table, as if looking at me, knowing what he now knows, will be too much to bear. Based on his stricken expression, I can't quite decide if he is physically ill, or just at a loss for words. "Jesus," he mumbles into his hand.

"So now you know." My words are nothing more than an empty platitude, but I feel compelled to say something — anything, just to fill the silence.

"I hope he rots in jail." Lauran, his teeth gritted, practically spits that sentence out.

"Who? Gab?" I am caught between feeling touched by Lauran's fierce desire to protect me and surprised that he didn't catch the subtleties of what happened that night outside of the factory. "Oh, no. We were going away together, don't you see? After he aimed his gun at me, he turned it on himself. He's been-" the words still hurt when I speak them aloud, "dead for three and a half years."

This revelation is followed by another long silence. I signal to the bartender for more wine and he fills up my plastic cup while my ex-boyfriend glares down at the Formica table, brooding.

I wait. I count the farmhouses passing outside the window, tapping my left foot nervously on the floor. I'm positively dying to reach for a cigarette – just to keep my hands still – but my *Gauloises* are back at my assigned seat and a red *Défense de fumer* sign hangs stubbornly overhead.

I wait. Fourteen farmhouses, each in a unique state of disrepair, pass by outside before Lauran says quietly, "I don't understand, Sophie."

"Which part?"

"After everything that The Organisation has put you through in your life," my ex-boyfriend finally looks up at me, his eyes pleading for some scrap of information, some unifying string that will allow him to tie together the facts of my disastrous existence, "what would possess you to join them?"

"None of this can be blamed on The Organisation," I explain. The look of doubt that clouds Lauran's face tells me exactly how impossible he considers this truth. "It took me a lifetime to learn that, but it's true. They are easy to blame because of their reputation for violence, but the truth is that if it weren't for the Spanish government's systemic oppression of our people, there would be no need for The Organisation. I know, I know, you want to point out that we have been granted autonomy – but it is autonomy without freedom. I spent my summers in a village where everyone felt so trapped, so cloistered, that by the time they reached school age, they were sure that their only option was to shoot their way out. It wasn't The Organisation that trapped them. The Organisation was the only place they felt they could turn."

"But, Sophie, they're–"

"If you're going to finish that sentence with terrorists," I cut Lauran off, "don't bother. Ilari and I are the only Sagastizabals left standing. My whole family; my parents, my uncles, even my grandparents – gave their lives because they saw no other way. They were poor, uneducated people. The only thing that gave them power was violence. Alleged independence offered them so little hope for the future that they lived as if it didn't exist. At least The Organisation tried to help them. The validity of their methods can be argued all day long, but their motivation was pure."

I pause to catch my breath. At times it even surprises me, after all of the years that I spent condemning it, that I speak so passionately in favour of The Organisation. But there is nothing that I believe in more strongly than what the organisation has done – and can do. Not even my beloved Gorbachev. "If you're wondering if I carry a gun, the answer is no. We declared an indefinite ceasefire more than three years ago – I made it a condition of my membership – and we have honoured it. We spend most of our time disarming poor, desperate teenagers. Soon, we want to open a school where we can unteach everything they have learned about life growing up in occupied territory. For now, we monitor them. Visit them. Talk with them. Teach them what little we know. Help them to find jobs. We believe – I believe that if they know that they are deserving of freedom, they will find constructive ways to achieve it. The work is messy and dangerous, it's true. But if it means that just one person won't end up the way Gab did, it's worth everything to me."

"Sophie!" Lauran looks like he wants to reach across the table and shake sense into me. "Someone tried to kill you! Do you honestly think that the best way to celebrate survival is to leap back into the line of fire?"

I sigh and run my fingers through my hair. "Do you want to know what Gab did for The Organisation, what he specialised in? He was a marksman. He could hit a moving target at a thousand yards like it was a tin can on a fence. When they were little, he taught Ilari how to aim left – so that he could shoot first and still ask questions. In another life-" my ex-boyfriend cringes at the suggestion, and even though I am telling him these things because I love him – because I so badly want him to love me – for a brief instant, I hate him, "he might have been a military sniper. He was a person, not a murderer. I can see you don't believe me, but it's true. And if he had meant to kill me, I wouldn't be sitting here with you now. But he aimed left. I have chosen," I emphasize the word, "to interpret that as a sign that I still have work to do. Maybe it would be more palatable for you if I didn't work with The Organisation, but it just made more sense to join an established organisation than to start from nothing. There are a lot of things I want to accomplish in a short time — this is the best way. I'm not asking you to come along for the ride, but I would appreciate if you could accept that this is my choice — at least for the duration of the train ride."

As if on cue, *Gare Montparnasse* appears on the horizon just as I come to the end of my monologue.

"Well," I stand up, "that made it nice and easy for you."

I stride back to my seat, not bothering to wait for an answer that isn't coming.

§

My seat is abandoned, just as I left it. I am tipsier than I realised, and gathering my things while privately raging at Lauran is a complex chore — it takes three attempts for me to throw my *portable* into my purse. When I finally manage to get myself in order, I sling my bags over my shoulder and whirl around in a huff.

I find myself face-to-face with my ex-boyfriend. He has been standing in the aisle, watching me. We look into each other's eyes for an instant and all of my anger vanishes, leaving behind a profound, aching sadness. "Good-bye," I whisper, and walk past him towards the door.

All along the aisle, I hear my ex-boyfriend's footfalls behind me. When I step off the train onto the platform, the sound of Lauran's shoes scraping against the metal grate steps is inescapable. I keep walking, pulling my suitcase behind me.

I take less than ten steps before I feel compelled to turn back. "Lauran?"

My ex-boyfriend stops and looks up. "Yes?"

"There is just one more thing I want you to know. I never told Gab that I loved him. And I have to live with the fact that he died without ever hearing those three simple words from me. I made a promise to myself that I would never waste a chance again — you never know when it might be the last one," I swallow hard. "Even if we never see each other again, please know that I love you. I always have."

I don't wait for his reply — I'm too afraid of what it might be. Fighting tears, I turn on my heel and rush out into the night.

Only when I've put three blocks between the train station and myself do I dare to stop. I sit down on a green-lacquered wooden bench and cradle my face in my hands so that passing tourists can't see me weep.

All of my years of waiting and wishing... And I walked away again. I can't believe that all along, this was how our story was meant to end.

## Chapter 22

I am dry-eyed and composed by the time I reach the blue lacquered door to the apartment I share with my brother. I don't hesitate for a second before putting my key in the lock — my feet are tired and my shoulders feel like they've been carrying the weight of the world. All I want to do is crawl into bed and forget that the past two days — no, the past two months — were real.

But when I shove the door open, I find Luc standing on the other side of it, a silly smile on his normally serious face. "*Bon soir*, Sophie!"

"Were you," I raise an eyebrow, "waiting for me?"

"No!" I can practically hear the exclamation point behind that one-syllable world. "Just happened to hear the door, that's all!"

While Luc cannot be described as emotionally stunted like my *anaia*, he rarely qualifies to be called expressive, either. I am instinctively suspicious. And suspicion only makes me more tired. I just don't have the wherewithal to do this, whatever it is, right now. "Well, I'm home. And now," I step around my brother, "I'm going to bed."

Luc sidesteps to block my path. "How was Bordeaux?"

My brother never asks about my trips — his question makes me nervous. "You never ask about Bordeaux."

"I'm asking now. How was it?"

"Fine." I step around Luc, wheeling my suitcase over his foot deliberately. He gives no sign of having noticed. "Good night."

I make it only two steps down the hall towards the refuge of my bedroom before Luc calls out, "I'm in love with Madeleine!"

An audible sigh escapes my lips. I am tired and sad but if I let on, it will only lead to more questions that I don't want to answer. Besides, my brother has taken care of me all these years; he deserves a life of his own, and a little happiness. He's lived without them for my sake since I was injured. I can't be the one to stand in the way when they're finally within his reach.

Against my better judgement, I turn around. "You have been since she first walked through our front door. What else is new?"

"She – I –" My brother looks down at the floor and mumbles sheepishly, "I think she's in love with me, too."

A vision of Luc standing at the front door for hours, just waiting for it open from the other side so that he could share his temporarily life-altering joy runs through my mind. I immediately feel guilty. My world may have stopped, but the axis still spins for everyone else. "That is an interesting development."

Those words are all the encouragement my brother needs.

"We went to the *Septime* on Saturday night and..." The whole story spills out of his mouth in a jumbled, chaotic mess of run-on sentences and happy digressions. I listen politely, exercising all of the self-control that I have, to force my expression to stay happy, even when I wonder just how much of Luc's giddy love is actually reciprocated. And especially when Luc says something that reminds me of something Lauran has said about me.

When my brother comes to the end of his story, I tell him, truthfully, "I'm happy for you." The words come out sounding more melancholy than I intended, but Luc doesn't seem to notice. "*Bonne nuit.*"

I pad slowly to my bedroom. I hang up my coat and lift my suitcase onto my bed, careful not to let the wheels touch the pale quilt. Motion by motion, I move mechanically through my life without thinking or feeling a thing. If I let even one thought cross my mind, that will make way for all of the others to follow. I'll have to think and feel everything at once and I just... can't. Not now. Not yet. Instead, I fold my sweaters neatly and stack them in my closet.

I am standing on tiptoe, reaching for a hanger when Luc pops his head in my open door. "Is everything all right, Sophie?"

"Fine," I lie, and wait for him to shut the door behind him.

§

Alone at last, I sit down heavily on the end of my bed and reach for my *portable*. My *anaia* has a lot of explaining to do. I am sad and defeated, true, but mostly I am furious with Ilari — and I intend to make that very clear.

But when I turn on my phone, I find an SMS from Madeleine. Four, in actuality. My research partner is vocal to say the least — the one hundred and sixty character limitation imposed in text messages cannot constrain her self-expression. I am used to seeing series of messages pop up one after the other — but never before has she begun with *I confess; I am in love with your brother.*

Taken aback, I rub my tired eyes and try to refocus. Still, the message remains. *I confess; I am in love with your brother.* Baffled, I can only read on.

*I still don't believe in your love nonsense. Pragmatism will not allow me to place the responsibility for my happiness in the hands of an unwitting man. But the facts are plain and I have run out of counter-arguments. Luc is charming and kind and quite possibly even more interested in the study of me than I am. I have never met anyone else like him and am forced to recognise that he may not wait forever for me to acknowledge that. And so, here we are. This is new and frightening territory for me. I promise, there will be no giddy stories about our dates and no breathless exclamations about how wonderful he is. In fact, I will likely never mention any of this again. But I thought you might like to know. Bisous, ma belle.*

When I come to the end of the messages, I have to shake my head. It seems particularly cruel that on this of all nights, my research partner and my brother should have finally fallen into each other's arms. I lie back on my bed and pull my knees into my chest, pondering what might have been.

After Gab died, I went through a brief phase of obsession with universal connection — I was plagued by thoughts of how just one subtle change at one moment in time might have changed every moment after it. When I began to consider all the little things that might have been different, that might have somehow kept Gab alive, I always remembered a Chinese puzzle box that *mamie* bought me when I was little girl. When the box was closed, it was static — nothing moved, nothing changed, but the possibilities that lay within it were infinite. All it took was one little push with my index fingers to transform the box completely — and then a small twist of the left corner to transform it again.

If my *anaia* hadn't pushed the proverbial box with his index finger, I might be with Lauran right now. We might have gone to his apartment after the train arrived at *Gare Montparnasse*. Or, better still, I might have brought him here, to see the view from my window ledge. We might have stood out there together — me leaning against the railing with him behind me, his arms around my waist, chin resting gently on top of my head.

It's too late, of course. The puzzle box is open now. All of the possibilities that lay inside have disappeared, giving way to only one reality... Me, alone on my bed, with tears overflowing my eyes. When I lost Lauran the first time, it was my own fault — no, it was my choice. But this time...

I sit straight up. This time it's Ilari's fault. And I want to know why. Ignoring all security protocols, I pick up my *portable* and dial my traitorous *anaia*'s home phone line.

§

"Hello?"

When Ilari answers the phone, I skip right over pleasantries and demand, "What did you say to him?"

"What the fuck?" my *anaia* is taken aback. "Who is this? Amaia, is that you?"

"What did you say to him?" I repeat — I can hear the venom in my own voice. Or maybe it's desperation. I feel like shaking my *anaia*. "What did you say?"

"Jesus fucking Christ, Mai — calm down. What did I say to who?"

"Lauran!" I scream his name into the receiver, pacing the floor of my bedroom in a fury. "This morning he was in love with me. I left him with you for two hours and now he doesn't want to be involved with my sordid little life!"

I hear my *anaia* mutter a string of obscenities away from the receiver. When he comes back, he says quietly, "Oh. That."

"You ruined my first relationship in almost four years and that's all you have to say for yourself?" My cheeks burn with rage. If any of our neighbours were asleep, I've woken them.

Ilari doesn't have the Sagastizabal temper. I have never seen him move from absolute calm to wild rage in a two-second interval; he doesn't throw or break things in his path when he is upset. But he will only let me scream at him for about three minutes before he reacts. "Just one goddamn minute," he snaps back. "All I asked was what he knew about your chosen vocation. Imagine my fucking surprise when his answer was, 'Well, based on her field of study, I'd say she wants to be an economist, or maybe pursue a career in diplomacy!'"

"What would have possessed you to even ask that question?"

"He doesn't even call you Amaia! What in the bloody hell possessed you not to tell him?"

"I was going to tell him!" A hiccupping sob escapes from my mouth, and when I shout, I don't know any more whether I'm mad at my *anaia*, or myself. "Just — not yet! He wasn't ready!"

"You shouldn't have brought him to Bordeaux if he wasn't ready, Mai," Ilari tells me gently, the same way he used to remind me that Gab wasn't really there just because I was talking to him and imagining how he would answer. "I think," he adds – the same way he always added when he talked about Gab, "that you know that."

"Don't patronise me! I came to visit you!" What little ground I had to stand on has crumbled under me, and we both know it. My attempt at protest is pathetic and futile.

"No – you came to meet with Thierry. If he wasn't in Bordeaux, you would still come to visit us, I'm sure. But you choose the dates of your visits based on when the commandant wants to see you. There's no sense in pretending. If the commandant had told you there was an enclave of armed young men hiding out in Estérençuby, you would have changed your plans and gone there at a moment's notice."

"Yes, but-"

"No," Ilari cuts me off, "there is no but. Imagine it, Mai. You and your boyfriend buy tickets for a weekend in Bordeaux, then Estérençuby comes up. What would you have done then?"

"I..." I don't know.

"Would he have been ready to know what you do?"

"No – not yet. I needed more time!"

"But if not now, when? What kind of catharsis could you have possibly forced on him that would have changed the opinion he spent his whole life forming? Especially when he was still labouring under the mistaken impression that you and the fifteen-year-old Sophie he met in Saint-Antoine were essentially the same person?"

"I could have done it, Ilari. Honestly. I just needed to say the words right. But instead he heard them from you."

I can hear my *anaia* sigh and pull out a chair to sit down at his kitchen table. 'You forget. I can't fucking believe you actually forget."

"What? What do I forget?"

"That you spent your whole bloody life up until you got shot deriding The Organisation. Calling us all terrorists. Remember how strongly you believed that we were wrong?" Of course I remember. I wore my beliefs like a badge of honour.

"Something extraordinary happened to you that changed your life — and perspective — forever. What could possibly have happened to Lauran that would have had the same impact?" I was going to happen to him. I could have. But the words get stuck at the back of my throat and when I open my mouth to force them out, all that escapes is another sob. "I'm sorry," Ilari goes on, "that he had to hear it from me. But it wouldn't have made any difference."

"It could have!" I choke.

"Come on, Mai. You had to draw a line in the sand sooner or later — and whether it was now or a month from now, he would still have been on the same side."

I open my mouth to agree but again, there are no words — just a ragged sob. I know that my *anaia* must be right. I know that I never should have fooled myself into believing that I could make things work with Lauran this time; that just because I was different, I would automatically be the kind of different that he wanted.

"Mai? Are you still there?" The best answer I can muster is a barely audible mumble. "Try to get some rest," Ilari advises in the gentle tone he reserves for moments when I am at my most disturbed and damaged; the tone that at once infuriates and calms me. We hang up without saying good-bye.

§

Paris gets cold on November nights. When I step out, barefoot, onto the window ledge, the air seems to cut right through my t-shirt. I sit on the stone platform in the dark and look out into the open sky.

I want to see Gab. I want to be able to picture him, sitting on the wrought iron railing, waiting for me to tell him about my day, the same way I have every night that we have lived in this apartment. Every night, at least, until I started having coffee with Lauran.

But when I look out, I see nothing. The railing is empty. I close my eyes and try to picture Gab, but his face is blurry — no matter how tightly I squeeze my eyes shut, I can't force my memory to show me his features clearly. I sit in the dark, shivering, for what seems like hours, but Gab's face is still cloudy and unclear.

Finally, the wind gets the better of me. I stand up, turning my back on Gab-who-is-not-there, and go inside to sleep.

## Chapter 23

I can't breathe. I lie in bed, coughing and gasping for oxygen, but no matter how much air I suck in, it doesn't make it to my lungs. There is someone on top of me, his knees crushing my chest so that it feels like it's on the brink of caving in. Again, I try to breathe in, but no air comes. My eyes fly open, panicked. I try to reach for the cord to turn on the light, but I'm pinned to the bed.

It's Gab. He kneels on my chest, two chunks of my t-shirt balled up in his fists. I can only watch in horror as he begins to shake me, tugging harder and harder on the thin fabric. He yells at me – "You should have known you would never find anyone else!" – and I realise, in a moment of terror that makes my heart seize in my chest, that where the words are coming from, there is nothing. Gab kneels on me, shaking me, with his face blown open, blood streaked across his cheeks and a ragged, gaping hole where his beautiful mouth used to be. "You should have come with me like you promised!" he rages, yanking on the layer of cotton that covers my chest, pounding my limp body against the mattress over and over. "You promised, Amaia!" The words come from nowhere – when I look at Gab's face, I can see straight through to the wall behind him. I try to look away, but he grabs me by the jaw and forces me to face him straight on. "You promised, Amaia! You promised!"

§

I wake up screaming. Gab is gone. My room is dark and empty. I sit bolt upright and look around, my eyes darting across the space, waiting for someone to leap out of the shadows, but there is nothing.... Sweat pours down my forehead, running into my eyes... still nothing. Just the shadow of Luc, his hand on the doorknob, leaning in. "Sophie?"

It takes a moment for me to realise that I'm still screaming.

My brother rushes into the room, arms waving. He has faced so many crises in the time we've lived together that he is normally calm, but it's been so long since I've had a nightmare that tonight he is surprised and overwhelmed. "Sophie, Sophie! You're awake, it's all right!"

I clamp my hand over my mouth to dampen the sound of my scream, which slowly dissipates into a muffled sort of sob before stopping entirely. My eyes, still panicked, are wide open — my focus races around the room. "Sophie." Luc pulls the beaded cord down to turn on my bedside lamp, then sits down on the edge of the bed, facing me, his hands on my shoulders. "Look at me." Still, my eyes race back and forth, running from corner to corner, door to door.

Luc tightens his grip on my shoulders. "Sophie. Look at me." The force of my brother's hold on my body pulls me back into the world. I look him in the eyes. "Are you all right?" I nod, tentative, although the truth is that I feel nothing like all right.

I used to have a lot of bad dreams. They started when I was first in the hospital; I would dream of the moment that I realised Gab had a gun. In those dreams I was frozen, waiting for a shot that I knew would come... but it never came. I would wake up screaming, and the nurses had to sedate me just to keep me in bed; the only other option was to use straps to hold me down.

The bad dreams went away, eventually. But then, when we moved to Paris, they started again. It was a different dream, but the same thing every night — Father Philippe came to me. He told me that he knew my sins, that God knew my sins, that

I needed cleansing. I never found out what he meant when he said cleansing. The sound of his voice in my dream was so lifelike that it felt like he was standing next to my bed, whispering in my ear. I always woke up before the threats became real.

Over time, the dreams came less frequently... once a week... then once a month... and finally, not at all. This is what *Docteur* André calls "responding to medication." At least, that's what he wrote in my file. Getting better would be too much to hope for, I supposed, sarcastically, at the time.

I have just proven myself right.

"What happened?" my brother asks, his voice full of concern.

I shake my head, in a feeble attempt to clear my mind. Every time I blink, an image of Gab, his face brutally wounded, flashes through my mind. "Just a bad dream."

"Are you okay now?" Luc puts the back of his hand to my forehead, checking the empirical evidence in case my answers are less than truthful. "You're burning up. Do you feel well?"

"I don't feel..." I swallow, "...quite like myself...?" There is no need for additional adjectives — I lean over and vomit into the wastepaper basket next to my bed, which illustrates my point in the most concise way possible.

My brother holds back my hair for me. We have spent more nights than I can count together like this and even though the overriding terror is worse than I remember every time, it helps to have Luc here. When I can sit up again, it's all I can do to murmur, "Thank-you."

"Come on, Sophie," Luc helps me to my feet, "let's get you cleaned up." With one hand, he grabs the wastepaper basket from the floor, while deftly steering me toward the door with the other.

I allow myself to be led. Putting one foot in front of the other seems like a colossal effort, even with help. When we get to the bathroom, even though I am inside first, I stand in the dark until my brother reaches for the light switch. He moves around me easily, pulling my pink toothbrush from the porcelain holder and squeezing a dollop of blue gel onto it from our half-empty tube of *Prodent*. "Now," he instructs me, placing the toothbrush in my hand and closing my fingers around it, "you brush your teeth and clean up. I'm going to make us some tea. I'll be back in just a minute."

When Luc leaves, I take a long look at myself in the mirror. My forehead is wet with sweat and strings of matted hair stick to it. My skin is a pallid, blue-tinged white, but my cheeks burn bright, flush red and my eyes... my eyes have a wild look, like they belong to someone I don't know; like the girl standing on the tiled bathroom floor and the girl looking out of the mirror are two different people.

With a sigh, I lean down to turn on the faucet and wet my toothbrush. As I stand back up, brush in my mouth, I cast a sidelong glance at our deep white bathtub. I can almost hear the water calling me.

It would be so easy. I could just run the tap and slip into the warm water – I wouldn't even have to take off my t-shirt. Two quick vertical cuts with the blade of *papie*'s old straight razor... the one Luc still uses once in a while, before a big meeting... on each wrist, is all it would take... I could just lay back and slowly float away into nothingness. I could see Gab again. I could be with Gab again. I could be with Gab forever. No questions, no disruptions, no one to tell us no.

All I have to do is run the water...

I lean forward and spit my mouthful of toothpaste into the drain of our cracked white sink. "Luc," I call out, my head down, eyes still on the tub, "I think I'm going to take a bath...!"

When I look up, I see a reflection in the mirror behind my own. For a second, I think its Gab, and I start – but it's only Luc. "It's three am, Soph. Too late for a bath." He puts one hand heavily on my shoulder. "Come on, I made tea."

§

We sit up in my bed, backs against the headboard. The glow of the bedside lamp casts shadows over our knees. We are quiet – the only sounds in the room are the sips of tea we take from our mismatched mugs.

"Do you want to talk about it?" Luc asks.

I look deep into my tea, avoiding his concerned gaze. "No."

And so, we go on sipping in silence. I try to avoid blinking as much as I can — every time my eyes are closed, even for a second, the image of Gab's shattered face appears in my mind.

It's on nights like this that I find myself contemplating my life as if it were my little Chinese puzzle box from *mamie*. It's still in my bedroom, sitting closed on my dresser, its red lacquer finish covered by a thin layer of dust, just waiting for an errant finger to brush against it and realise its endless possibilities. I can't help but wonder where, or when, I pushed too hard on my life and released the chaos of the past three and a half years.

I would give anything — almost anything — to be able to go back to that moment in time and give the proverbial puzzle box another push, to twist my fate in a different direction. Anything, even a lifetime spent as a clerk at *Épicerie Carbodel* in Saint-Antoine, would have been better than this.

"Did you ever think we'd end up here?" I ask my brother absently.

"What do you mean, here in Paris?"

"No, no — here. Together. You, a bank manager, taking care of me, your crazy sister... Is this how you imagined your life would be?"

Luc laughs. "Of course not! I thought I would be halfway to the senate by now, banging every blonde in my path along the way. I hate to say the word banging, but that's exactly the verb I would have used when I was at *lycée*."

I roll my eyes. "I know."

"But I was a completely different person back then. Things change. I'm happy this way. I wouldn't trade my job, or our apartment, or even," Luc reaches over and ruffles my hair affectionately, "your moments of slight insanity. Why?"

All I can do is shrug — I have no real answer. At least, not a good one. "Do you know what my big dream was? I wanted to be a novelist."

"You still could be — you have your whole life ahead of you."

"But how? Nothing that I invent sounds even half as unbelievable as the stories that I have lived." My brother has to admit that I have a point. "I just wonder, sometimes, how my life veered so far off the course I had planned. I wonder if I could have done something to stop it."

"Would you have wanted to?"

"I don't know," I admit. "Most of the time, probably."

Luc takes one last sip of his tea then puts the empty mug down on the bedside table. "I worry about you, you know."

I raise an eyebrow. "Why? Haven't you ever been in love before?"

"What do you mean, exactly?"

"If you've been in love, you must know what kind of crazy things it can do to you."

"I don't think I fall in love quite the same way you do, Sophie," my brother laughs.

"Luc!" I reach out and shove him with my weak hand; he hardly moves a millimetre. "I'm serious! Haven't you ever loved *anyone*?"

My brother looks down at his hands – his voice is barely audible when he admits, "Only Madeleine."

"Really?"

"Really. When I was younger it was all just sex – as much as I could get with as many women as I could talk into it. I rarely knew their names, which, believe me, decreases the chance of falling in love exponentially. And then you got hurt and I stopped thinking of anyone but you. I don't think I ever considered the possibility that I might eventually fall in love with someone until that day you brought Mado home to work on your economic theory project."

I remember that day. It was the second week of our first year at university. Madeleine let herself into our apartment huffily – she was in a rush to go out with her friends and do something more conventionally fun than economics homework with me, the *commune* bumpkin. I lagged behind, weighed down by textbooks, having been somehow compelled to carry Madeleine's in addition to my own. Luc walked out of the kitchen with a cup of hot coffee in hand — and the second he laid eyes on her, he dropped it. The porcelain smashed on the parquet — my already sulky research partner got coffee on her suede pumps, which launched her into a full pout. Both she and my brother were utterly useless for the rest of the afternoon.

Come to think of it, that sounds like the beginning of a love story.

"What was it about her? I mean, how did you know you were in love?"

"How could I not know?" Luc can't help laughing at himself. "I couldn't hold onto anything for the next two days!"

It's true. "I counted how many things you broke that week, you know. Six cups, two plates, a vase and the teapot."

"She changed my life and my dishes...!"

"Do you still feel that way?"

Luc's face lights up like a sparkler on Bastille day, giving him away before he answers, "More than ever."

"I've been in love twice and both times, it's been completely different. The first time, it was instant — we ran into each other in the school hallway and the moment I looked into his eyes, I knew. But the second time, I had no idea. We were always fighting. He was a Stalinist; I was devoted to Gorbachev. Day and night, we argued. I thought he was a narrow-minded, uneducated warmonger. His vocabulary wasn't quite as extensive as mine, so he just called me *potxa* — it's the Basque word for cunt. Would you believe I once got so angry with him that I hit him in the face? It's true. He once told me that it was when he touched his face and saw blood on his hand that he realised he was in love with me." It occurs to me, as I speak these words, that so many of my favourite stories about Gab are ones that he has told me since he died. The tragedy is that I'll never really know if they're true... but I remember them so vividly that it feels like they are. And I'll always hope that I'm right. "He actually had to show me that I was in love with him. I had no idea until he kissed me.... But then it all happened so fast. The truth is, I'm still in love with both of them. And I'm spending the night in bed with you!"

"Speaking of that," Luc smiles, "why don't you turn off the light? Its four-thirty. We should get some sleep."

I pull on the beaded cord to turn off the lamp, but I lie awake in the dark next to my brother, eyes wide open, just waiting for daylight.

## Chapter 24

When I wake up, my mouth feels like it has been lined with sandpaper. I am curled in a shivering ball in the middle of my mattress, the tangled blankets pulled over my head. Disoriented and dizzy, I push my hair away from my face as I crawl out of my protective cotton cocoon. Soft white light filters into my bedroom, slipping beneath the window blinds to illuminate the carpet. The sun is shining over Paris. It's morning. I survived.

The sudden creak of door hinges behind me is so startling that I nearly leap into the air. Clinging to my sheet for safety, I turn around slowly to find Luc standing in the doorway. He is dressed for work in a tailored gray suit – and he is still knotting his tie around his neck when he says, "Good morning, sunshine."

"What time is it?" I manage.

"Just after eight. You had a hard night."

"I was there." I blink, and the image of Gab's beautiful face, bloody and broken open, flashes behind my eyes.

Luc knots his tie with finality. "I'm going to be late. There's coffee brewed and you're seeing *Docteur* André at one o'clock. Martine will come at lunch to take you to his office. Stéfane is home this morning, so if you need anything, just go next door, *d'accord?*"

I wonder, sometimes, what these days are like for Luc; days when he has been awake all night because I can't sleep but when he still has to drag himself out of bed and get dressed for work when the early alarm rings. Days when employees knock at his office door while he is on the phone with the psychiatrist and the pharmacy and he has to wave them away, finishing his conversation more quietly. I wonder if he knows that his staff raise their eyebrows and whisper about *Monsieur* Cassou's crazy sister when they think he won't hear them. I wonder how he can live these days and give no indication that he is bothered by the lack of sleep, or the inconvenience, or even the social judgement, while I, the root of all the problems, sit in bed seething just contemplating it.

But all I say is, "*D'accord.*"

"Try to get some rest this morning."

I nod. My brother waves a final good-bye and closes my bedroom door behind him. I listen to his footfalls on the parquet, a cracking decrescendo to the door. Still, I listen, as he lifts his keys from his pocket, turns the squeaky lock to let himself out and, standing in the hall, turns his key in the lock to safely bolt me in.

Then — only then, when he is safely out of earshot, do I lie back in bed. I can't close my eyes. I know what — or rather, I suppose, who waits for me behind them. There can be no rest for the haunted. I heave a sign, and weep into my pillow.

§

When I look out over the rooftops of Ile Saint-Louis, I always remember Saint-Antoine. I stand barelegged on the window ledge, my thin t-shirt and a pair of black cotton shorts my only shields from the brisk autumn air, and lean my elbows on the rail, a lit cigarette dangling between my fingers. The morning sun dries my tear dampened cheeks. I don't often think of home, but this morning, it is preferable to think of anything if it means I can avoid thinking of Gab.

I don't miss my parents. I'm not sure that I ever had parents — just a group of adults who wanted to claim ownership over me to satisfy their own selfish needs.

And *ama*. I knew so little of her until the very end but I will always empathise with the terror in which she must have lived every day. I don't miss Father Philippe, and the way he could make me feel, just by looking at me, as if I was to blame for my own poorly executed birth. But sometimes I wonder what it might have been like to be a biological Cassou; a born and bred provincial *minette* who sang in church and lived happily ever after with the grocer's son; not Patrice, of course, but his older, taller brother, Yannick, who stayed in Saint-Antoine to take over the store from their *papa*. Sometimes, on mornings like this one, I wish I knew.

I wonder where Patrice is now. I still maintain that my reaction to his impromptu *I love you* was justified, but I'm sorry that I hurt him. And I think, knowing what I know now, that I should have kissed him back. Not because it meant anything – a kiss is just a kiss, after all – but because, for that one brief moment, I would have known for sure what life in Saint-Antoine would be like if I fit in. That way, when I left it behind forever, that very same evening, I would have known for sure that I made the right choice.

But it's too late, and now, I'll never be sure.

I take a final, lingering drag on my dying cigarette, then drop the still burning butt over the iron railing and go inside to wash up.

§

The bathroom mirror does not lie – I look like I've spent the night under a naked light bulb with my eyes held open against my will. Deep, bruised circles ring my bloodshot eyes; matted tufts of tangled hair cling to my clammy forehead; my dry lips are riddled with savage bite marks from my own teeth. With a sigh, I turn on the tap and run warm water to wash my face.

It occurs to me, as I hold my hand under the stream of water, waiting for it to heat up, that I should be thinking about Lauran. It was only twelve hours ago that he left me, but that terrible moment on the platform at *Gare Montparnasse* already feels like a lifetime ago. All I can think of is Gab, his knees compressing my chest;

the desperate feeling of lying, gasping for air, beneath his weight, unable to look away from the wreckage where his mouth used to be.

A cold feeling comes over me, the same one I had late last night, and I look over at the porcelain bathtub, contemplative. It would be so easy. I've thought of it so many times before that I know exactly how it will go... All I have to do is run the water up to the rim and slip into it. Two vertical cuts to my wrists with *papie*'s antiquated straight razor and I'll quietly fade away in the warmth of the bath. I would leave my underwear on — it's less romantic, I think, but it wouldn't be fair to Luc to have to find me with everything exposed —

There is a knock. The sound at the door cuts off my train of thought. I turn off the tap and make my way down the hall to see who is there, calling, "*J'arrive!*" as I go.

§

On the other side of the front door, I find Stéfane, holding the largest Pierre Hermé box I have ever seen. "I heard you were feeling unwell." He pushes his glasses up on his broad nose, adding, "Martine says that chocolates are a Band-Aid, not a solution, but on that matter, we disagree."

I have to invite him in — I have never turned away anyone bearing chocolate. We take the box to the kitchen, where I put on a fresh pot of coffee. "I expect," Stéfane says, as I spoon out the grounds, "that you will brush me off if I suggest that it might help to talk about it?"

"I'll meet your expectations in half a breath," I agree.

"Well then, what shall we talk about?"

I carry two empty mugs to the kitchen table where my neighbour sits, the box of chocolates open but untouched in front of him, and I pull out the chair opposite him to sit down. I have a chocolate in my mouth before my thighs touch the wooden seat. "I've never had a problem that one or two *chocolats* couldn't fix."

Stéfane indulges me and does not point out the truth. We both know that my purse makes a rattling noise when I lift it because of all the pill bottles I have to carry around.

"I have this Rubik's cube," I start.

"Isn't that more Martine's area of expertise...?"

"This one requires creativity. It's solved — except for two squares. There is one white square stuck on the red side..." I pop another chocolate in my mouth, "and one red square on the white side. No matter where I move them, they wind up back where they started."

Stéfane rubs his eyes under his glasses. "That sounds like a metaphor."

"A metaphor?" I question my neighbour through a mouthful of caramel. "For what?"

"I'm an artist. You asked me about solving a Rubik's cube. That's the best I can do. Besides," Stéfane looks at his watch, "it seems to me that you have an appointment with *Docteur* André soon. Shouldn't you get dressed?" I shrug and reach for a praline. "You know Martine will just make you get dressed when she gets here, don't you?"

"*Bien sûr*," I admit, chewing.

"Then why not just go now?"

"Fine, fine," I agree grudgingly, standing up, "but I'm taking the chocolates."

"I expected as much."

With practically a party tray of chocolate confections under my arm, I meander off down the hall to my room. "And put on the brightest outfit you own!" Stéfane calls after me. "I won't be satisfied unless I see at least two colours! Your wardrobe gives away your politics every time!"

## Chapter 25

I arrive at *Docteur* André's office wearing a blue dress, the shade of which is not found in nature, and yellow pumps. I did not even know that I owned yellow pumps — they must have been cast-offs of Gen's that I accepted with gratitude all the while wondering in precisely what context it might ever be appropriate to wear yellow shoes. After my first attempt at a colourful outfit was unsatisfactory, Stéfane found them at the back of my closet, buried under Gab's old sweater - I asked him the context question to hide the fact that the sensation of holding my last tactile memory of my dead boyfriend in my hands was causing my already fragile heart to contract under the weight of its thin fibers.

"To the doctor's office, of course," he replied, and it was all I could do to grip the sweater between my fingers and nod in resigned agreement.

*Docteur* André made me stop wearing the sweater at the end of my first year of university; he said that clinging to a physical manifestation of my past was holding back my progress. I suffered separation anxiety for weeks. Whenever I was at home, I would run back to my room every ten minutes just to make sure that the sweater hadn't vaporised. The pain eased, slowly, just like the doctor promised it would. The sweater took up residence in the closet with the rest of my clothes — I still used to pull it out sometimes, when I talked to Gab. But I hadn't given it a second thought until this morning; not since I started seeing Lauran. When Stéfane found it in the closet, seeing it folded in a tired square only hours after I saw Gab wearing it in my nightmare made me feel unbearably sad but also somehow safe... like as long as the sweater was still with me, the Gab in my dreams couldn't be real enough to hurt me.

At the office on *boulevard Richard-Lenoir*, Martine practically has to push me out of the car. In addition to the usual trepidation I feel before an appointment with *Docteur* André, I feel certain I look like a clown. I wish I had put on Gab's sweater instead of this stupid garish dress.

Inside, I am greeted, if looking up from paperwork can be called that, but Marianne, *Docteur* André's exceptionally devoted and diligent secretary, who works herself to the bone all while reapplying lipstick thirty times a day in the vain hope that one of these endeavours might make the good doctor notice she is alive. She is a petite blonde with a Ph.D. who is utterly wasted in her role transcribing files and recording phone calls, but it is evident that she cannot imagine herself anywhere else; that she would throw her whole life away for one fleeting moment when the Doctor's eye caught her in the right light. When she points me, wordlessly, to the office door with an envious glare that could burn my skin, I almost sympathise with her. I have hated angels the way she hates me now, for every second with Gab that they have robbed me of.

§

*Docteur* André's office betrays his serious personality. He is a young man, with a close-clipped beard and glasses, always seated behind his oak desk, always with his intimidating fabric-bound copy of the *Diagnostic and Statisical Manual of Mental Disorders IV* open in front of him for reference. "*Bonjour, mademoiselle* Cassou," he says when I cross the hardwood threshold, his thin lips curling into his best impression of a smile.

I dislike *Docteur* André. I feel as though he is always trying to catch me out — and that's because he is. When I moved from Bordeaux to Paris, I was well known by the *Bordelais* doctors as a compulsive liar. I have only ever lied because I knew that the truth of what I thought and felt sounded utterly absurd. Psychiatrists do not approve of patients who do not give full disclosure. If I had a *centime* for every time I've been told I am holding back my own recovery, I could have put myself through medical school and become my own doctor. Since I do not have those *centimes*, I was referred to *Docteur* André, who is renowned for his work in the field of post-traumatic stress disorder, particularly as it affects young women.

"*Docteur*."

At best, our relationship is conflicted. We disagree often. But I cannot deny that he has helped me to function more like I did before Gab died.

"What brings you here? I was under the impression that we had our regular Thursday session this week."

"We do." I sit down on the sofa facing *Docteur* André's desk and cross my legs. My shoes look like I coloured them with a highlighter.

*Docteur* André scratches his beard. "Has something been troubling you?"

"A nightmare." And I describe for him, in every painful detail, the way that Gab attacked me in my sleep, screaming at me and holding me down; alternately shaking and asphyxiating me with his hands. I describe the words that he said, and the way that they came from his broken mouth. I detail every jagged, shattered tooth; every blood stain that dotted his cheeks, and the cavernous space where I knew the rest of his mouth once was; the way I could see through it all the way to the wall. "Every time I close my eyes," I sob, tears running down my face in devastated torrents, "every time I blink, I see him that way. I can't sleep, I'm so sure he'll come back again. If I could manage it, I would stop blinking."

*Docteur* André hands me a tissue. "Do you have any idea what may have precipitated this nightmare? Have you experienced any recent changes in your personal life?"

"No," I start, but the doctor just glares at me sternly until I admit, "A break-up."

"When did this happen?"

"Yesterday."

"I can therefore safely assume that the nightmare occurred last night?"

I can only nod. *Docteur* André swivels in his overstuffed desk chair, pondering this new development. I have been stable for well over a year now — a new, violent delusion was the last thing he expected when I walked through the door. But my doctor has never been the type to shrink from a challenge. "I can see that this is causing you profound distress. Have you had any thoughts of suicide?"

"No."

My answer is too quick, too emphatic to be believable. *Docteur* André knows my history. He looks at me like he would a naughty child, his gaze trained over the tortoiseshell frames of his glasses. "*Mademoiselle* Cassou, we have discussed this time and time again. The only way to facilitate your recovery is by being truthful. Lying will hold back your treatment and, in this case, may put your life in danger. Now, I'll ask the question again. Have you had any thoughts of suicide?"

"Yes," I hiccup, an errant sob still caught at the back of my throat.

"You're familiar with the series of questions I'm about to ask you — please remember that this is for your own good, and not my enjoyment."

*Are you contemplating suicide now?* No.

*When was the last time you actively contemplated harming or killing yourself?* About three hours ago.

*Was the contemplation passive — thoughts only — or active — gathering necessary supplies?* Passive.

It goes on. *Docteur* André asks what triggered the thoughts, what stopped them and if I had, at any time, contemplated harming others as well as myself. I answer in the docile manner he expects; yes, yes, no, a detail here and there. Whenever we go through this list of questions, I can't help thinking of what would have happened if anyone had ever subjected Gab to the same series of inquiries — and he had deigned to tell the truth of what was happened in his head.

"I appreciate your candour, *mademoiselle* Cassou," *Docteur* André tries to smile when we finish, but the change in his stiff facial expression is scarcely perceptible. "I will write you a prescription for a low dose of Seroquel, a mild anti-psychotic. One tablet a day for two weeks should be enough to take care of your nightmares. And you know, of course, that I will be in touch with your guardian to advise him of your current mental state so that he can properly monitor your safety."

I can imagine Luc in his office at the bank, carefully pouring over budget reports, his blue tie loosened and his suit jacket slung over the back of his chair haphazardly, when the phone rings. I know that he will answer the call in his quiet professional voice, expecting a colleague — and, after a moment of surprise, accept *Docteur* André's news soberly. But once he hangs up the phone, the panic will set in. He will knot his tie so tightly that he can't breathe properly, throw his jacket over his shoulders in a rush and make an excuse to his assistant about an urgent meeting with the board of directors before he dashes out the door to run the two blocks home.... Envisioning me sitting on the couch, crafting a noose out of bed sheets all the way.

I hate to do this to him. If I had any power to stop my psychosis, I would do it just for Luc. No one has suffered more because of it than him.

"*Docteur*, are you sure that's absolutely necessary?"

The doctor grits his teeth. We've done this dance before, and I always stomp on his toes at the same beat. "Alternatively, I can place you in a psychiatric facility for seventy-two hours… or until it can be confirmed that you are not a danger to yourself. What would you prefer?"

I agree to the phone call grudgingly and leave the office with my prescription, digging my hideous yellow heels into the plush Persian rug in the waiting room as I go.

## Chapter 26

In the car on the way home, Martine asks about my Rubik's cube.

"I'm stuck," I admit. "I haven't been able to make a move for weeks. There is one white square on the red side, one red square on the white."

"That's mathematically impossible."

"What do you mean?"

"I mean that it can't happen – the cube has six sides with nine tiles each, stacked in three rows of three. If a tile is out of place, unless it's the last one, it moves two other tiles with it. It is categorically impossible for you to be left with just two tiles out of place. It's either three or one."

I am adamant. "It's two."

For a long moment, we are both quiet. Martine maneuvers her petite white *Renault* calmly through the slowly moving chaos of rush hour traffic in Paris, ignoring the repetitive chorus of honking horns that resounds around us. She always seems to know exactly what to do – when to cut in, and when to hold back; when to charge and when to stand down. I can't help but envy the sense of absolute certainly – the confidence that there is always a correct answer, just waiting to be found – that her chosen career has given her.

"Everything I ever thought was impossible has happened," I say quietly, more to hear the words than because I want Martine to hear them. I remember the second afternoon after Ilari brought me back to Euskal Herria, when I sat with Gab on the hard floor behind the executive desk in the *despachos*. We faced each other, our knees bent into our chests but pressed together; our arms stretched out to envelope each other's shoulders, silently weeping for what we had lost. I felt something that day, while I clung to Gab, which I had never experienced before and never have since, until this afternoon; the curious sensation of having let everything out until there was nothing left in me — no more sadness, but no more life, either. "A Rubik's cube that defies mathematics is nothing. I don't think there is anything left that I could disbelieve."

## Chapter 27

I am on the couch when Luc comes home, still dressed in the outfit that Stéfane chose for me. I have my yellow-heeled feet planted firmly on the living room rug and I am staring straight ahead at the muted news program on the TV, waiting for my first Seroquel to give any sign that it might be working so that I feel safe to blink.

So far, nothing.

"I have good news." My brother is all smiles, his tie still neatly tied and his hair as perfectly in place as when he left this morning. He juggles his keys playfully, and I can almost hear the tune he's humming under his breath. I expected the riot police, and instead all I've got is a happy-go-lucky banker...!

He didn't get the call – the realisation crosses my mind in a flash. Somehow, *Docteur* André wasn't able to reach him or, better still, forgot to try. He knows only as much as when he left home this morning. He knows I had a nightmare, that's all.

I try not to give away my sense of relief. "Oh?"

"Madeleine is coming for dinner," Luc takes a step, crossing through the doorway to that he can see me completely over the end of the couch. "What on earth are you wearing?"

"It's Stéfane's fault," is the best excuse I can muster — and most surprising of all, it's actually true.

"Whatever it is, go change into something you can wear to cook."

I raise an eyebrow. "You know I'm fine with cigarettes for dinner, right?"

"We have a guest coming, *niaise*. I want to impress her and, well, soup that I've boiled over isn't going to do it."

Since I can only concede that my brother has a point, I grudgingly make my way to my room to change.

§

To say that I don't cook is a gross understatement. Unlike Gen, I do know how, I simply haven't the slightest interest in preparing food, even if I'm hungry; left to my own devices, there is no doubt that I would subsist on nothing but *pain au chocolat*, coffee and *Gauloises*. But I have to admit, it helps. Luc puts on a Calogero record and we work side-by-side at the kitchen counter — he peels, I chop. The rhythm of the knife against the cutting board is dull and even. If I just concentrate on the sound, everything else seems to leave my mind.

The problem, of course, is that we only need so many carrots.

Once the job is done, I wander the kitchen, listless, my eyes wide open. The longer I can keep from blinking, the easier it is to hold back the scream at the back of my throat. Luc notices my odd behaviour more quickly than I expect. "Are you all right?"

"Fine — just a little restless," I lie. I don't know why I hide things from Luc. He's given me every reason to trust him, but, well, I tried to tell Lauran the truth and look how well that went.

"Why don't you pick a bottle of wine? Something that goes with chicken."

"Sure," I agree. It's worth a shot. At this point, anything is.

§

Madeleine arrives like a hurricane, expected but feared. When the doorbell rings, Luc panics — he still has his apron on and, nervous, he runs his fingers through his hair, immediately undoing all of his hard work in combing it. "*Merde!*" he curses, flailing his arms in a desperate attempt to free himself from the simple knot that fastens his cooking uniform. "Sophie, can you...?"

"Calm down, would you? I'll get the door but seriously.... It's just Mado."

No sooner do I spit out those irritable words than a memory of a classroom conversation with Madeleine flashes behind my mind's eye. "He's just a boy, you know," she pointed out to me, scoffing at my love for Lauran.

But to me, he wasn't *just* anything.

I swallow hard, trying to forget. "I'm sorry, Luc. I'll let Mado in. Take all the time you need."

The truth, I have to admit, is that Madeleine isn't *just* anything to anyone. When I open the door, she is a vision in white on the other side, her blonde waves hanging long and loose over a sheer blouse, only just concealing a black lace bra she very deliberately chose to put on under it. "*Bon soir, ma poulette!*" she greets me with uncharacteristic enthusiasm, planting a kiss on each of my cheeks.

"So this is what happiness looks like on you," I marvel, closing the door behind my research partner.

"I suppose it is," Madeleine shrugs, slipping off her tan booties. "But never mind me; I'm sure that Luc has filled in all of the blanks already. I want to hear about you!"

I raise an eyebrow. "What about me?"

"You missed linguistics today... and so did your friend! How is your great love?"

Madeleine's question goes on, I'm sure, but I don't hear it. Since last night, all I have thought of is Gab with a hole torn through his cheeky smile. But now, in this terrible moment, Lauran's words come back to me as if he were standing in the hall next to me, whispering them in my ear. My hands start to shake. "I'm sorry,

Sophie." A lump expanding in my throat, forcing out a jagged breath. "I don't know how to handle this."

§

I'm sitting cross-legged on the parquet in the hall, a heaving sob rattling my rib cage. I don't remember how I got here. Madeleine is crouched in front of me, her hands on my cheeks. "Sophie? Sophie, I'm so sorry, I don't know what I said. Sophie, can you look at me? Please. Luc...!"

"*J'arrive*, Mado *chérie*...!"

"We-" I can just manage to gasp the words. "He — it's over."

My brother makes his grand entrance, hair neatly combed and shirt freshly ironed, to find his girlfriend sitting on the floor with me in the front hall. We are both crying. "I'm so sorry," she is telling me over and over. "My *maman* always says I need to learn when to be serious!"

"Mado?" Luc is confused at first. "Sophie?" And then concerned. "What happened?" He crouches down with us, places a heavy hand on each of our shoulders, looking behind our hands to carefully examine our tearstained faces. This is my brother, so accustomed to crisis that after one reprisal, it has once again become his calm. There is no arm waving, no pacing. He hardly blinks. "Are you both all right?"

Madeleine looks up first, wiping away mascara-blackened tears with the cuff of her white sweater, while she holds onto me protectively with her other arm. "Sophie split up her with her boyfriend," she explains quietly. "Maybe the love of her life."

"What? Sophie, you were seeing someone?" Luc sits down on the floor with us, resting his elbows on his knees. "Why didn't I know about this?"

"There's so much you don't know." I say the words, but they are inaudible through my tears.

Madeleine acts as my interpreter. "It was Lauran."

"The one from Saint-Antoine...? I thought she told me they were just friends."

"She might have," Madeleine concedes, still holding me close to her. "But trust me, there was a lot more to it than just that."

§

I recover. I always do, in the end. The idea, of course, is to get to a stage where I don't have to recover... where I don't collapse in the middle of the hall at the mention of a name... but I'm obviously not there yet.

Luc serves salad and roast chicken and a *tarte au citron* from the *pâtisserie* down the road. We all make quiet conversation as though this were just another meal among friends, but I can still feel tears weighing down my eyelashes and I hear every scrape of fork against plate, every tooth tapping the rim of a wine glass, every bump of the salt shaker against the pepper screaming in my ears, as if the volume of those sounds were amplified by my sadness. When I blink, I see Gab, or at least what is left of him, flash behind my eyes. When my eyes are open, all I can think of are the agonising moments when I walked alone across the platform at *Gare Montparnasse* last night, away from Lauran.

*Docteur* André has told me over and over not to assimilate imagined conversations and dreams into my memory; he says that by doing that, I blur the lines of reality and make it harder for myself to move on through recovery. But I was there in the hospital room when Gab told me that they would send someone to be with me because he couldn't; I know that it didn't happen but I also know that the words were true, even if they were only a reassurance from my subconscious. I was sure, so sure, that Lauran was that someone.

The idea of facing my life, and my work, alone, is painful. But the idea of having to look for someone who is not Lauran is more than I can bear. I feel the fact that I am the third person in the room acutely. Luc and Madeleine share secret smiles, their hands brush accidentally when they reach for the same dish, they laugh when no one has told a joke. They are obviously in love and I am just here, absently picking away at my chicken.

I stay quiet, keeping my eyes on my plate unless someone asks me a direct question. My brother is so happy with Madeleine. For the first time, she seems genuinely happy with him, too. The last thing I want to do is spoil this beautiful night for them with another one of my sad stories. I wish I wasn't a girl who sad stories follow around, but I don't believe in miracles tonight; the best I can do is stay inconspicuous.

After coffee, I excuse myself as quickly as I can manage without appearing to be running away. Luc and Madeleine pretend not to notice that I am on the brink of another breakdown, and I appreciate it — when you're alone, sometimes that's all you want to be. They are at the table long after I leave, talking. Just talking.

I pretend not to notice when Madeleine doesn't go home.

## Chapter 28

There is a small red light flashing in my bedroom. It's the first thing I see when I open the door to my darkened space and I start, my hand poised but frozen on the light switch. I clamp my free hand over my mouth to stifle the shriek of terror I can feel rising in my throat. They tell me I didn't scream when I faced down Gab's gun; I just stood there and braced for the impact. Now, everything scares me. Part of me is always half-expecting to find a bomb on the nightstand.

I turn on the light — there is only one reasonable conclusion, and it's not a bomb; it's my *portable*. I'm sure I'm going to find an under-the-table text from Madeleine, something about how she knows I will call her crazy but she can't believe that she waited this long to give in to Luc's increasingly pitiful advances. I almost smile, anticipating her self-deprecating words. But when I turn over my *portable*, there is no message from my research partner. Instead, a white exclamation mark points out that I have missed a call. The ten digit number beneath the notice isn't initially familiar, and then...

I sit down heavily on the edge of my bed. Lauran.

I am stunned. For a second, I feel nothing — all I can do is stare at my *portable*. And then a storm of questions races through my mind at hyper speed, passing so quickly that I have no time to even fully grasp one before another comes along. My hands shaking, I dismiss the call notification, only to have another exclamation point pop up on the screen. One new voicemail.

I instantly reject the hopeful idea that he might have changed his mind. It's impossible to even contemplate it without feeling my chest heave.

But then, why would he call?

Should I listen to the message?

Is it worth feeling my heart shatter inside my chest cavity again just to hear his voice one last time?

What if he only called to tell me that he's reported my work to the police?

I sit still on my bed, staring at my *portable* in my shaking hand. The questions stop racing through my mind as quickly as they started. My jittery hands sit still in my lap. I feel... a sensation that is unfamiliar at first - and then I realise that it is the fabled calm that people talk about so often. I feel calm. It strikes me that I have spent almost three and a half years trying to wish Gab back to life, and the past two months trying to fit Lauran into a mold that wasn't made for him, because I thought that I needed to do my work *for* someone, and then *with* someone. But neither of those things is true. I work with The Organisation but not because Gab shot me, but because *when* he shot me, I woke up with a new perspective on life. I woke up with the sense that my people have greatness in them, and that I can help inspire them to unleash it on the world. I don't need to talk to Gab to remind me of it; it beats in my heart, the unruly organ that races and heaves and occasionally lies down and plays dead. I don't need to be with Lauran for moral support. I am doing my work for me and only me – and for the first time, I feel fully prepared to walk the path that I have laid for myself. Alone.

There is no hesitation. Using my index finger, I delete Lauran's unheard message with the push of two buttons. And I feel at peace.

I put my *portable* face down on my nightstand. At least for this moment, I am the master of my own destiny. I am alive and free and ready to take on the world alone. I wrap my bed quilt around my shoulders and step out onto my window ledge, into the night.

§

Gab isn't waiting for me on the railing, and I don't expect him. I light a cigarette, blowing out a cloud of smoke that blurs the jewel-coloured reflections on that Seine into sparkling chimeras. *Notre-Dame de Paris* stands watch over Paris tonight like all nights and I stand behind her, resolute. For the first time since I moved into this island apartment, my time on the window ledge is completely silent. Thoughts come and go, but I hold them inside of me. There is no one to share them with.

I don't need anyone to share them with. I am enough.

When my cigarette burns down to a smoldering ember, I put it out on the railing and go inside to sleep.

## Chapter 29

I can't breathe. I lie in bed, coughing, gasping for breath, but no air can reach my lungs. I'm drowning in my sheets. My arms flail in desperation, but I can't move. I'm pinned to my mattress, held down by something... someone... I shudder, trying to find oxygen. It's him. I know it's him.

When I open my eyes, he is on top of me, his knees pressed down on my chest. Gab. He shakes me by my shoulders, screaming at me through the open wound where his mouth used to be. "Did you really think you could leave me? Did you really think you could just forget me, Amaia?"

My heart throws itself against my rib cage, pleading hysterically to be set free from the torture chamber my chest has become. But I am stronger than this nightmare is. Gab is in my head – and maybe I can't just force him out in one night, but I don't have to look at him. Determined, I take a ragged breath and close my eyes.

Gab grabs my shoulders hard and slams my head into my mattress. "*Potxa!*" he curses at me. "I did this for us! For us!" He yanks my eyelids open and holds the flesh taut against my skull so that I can't take my eyes off him. "Look at me!"

I want not to scream. But there are spots of blood on Gab's cheeks and tattered flesh hangs in threads from his chin; broken pieces of what were his front teeth jut out from beneath his torn upper lip... and when I look at him, I can see straight through his face to the floral paper on the wall behind him. It's too much. I lift my hand to cover my mouth, but Gab grabs my wrist and holds it down. "Look at me!" he roars.

And I scream with every molecule of oxygen in me.

§

The pink lamp on my nightstand is on when I wake up. Luc and Madeleine are both there, kneeling beside my bed. My hands shake. My black *Zadig et Voltaire* t-shirt is torn at the neckline, revealing the scar on my chest. I can't focus my eyes — they dart around the room, from corner to corner and back again, searching for Gab.

"Sophie," Luc puts his hands on my shoulders. "Sophie, I need you to look at me now."

"Please," I hear the words tumble out of my mouth in a rush, "tell me he's gone."

Madeleine stands up and comes to sit beside me in bed, wrapping her arms around my waist. "Who was here, *ma poulette*?" she asks gently, stroking my matted hair.

My brother holds my gaze and grips my shoulders — he has read every book, perused every pamphlet and, perhaps most depressing of all, he has had hundreds of opportunities to practise bringing me back from the brink. He could perform this scene with his eyes closed. "Who was here, Sophie? Who did you dream about?"

"Gab." A violent shudder wracks my body when I say his name out loud.

Luc doesn't know that name, but it doesn't matter: "Did he hurt you?"

I can only nod a yes in answer to the question.

"You're safe now." My brother strokes my trembling hand. "Madeleine and I are here. We're your family. You can trust us. You know that, right?"

I nod again. The tremors running through my body slow down from the speed of an earthquake to minor seismic activity. "I know that." The words are strained, but I manage to get them out; Luc needs to hear them.

"Do you feel safe enough to stay here with Mado while I go to make us all some tea?"

"Yes."

"That's my girl." Luc ruffles my hair lovingly and stands up. "I'll be right back."

When he's out of the room, Madeleine leans in close to me, pressing her lips almost right against my ear. "You don't have to tell me, *ma belle*, if you don't want to, but I'd love to know who this Gab is."

I turn to face my beautiful friend in the midnight darkness and tell her, "He isn't, anymore. He died more than three years ago."

§

When Luc comes back, juggling three mugs in his two hands, I am laughing with Madeleine as if it were a Saturday afternoon in the sun at the *Jardin du Luxembourg*.

"Oh, my little *minette*," Madeleine giggles, shoving me playfully, "if only I had known you had such a dangerous past, I would have been far less mean to you in first year!"

"You would not have!"

"Okay, you make a point. But I would have been impressed."

"Who needs impressed?" I scoff. "I knew my brilliant personality would win you over eventually. Friends should like you for who you are, not how many bullet wounds you have…!"

Madeleine laughs so hard that she tips over sideways and has to prop herself up on my bedside table, knocking my lipstick and my dog-eared copy of Gorbachev's biography onto the floor. The accident makes us both giggle more. Tears run from the corners of my eyes. My brother just stares, baffled. "I, uh, brought tea...?"

"Thank-you, *chéri*," Madeleine stifles a chuckle.

"Seriously, what the hell happened? When I left, Sophie was one millimetre away from a nervous breakdown. I'm gone for five minutes and I come back to this?"

"Come sit with us." I reach my hand out to Luc, "Come!"

After a moment of hesitation, Luc grudgingly relents and comes to joins us on the bed, handing cups of tea to Madeleine and me. We sit three in a row, shoulder to shoulder with our backs against the wooden headboard, sipping from our hot, sweet tea in silence, the occasional snigger escaping from Madeleine (or, in spite of my best efforts, me.)

My brother can't take it for long. "Can one of you please let me in on the joke?"

"Do you know what happened to your sister?" Madeleine leans over me to ask the question, still half-delirious and giggling from the combination of lack of sleep and total disbelief. "I mean, *really* know?"

"I saw the police report," Luc deadpans. "I know."

"The police report?" I almost choke on my Earl Grey. "That's where you got your information?"

"You never volunteered anything much more significant."

Madeleine leans forward again, this time utterly serious. "And you never *asked*?"

Luc sighs and looks me straight in the eyes. "I'm asking now."

"Really?" my thirteen-year-old self asks; she is still defensive and used to being hurt. My brother nods. "Then I'll tell you."

§

My story is shorter when I tell it this time. I leave out the background information about terrorism and poverty and my dysfunctional upbringing during my summers in Euskal Herria. But I explain how I hated Gab... and then how I loved him. And how I lost him.

It's easier than I expected it would be... until I have to hear myself explain, for the second time in an hour, what he did to try to get me back. My hands start to shake.

Luc gapes. "Please, don't take this as me saying that I thought you were just crazy before, because I didn't, but... I understand so much more now, why you're still so sad, and why you have these nightmares. When we talked last night, it never occurred to me that you might have been in love with Gabrié Duarte. The police report called what happened to you a terrorist attack. I thought you were a target, and they used him to lure you into the trap."

"Fucking *txakurra*," I mutter under my breath. Just typical.

My brother doesn't hear me over the sound of his astonishment. "Why didn't you ever tell me?"

"I've never really told anyone, honestly," I admit. "Besides *Docteur* André, I mean. And all the talking I've done doesn't stop me from needing to take enough pills to tranquilise an elephant just to make it out of bed in the morning, or from having nightmares where Gab attacks me because he thinks I'm forgetting about him. I guess I just didn't think it would help. And," I sigh, "I promise, it was so, so much easier not to."

Luc yawns and rubs his eyes. He is obviously exhausted and now sad, too. Words don't come easily. "Can I just ask one thing?"

"What is it?"

"What made you tell Mado, just now?"

"Honestly? She asked."

"Jesus Christ," my brother curses, not exactly under his breath. "Sorry, I — we need to talk more about this but... tomorrow? Are you all right to sleep alone?"

Madeleine, who has been quiet through our awkward exchange, speaks up before I can answer. "I'll stay with Sophie."

This time, my brother and I both stare. "Really?"

"Really."

I expect to have to see Luc's heart break a little, but this is a night of surprises. He leans down, kisses Madeleine on the forehead, whispers, "Thank-you," and wanders groggily back to his room, mumbling about the bank.

§

Madeleine and I lie side-by-side in the dark, her arm around my waist. It is four o'clock in the morning. Paris is silent. Down the hall, Luc has stopped tossing in bed and is breathing himself gently into a deep sleep. My research partner dozes beside me. And I am awake, eyes wide open onto my unlit room, doing everything I can to avoid blinking.

"Sophie?" the girl next to me whispers.

"What is it, Mado?"

"Are you asleep?"

"Do you think I would have answered you if I were?"

"Can I tell you something?"

"I'm listening."

"I have a sister."

I raise an eyebrow. Madeleine and I have experienced the better part of our university years together; through research projects, presentations and nights of emergency study, we've discussed almost every topic available, in one context or another, and argued about most of them. And not once has she ever given any indication that she was not a spoiled only child. "You never told me."

"I know. That was on purpose."

"But... why tonight?"

"When you were telling me about your Gab, my little *minette*, it reminded me of my sister. He name is Juliette. She's a quadriplegic."

I can't help but gasp a little. "What happened to her?"

"Great love."

For a long minute I lie quiet, remembering all of the times that Madeleine has callously mocked my love nonsense, or berated me when I described my emotions for someone as love, or retreated from Luc's advances with a scoff, claiming that she doesn't believe in anything as plebeian as love. The blurred picture becomes alarmingly clear. "Mado, you don't mean...?" My research partner nods, her hair rustling against the pillow. "Do you want to tell me about it?"

"Not especially, but I'm going to. Juliette is ten years older than me. My parents won't admit it, but I was a little surprise — not an unpleasant one, I don't think, but still. Juliette already had her own life by the time I was born. She was so, so pretty. I adored her. She was always sweet to me, when she was around, but I think I loved her more because she was always so busy and that made the time I got to spend with her feel special. I only saw the smallest piece of who she really was, and that piece was beautiful and fun and shared her cassis-flavoured *Anise de Flavigny* candies with me. When I was eight, she went to university and at Christmas, she came home with the most awful boyfriend — he chewed with his mouth open and argued with *papa*, but Juliette loved him. I remember my parents were so relieved when they broke up; they practically danced in the living room.

"And then Juliette met Maxime. The law student; so handsome, so well-spoken, so polite. He seemed so perfect, it should have been obvious that he wasn't, but no one ever guessed — especially not sweet Juliette. He got her pregnant when she was twenty-one. She never told him, in the end; it was the same week that she found out he had a girlfriend at home, and she had been the other woman all along.

"She came home. She was such a mess. *Maman* and *papa* did everything right. They said they would help her; they even offered to raise the baby. They convinced her to go back to school to finish the term. She was alone in her dorm when she put a gun in her mouth and tried to kill herself."

"Oh, Mado..." There are tears welling in my eyes.

"Well, the thing is, she missed. No one has ever been able to figure out where she got the gun, and she's never told, but she had never so much as held one before that. She severed her spinal cord, and her vocal cords. The baby died. But she survived. She lives at home with my parents; she has to get around in a motorised wheelchair, and a keypad helps her communicate. She doesn't say much, but she reads a lot."

"Mado," I lean in close to my friend, "what made you tell me all of this?"

"When you woke up tonight, screaming and shaking," Madeleine runs her fingers over my hair, "you looked just like Juliette when she came home. And I knew she would want me to tell you. We're not close, but when I was fifteen she told me something I've never forgotten. I had just brought my first boyfriend him for dinner. It was nothing serious, I don't even remember his name now. He barely looked up from his plate during the meal he was so uncomfortable. But after he left, Juliette sat me down and typed so earnestly, so slowly... *Look at me.*

"So I looked. But I didn't really see the point. My sister spelled it out for me with her stiff, barely mobile fingers. *I did this to myself to hurt Maxime. But he's gone on to marry his girlfriend and live a happy life in the country without giving me a second thought. The only person I hurt was me. Never let love get the better of you.*"

"But... she didn't mean not to love anymore."

Madeleine shrugs, "She probably did. Juliette is a very sad, bitter person. I don't really believe that... but I did learn from my sister's example. She made me want to be very strong, and very careful who I let in."

"And Luc...?" I can't help but ask.

"Luc is the best man I've ever met. And don't you dare tell him I told you."

I smile to myself in the dark. "Agreed."

Madeleine hugs me hard from behind. "Promise me something, *ma minette.*"

"What?"

"Promise me you'll be strong. I need you."

"I promise." And for once, I really mean it.

## Chapter 30

I stay home from school again. It's not that I'm actively avoiding Lauran — the prospect of running into him and wracking my brain for the right words, for any words that don't give away the uniquely uncomfortable combination of sadness, resignation and desire that I will feel when I see him again, all while trying to meet his eyes and not blush while I sort out what to do with my hands, doesn't thrill me. It wouldn't keep me in bed, though. But another night spent with my eyes wide open, this time with Madeleine snoring softly beside me, has left me worn to a thin, shadowy version of myself. When the alarm rang, I could hardly lift my head to see the sun shining through the blinds, making golden geometric patterns on the carpet. My research partner got up quickly and I pulled the quilt over my head, silently begging Gab to leave me in peace for a few hours so I could get some sleep.

Apparently, my dead boyfriend is in a generous mood. I sleep peacefully through the morning, only rolling over to greet the afternoon.

And then the front door opens. I wake with a start and sit up in bed with an anxious jolt, afraid that this sound, this wakefulness, might just be the beginning of another terrifying dream. "Hello?" I call out. "Is someone there?"

Luc barges through my bedroom door, his tie half-undone and his hair dishevelled from nervous finger-combing. "That's it, Sophie," he announces, "I'm not playing anymore."

Confused, I shake my head, trying to clear the sleep haze from my brain. "What are you doing home? What aren't you playing anymore?"

"This game we've apparently been playing for the past three and a half years where you only tell me things if I ask specific questions. I don't know what questions I have to ask if you don't even give me a hint what the answers might be!"

I rub my eyes. I'm tired, and still baffled. "I don't understand. Is this about what I told you last night?"

My brother sighs and sits down beside me on the edge of the bed. "*Docteur* André called me at work."

"Shit," I mumble, and look down at the quilt, scrunched between my suddenly tense fingers.

"I have to call Ilari to let him know what's happening, but after that, you and I need to have a long talk."

I mutter something that must sound like agreement to Luc, because he stands up and leaves the room. It is only after he is out of sight that my brain fully processes what he said. Call? Ilari? "Wait," I leap out of bed and chase after him, barefoot, down the hall, "what?"

My brother stands in the kitchen, hand poised to dial out to Bordeaux. "I said, I have to call Ilari."

The betrayal is acute, and it cuts me along an old wound. I am alone. There is no one I can really trust. I feel rage rising in the back of my throat. "Why? Why would you do that to me?"

Luc is taken aback by my reaction; his face gives him away. But his voice is calm when he says, "I have to. Ilari is your guardian when you're in Bordeaux, the same way I'm your guardian in Paris. I have to let him know anytime there is a change in your condition."

My breath comes in furious bursts, and I clench my fists until my nails slice open my palms. "You two have been talking to each other," I rage, "for three and a half years, about me, and neither one of you have ever told me?"

"Well..."

"Well, what? What do you have to say for yourself?"

"We both love you," my brother can only shake his head. "We both want what's best for you. Honestly, I never thought it would bother you. I know how uncomfortable we made you when you were in the hospital, always posturing, always trying to prove something. I thought you would be happy that we've learned to work together."

"Not if you're working against me!"

"Against you?" Luc turns pale. "I use all of my vacation time taking you to doctor's appointments. I fill your prescriptions on my lunch breaks. Every single thing I do is to help you be healthier so that you can go on with your work! How dare you say that anything I do isn't for you?"

I stare at my brother, my mouth wide open. The last words I heard him say were *your work*. "You... you know?"

Luc nods.

My knees go weak. I have to sit down, and the floor is the closest place. I sink into the doorway and hug my knees into my chest. "How did you... who told you?"

Luc sits down on the kitchen floor, facing me. "When you were leaving the hospital, Ilari took me for a cup of coffee. I thought it was a sort of goodwill gesture, which it was... but he also told me that you had made the decision to fight for Basque nationalism. I'm not going to lie, I thought it was way too dangerous and just plain stupid. But I realised that I had no idea what there might be to fight for... I still don't know anything about the life you lived outside of Saint-Antoine. I probably should have asked. But at least I've always respected that it is your life and your battle. And I have always — and I will always — support you in any way I can."

"Bloody hell," I run my fingers through my hair. "I'm sorry, it's not you, it's Ilari. He tells people about what I do like he has a quota to make."

"He's proud of you."

"Maybe," I hiss, my angry venom not completely gone, "but that isn't why he tells people."

"Yes it is. Every time I call he tells me about some poor illiterate kid you've dragged up out of the muck and how now the kid is working at a constructions site or in a warehouse like it's a miracle. And it is." Luc reaches out and takes my hands, "I'm proud of you, too."

It's all too much – I'm tired and heartbroken and angry and touched all at the same time and the only way I can find to express that is with tears. "I just wish," I sniffle, wiping my eyes with the back of my hand, "that once, you would have asked me what my plans were for my weekend in Bordeaux. I wish I had known that you knew and that it didn't bother you," a hiccupping sob escapes me. "I'm always so afraid…" I feel like I should follow that up with something, but the truth is, I'm afraid of everything. There is no word to sum up the gnawing terror that I live with; that I might be kidnapped or killed or lose more of the people I love or that I'm not strong enough or good enough or that Father Philippe might have been right about me all along. "Why didn't you ever ask me?"

"I'm so sorry, Sophie. I had no idea how much it meant to you. I always thought you would tell me, if you really wanted to."

I swallow hard. "I would have taken that secret to the grave rather than risk losing you."

"Good grief," Luc gazes at me in disbelief. "We've lived together for three years and the things we don't know about each other could fill volumes. We have to talk more. We're family! No more secrets."

"No more secrets," I agree. And I think I might really mean it.

"And that starts now – but before we talk, I have to call your brother."

"I understand." And I stay sitting on the floor, watching Luc as he dials the phone.

§

"Yes, yes." I am still watching from my place on the floor as Luc finishes his conversation with Ilari. They don't laugh or joke, but their discourse is surprisingly free of tension. They work well together. "Of course, it's not a problem at all. Yes, she's here with me now. She seems to be on the mend. I really think it was irresponsible of the doctor to wait so long to get in touch with me... Exactly. I'm glad you agree. Of course, you're welcome to speak to her, just a minute." Luc takes the phone away from his ear and looks down at me. "Sophie, your brother wants to talk to you."

I reach my arm up to take the phone from Luc — the cord is just long enough to reach to where I sit. "*Kaixo?*"

"Hi Mai," Ilari's words are quiet and gentle. "How are you?"

"I'm all right."

"Jesus..." I can practically hear my *anaia* stabbing his kitchen table with a pen in frustration. "You know I suck at this. Help me out here."

"I'm not going to kill myself...?" I offer. I feel okay saying it even with Luc in the room. And I say it in French, because I think he needs to hear it, too. "I think about it sometimes, but I promise, I won't act on it. It's hard to live without Gab," my voice catches.

"I know, Mai. I think about him every day."

"So do I." I wipe a lone tear from my cheek. "But there's so much more that I still have to do..."

"We need you," my *anaia* struggles to get the words out. "Shit. I know I've never told you that, and I should have. You're the lynchpin — without you, it all falls apart. Me, especially."

"Ilari..."

"Just — let me fucking saying it, okay? I lost *ama*, I lost Gab, even *aita* is gone. You're the only family I have left. I need you to stay strong."

"I know... I know."

"*Maitatu*, Amaia."

This is the first time that I can remember Ilari saying those two simple words to me. I never doubted him, but to hear them... my heart is so full it feels like it might burst.

"*Maitatu*."

## Chapter 31

After a long night of talking — so, so much talking — with Luc, I stumble, exhausted, to my bedroom. My eyelids feel like they're weighed down by sandbags, they're so heavy and worn from hours of holding them open against their will, but I had to do it; opening up to my brother while a bloody and broken Gab popped up again and again, like a jack-in-the-box behind my eyes, would have been too much to take.

Luc knows everything now; as much as Lauran. I'm too tired to consider how so much truth might change our comfortable, if distant, existence. All I want is to crawl into bed and sleep. Really sleep, for once. As I curl up and reach to pull the quilt over my head, I notice my *portable* flashing on my bedside table. I pick it up and give the screen a cursory glance; I have another message from Lauran, which I delete without an instant of hesitation. I already know what the truth did to that relationship.

With the last ounce of energy left in me, I turn out the light and try to sleep.

§

Gab is here. I know it instinctively, without opening my eyes, because I can feel the pressure of his knee caps against my breastbone. Air trickles into my lungs like I'm sucking it through a straw; I breathe in low and slow, determined not to panic even as I feel Gab grab the torn collar of my t-shirt and slam my head back into my pillow once, twice, three times. This is a routine, and I know the paces now. The next thing will be the abusive screaming —

It starts just as I think to expect it, and each harsh word falls on me like broken glass, every shard of the sentence cutting me a little deeper — "You should have known no one else would love you! *Potxa*, you broke your promise!" — but I've heard all this before and I can listen to them again. As long as I keep my eyes closed, I can go on like this all night without screaming.

But — the realisation runs blazes through my mind as my head smashes into the mattress yet again — if I keep my eyes closed, this will go on all night. And every night after this. As much as I want to rationalise that the verbal abuse isn't that bad, the reality is that I can't live this way. I know I can't.

Taking the deepest breath I can manage with Gab kneeling on my chest, I steel myself and open my eyes. I stare my dead boyfriend down, looking straight through his shattered, bloody jaw to the pink floral paper on the wall behind him. I remember the man he was; his gentle lips, so often twisted into a know-it-all smirk; his cleft chin and the flesh of his cheeks, stretched tightly over his high-set bones. There is nothing left of that man, just a gaping hole to mark the place where, in a fit of desperation, he put his gun. What we had, however beautiful and brief, is gone. Nothing and no one can bring it back. I face that truth straight on, with my eyes wide open — maybe for the first time.

And I do not scream.

§

I wake up in a cold sweat. My sheets are knotted around me so that I can hardly move my arms. I sit up and scrape a matted clump of hair from my clammy forehead. I take a quick look around my bedroom, but there are no ghosts lurking in the dark, and I know it. All of the ghosts are in my head.

It was a nightmare. Just another nightmare.

With a sigh, I lie back down, pull the covers over my head and try, once again, to get some sleep.

§

It's instantaneous. The second my eyes close and my body drifts into the weightlessness of sleep, he's back. The pain of his boney knees bearing down on my bruised chest is visceral. I wince under his weight —

And then I'm angry. I sit straight up, throwing off my sheets and shoving my boyfriend's ghost to the side. "Seriously?" I demand, glaring at Gab; facial wound or no facial wound, he's acting like an asshole and I have no idea why it hadn't occurred to me until now to tell him exactly that. It will hardly be the first time. "Do you have any idea how incredibly obnoxious you've been for the past three nights?"

Gab's bleeding wound fades away, leaving the face I have so often argued with in its place. "I-" he starts.

"You can shut that off?" I should be relieved not to have to look at the blood splattered on his torn cheeks anymore, but instead I'm fuming. "You bastard! What the hell is the matter with you?"

"You never talk to me anymore!"

There it is — the simple but painful truth. I cover my eyes with one hand and shake my head. Everything else in my life is unbelievable, from my survival at birth to my place as second-in-command of an organisation that is considered the most serious terrorist threat to Spain. Now I have a ghost haunting me - a needy, vulnerable one. "Gab, I..." I try to explain, but he cuts me off.

"You're the only one I have, you know! If you don't talk to me, I'll just fade away!"

"And if I keep talking to you," I sigh, "I'll never be completely alive."

"Yeah, well," Gab counters, crossing his arms like a petulant child, "that's what happens."

"That's what happens when, genius? When your boyfriend who is married goes off the deep end and shoots you, then kills himself? In case it was unclear to you, I didn't exactly sign up for all of that."

Gab sighs and looks down at his hands, embarrassed. "I'm sorry. Honestly. I suck at being in love with you. I always did. First my strategy was that if I pissed you off, you would notice me. Turns out that actually works."

I can't help but laugh, remembering. "Yeah, it does."

"The problem was, I was too much of a pussy to do anything about it for three years. And when I finally did, I was so scared all the time that you might wake up one day and realise you were making a mistake. I never wanted you to know that, so I acted like it was just some stupid fling. I loved you so much I could hardly breathe when you were around. And I never told you. That's the thing I regret the most about my life."

"Me, too."

"What?"

"That I never told you, either. I always wish I had told the world. Even if no one had heard me, at least you would have known."

Gab reaches out and takes my hands, clasping them in his. "I always knew, my princess."

Princess. It makes me ache to hear Gab pronounce that two-syllable word. The village children called me that name behind my back; sometimes they taunted me in the street, shouting *Printzesa! Printseza!* while hurling clods of dirt in my general direction. I knew it was stupid, but even so, the exclusion stung. When we argued, Gab often punctuated his most biting comebacks with that name; it was more hurtful than *potxa*, and he knew it.

When we fell in love, the word princess took on a new meaning. In the days after we first made love on the executive desk, we were nervous when we were alone, avoiding direct eye contact and uncertain of what to do with our hands. I wondered, fleetingly, if we might have made a mistake. It was a quiet evening in town when we began a fake argument about the merits of communism — we were so afraid of being found out, we argued even more that summer to make everyone believe in our enmity. At least, it was supposed to be a fake argument, but it became very real in a matter of sentences and, furious, I turned on my heel, leaving Gab alone in my dust.

He caught up to me just as I reached the factory and grabbed me by my shoulders, pulling me into a shadow cast by the imposing brick structure where the darkness hid us from view. We faced each other. He took my face in his hand and looked directly into my eyes when he said, "You are my princess." I realised, in that moment, that his words were unabashedly sincere. *My princess* wasn't just a pet name; in the rarefied world that Gab inhabited, I was the sophisticated, cultured daughter of a leader he had been taught to revere and the closest thing to royalty that he could imagine. He was amazed and thrilled by every second of my time that I deigned to give to him.

Whenever I think of it now — whenever he calls me *my princess*, even if it's only in my imagination, I can't help but think of the world I could have opened up for him, and the life we could have lived together, if only we'd had more time. We didn't even have enough time for me to tell him how much I loved him.

But he always knew. And, "So did I."

"And then, of course, I shot you. I regret that, too, but only because it didn't work out the way I planned."

"The way you planned?" I raise an eyebrow. "You couldn't have strung together a complete sentence at that point. Don't try to tell me you actually planned out that fiasco."

"You know, when the *Ertzaintza* had me in prison, they kept me awake twenty-four hours a day. At night they handcuffed me to a metal chair and left me sitting under a bare light bulb. When my eyes felt like they were going to burn out and my arms went numb from being held behind my back, I used to talk to you."

"Gab..."

"It was the only time I still felt human. And okay, you're right, it wasn't a plan... I just wanted to grab onto that and keep it forever. Guns were all I knew."

I run my fingers through my tangled hair. "I know."

"It was you who got me through my time in jail. Even if you weren't really there, even though you had absolutely no idea where I was or what I was saying to you... just being able to say the words and imagine how you would answer me kept me from asphyxiating myself with my handcuffs when the guards turned their backs. Now that you have a hard road to walk, I want to be here for you the way you were there for me."

"No, you don't," I shake my head.

"But I just said–"

"Maybe you did want to, at first. But it's been more than three years and up until a few weeks ago, I talked to you every single night. I barely had any friends. I hardly even spoke to my brother, who I live with – just you. Even though I'm here, and you're not. When I finally realised that I'm still alive and that I needed to be part of the living world, you wouldn't let me go. You've been attacking me in my sleep, Gab!"

My dead boyfriend sighs. "I told you I suck at being in love with you."

"Listen..." I never envisioned myself breaking up with Gab. After he died, it seemed like a moot point. The truth is, aside from walking out on Lauran, I've never ended a relationship. And I'm still hesitant to close the door on this one. I love Gab. But I know what I have to say. "... I know that I promised I would always love you. And I do. And I will. But when you shot us both, you're the only one who died. At some point, I have to go on living my life. And this... this is that point. I can't talk to you anymore, Gab."

"What?" Gab backs away, stunned. "Is this because of what I've been saying to you? I didn't mean anything, honestly. I was just trying to scare you a little."

"It was a shitty thing to do," I snap. "But that isn't why."

"I don't understand. You promised, Amaia!"

"I promised," I sigh; I remember it so vividly, "that I would always love you, and that I would never forget you. I've kept my promises. This is about my life. I need to know that I can stand on my own two feet."

"But..."

"No buts." I can see Gab's heart breaking in front of me, but I have to keep going. "I'm alive, Gab. I have to live. I can't do that if I just spend every day waiting to tell you about what I've done, instead of actually going out and doing things. We'll be together again someday." I lean forward and kiss my darling dead boyfriend on the cheek. "For now, I have to say good-bye."

"I never thought you would do this to me," Gab's trembling voice is barely audible.

"Try to think of it more as something that you're doing for me." I wrap my arms around his neck and hold on for one last, long moment. "I'll miss you."

"I'll miss you more, princess."

When I let go, Gab has already faded. It's only a few more fleeting seconds before I find myself sitting alone in the dark.

§

Just as I'm about to pull the covers back up and go to sleep, there is a knock at my door. I can't help but jump, startled. "Hello?"

Luc pokes his head in the door. "Everything all right, Sophie?"

"What are you doing up so late?"

"I was just on my way to the bathroom. I thought I heard you talking to someone."

"Nope... just rolling over. Good night, Luc."

"Night, Sophie."

## Chapter 32

I'm at the kitchen table, eating a slice of burnt toast slathered with *Bonne Maman* black currant jam the next morning when Luc walks in, dressed for work in a gray suit, his green tie hanging unknotted around his neck. I'm in a good mood, having slept through the night after my talk with Gab, so I don't even flinch when my brother observes, "You're up early."

I take a bite of my extra crisp breakfast. "There's more toast on a plate on the counter."

"And you made breakfast!" Luc is suitably impressed.

"I put bread in the toaster and pushed the button down," I roll my eyes. "And I burned it."

"I'll take it," Luc picks up the blackened slice of plain toast and takes a bite. "Why are you up so early, anyway?"

"I have class today."

"Oh, I-" my brother is embarrassed and flustered, trying not to let on that he just assumed I would be staying home again. "Of course you do."

"Smooth," I can't help but laugh.

"Don't you have to get dressed or pack your textbooks or something?"

"Not for twenty minutes," I stand up and pick up my plate, "but I'll take my toast to my room if it will put you out of your unbearably awkward misery."

"No need," Luc laughs. "I'm late, anyway. Have a good day."

"You, too!" I call after my brother, but he's in a rush and has already made it halfway out the door, knotting his tie as he goes, before I even open my mouth.

Life goes on. And if you don't go on with it, it will leave you behind.

§

The school day chugs along uneventfully. I have lectures in economics and market policy, the philosophy of thought and finally, statistical analysis. It doesn't cross my mind to take certain hallways or leave through specific doors to avoid Lauran — the time will come for our paths to cross tomorrow during our linguistic theory lecture and when it happens, I will face him as coolly as I can. For now, I know that his classes are far from mine and I walk the halls with my head held high, almost as if I were just a normal girl in university, attending her regular courses on an average Tuesday.

For a few minutes, I actually manage to convince myself that I am.

And then I meet Madeleine outside our statistical analysis lecture hall; her blonde hair is pulled back in a tight ponytail, which seems to accentuate her flushed cheeks and flaring nostrils. She is patently furious. A knot forms in the pit of my stomach. I must have forgotten something, something important. "We aren't presenting our report today, are we?" I stutter, skipping right over hello. "I was sure that wasn't for another week."

Madeleine ignores my question. "I just ran into Lauran on my way here," she snaps, as if the meaning of that statement is obvious.

"I just stopped for a coffee...?" I offer. It's true. In fact, I could use a piece of gum now.

"He told me he's tried calling you — more than once!"

"Mado," I tilt my head and take a good, long look at my research partner, "I don't understand what we're talking about."

"We're talking about your great love, *grande niaise*! You've been blabbing on about this boy like the sun rises and sets on him for months — and, having spoken to him, I can now confirm that he is a truly exemplary specimen — but then, at the first little hiccup, you just throw it all away?"

"It wasn't exactly a little hiccup," I sigh. My emotionally stunted research partner is the last person I should have to listen to when it comes to love. "And besides, what happened to being strong?"

"I said be strong, not stupid."

"Sorry," I retort sarcastically, "it's hard to tell the difference when your instructions come from someone who calls love a corporate scam to sell chocolates to skinny people!"

"He's in love with you, Sophie!"

"And my brother has been in love with you for two and a half years — but I never once pointed it out!"

Madeleine throws her hands up in exasperation. "I can't talk to you when you're like this!"

"Like what? I showed up for our statistics lecture and you pounced on me — excuse me if I didn't just bend over and take it."

My research partner has no quick come back. She turns on her heel and storms off down the hall, the heels of her pumps clicking behind her. All I can do is shake my head and let myself into the lecture hall. I am strong, even if Madeleine has changed her mind about exactly what that means. If Lauran is really in love with me — with all of me, and all that I do, even the parts he was so quick to call sordid — he'll find a way to let me know that himself.

§

After the lecture, I walk home alone along *boulevard Saint-Germain*. The sense of general optimism that pushed me to get out of bed and make toast for breakfast this morning has faded away with the passing hours. A full day of classes combined with very little sleep, a strong new drug and the spat with Madeleine have left me drained; every step I take is a chore. When I finally make it to the front door of our apartment building, I barely have the strength to shove the door open and I have to drag my feet up all four flights of stairs. Finally inside the comforting confines of our apartment, I plod straight towards the refuge of my bedroom. Luc is in the kitchen, slicing vegetables for dinner; he is engrossed in the task and doesn't seem bothered by the fact that I have nothing more to say for myself than a cursory hello.

My body is exhausted and my nerves feel like they've been rubbed against sandpaper. I toss my purse haphazardly on the floor and stretch out on my bed, heaving a long sigh. I am still carrying the memory of Lauran describing my sordid little life around with me everywhere I go, and it makes my heart feel like there is a weight hanging from it, dragging it deep down inside of me. Add to that the cold conviction of his ex-girlfriend that he was still in love with me, so absolute that she packed up and left the apartment they shared… and the fact that Madeleine, perpetually unimpressed by the extraordinary, described him as a truly exemplary specimen… and I have to pinch myself so that I can rationalise my tears as a reaction to physical pain.

My *portable* rings, chiming from the bottom of my purse, and I start. It's probably Madeleine — and she may well be calling to give me another lecture instead of apologising like a sane person, so I'm not in a rush to answer. I sit up, wiping my eyes with the backs of my hands. By the time I reach my purse where it sits, spilling its contents onto the floor, the ringing has stopped. Out of a need to satisfy my curiosity, I dig past textbooks, pill bottles and my wallet to find it. The screen flashes three missed calls, and three new messages, none of which are from my research partner; the phone number on the screen belongs to Lauran.

This is too much for me.

*I am strong.* I repeat the mantra over and over in my head. *I am strong. I am strong. I can do this on my own, and I will.* And I delete the messages, unheard, one by one, until the screen on my *portable* is blank.

"Luc," I call out to my brother in the kitchen, "can we have wine with dinner?"

"Of course!" he shouts his reply. "Do you want red or white?"

"Whatever you choose is fine with me!" *As long as it has alcohol,* I add privately.

Just as I lay back down, my *portable* rings again. Exasperated, I sit up and grab it, intent on giving Lauran a piece of my mind. But the screen is blank. Still, I hear ringing… It takes my tired brain a moment to remember my second line, the one I use to make calls to Bordeaux. I fling open the drawer of my bedside table and grab the ringing phone in a rush; Thierry is calling.

"Hello, commandant."

"Good afternoon, *mademoiselle* comrade. I have an assignment for you."

I keep a red notebook and a reliable blue pen on my bedside table for these critical moments- I grab them now and, opening the notebook to a blank page, tell the commandant, "I'm ready to receive your instructions."

"We have received word that a group of eight men between the ages of fourteen and nineteen have been menacing the town of Urdazubi/Urdax in the name of The Organisation. They are considered armed and volatile. Based on the intelligence reports, they are not being lead or influenced by an older community member — the leader is one of the band members. I need you to get down there and infiltrate as soon as possible; at least one of the young men was part of a similar group we broken up in Larraun."

"Yes, commandant. I can leave as early as tomorrow afternoon."

"Right. Take the train to Saint-Jean-de-Luz. Ilari will meet you there with a truck and you will cross the border together. He will bring you a weapon but, as always, take care not to use it except in retaliatory self-defence."

"Of course, commandant. I would never shoot first."

"I expect a status report on Thursday evening. It is crucial that we get this situation under control before the week is out."

"Understood."

"*Beitan jarrai, mademoiselle* comrade."

"*Beitan jarrai*, commandant."

I hang up the phone, finish my notes then call out to my brother, "Have you washed the darks in the laundry yet? I'm going away!"

§

By the time Luc has dinner on the table, my travel bag is packed and my train ticket to Saint-Jean-de-Luz is booked for a departure in less than twenty-four hours. We sit down together, plates of pork, vegetables and buttered bread in front of us, at the kitchen table.

"Where are you going?" my brother asks. Now that everything is out in the open between us, he asks more questions than a journalism student.

"Northern Spain," I take a sip of my wine. "According to our security protocols, I can't tell you specifically where. There is a group of teenagers acting in the name of our organisation, causing trouble in a small town. One of them is a repeat offender from another group that we broke up over the summer. We have to disarm them to start... and then the real work begins."

"Isn't that," Luc raises an eyebrow, "a bit dangerous?"

I can only shrug. "It's important to me. That's all that matters."

§

I always fall asleep easily before an assignment. I put my head on the pillow with thoughts of strategy on my mind; recollections of the angry, uneducated teenagers I grew up with in the village and the few ways of successfully earning their tenuous trust... recollections of young, uneducated, angry teenagers I have met in villages like my own; their fear, their passion and the tragic way they cling to their weapons as physical replacements for courage. I have to gain their trust quickly and quietly. I never disarm anyone who is unwilling to be disarmed; it's too risky. I have to sell every would-be freedom fighter on a whole new concept of what freedom is, and what it can be. Running over my plans, step-by-step, I can never remember when exactly I drift off, but it happens quickly. It almost makes me wish I could go into the field more often, except that every assignment, every individual is different and some are much more threatening than others. Every assignment increases my risk of meeting a truly dangerous match — and ending my work just as it is really beginning.

It's not time in prison that scares me, or even death. But the idea of leaving this job unfinished has kept me awake more than one long night.

Satisfied that I am as ready for this assignment as I have been for all of the others before it, I cast a sidelong glance at my Rubik's cube, still sitting unsolved on my bedside table and pull the beaded cord that turns off my bedside lamp before I close my eyes.

§

In the middle of the night, I wake with a start. The lamp next to my bed is on, casting an amber glow over my quilt, and someone sits next to me on the bed, gently stroking my hair; sleeping on my stomach, the first thing I see when I move my head is a knee covered in black denim.

I roll onto my side and the rest of Gab comes into view; he is cross-legged on the mattress, facing me, his head on my head, smoothing my unruly hair. "Hi, Gab," I sigh.

"Hi, princess." The smile on Gab's face is wistful, and somehow sad, even though the corners of his mouth are turned up. "How are you sleeping?"

"I'm not, right now. I'm talking to you. Did you forget our agreement already?"

"No..."

"Then you know that you have to leave."

"I know. I just wanted to watch you for a while. You're so beautiful when you sleep."

All of my memories of Gab and I together – the fights, the sex, and even, on those rare occasions, the conversations – run through my mind in a rush. But they always end the same way; Gab points his gun at me before turning it on himself. And all of those moments we spent together end, after the shots. I live. He dies. We are over. It's taken me three and a half years to finally give in to that reality, but I have now. And when I said good-bye last night, I meant it.

"Look, then, but don't touch. And please, don't wake me anymore."

With a resigned sigh, I turn my head to face away from Gab and close my eyes.

## Chapter 33

Linguistic theory – this lecture is my final frontier. I have my travel bag slung over one shoulder, and a purse full of textbooks over the other; my hand sits poised on the doorknob that will let me in to the lecture hall. I have faced more of my fears head on than I can count on one that hand this week, and yet I'm still standing here; I know I've survived, but that doesn't diminish my anxiety at all. My heart beats a violent staccato on my chest wall, begging to be set free. My hands tremble. Lauran – Lauran who called my life sordid; Lauran who nearly accused me of terrorism; Lauran who alleged that my working with The Organisation after being shot by one of its members was the same as leaping back into the line of fire – may already be inside. I steel myself, taking a long breath in. I am strong.

"Excuse me," an unfamiliar voice behind me interrupts.

I turn around to face a girl I've never seen before. "Yes?"

"I'm trying to get into class. You're in my way."

"Oh. Of course." I step aside, embarrassed, to let her pass. Repeating the three magic words to myself one last time – I am strong – I take another deep breath and follow the stranger through the door.

The lecture hall is unchanged since the last time I was here. I walk straight to the middle of the room, my eyes focussed on my target – my usual chair. Not once do I allow my face to turn left or right. Lauran will be here. I already know that. There is no sense in seeking him out in the crowd — all that will achieve is an earlier start to the inevitable anguish of being so close to him, and yet so far away.

I take my seat. The lecture isn't scheduled to start for another ten minutes, so after I have my notebook open to a blank page and my pen poised, I reach into my purse, pulling out my unsolved Rubik's cube. I don't know why I packed it this morning, honestly. I noticed it on my bedside table as I was leaving and I guess maybe I thought it would give me something to do besides contemplate strategy and read my old dog-eared copy of *Gorbachev* by Martin McCauley while I'm on the train. Now that I'm trying everything I can to avoid looking around the room, it seems like a godsend.

I'm in the middle of rotating the left section counter-clockwise when Madeleine walks up, a new pair of gold booties sounding her entrance against the tile floor. "Listen, Sophie," my research partner puts an armful of textbooks down heavily on her desk, "I think I may have been a bit harsh with you yesterday..."

"You think?" I roll my eyes, my fresh wounds still stinging.

"I wasn't finished," Madeleine snaps, sitting down huffily beside me. "I was going to say that if you want to ruin your last chance with Lauran, that's your business."

"I'm so glad," I shove my Rubik's cube violently into a new pattern, "that I have your permission."

"I said I was sorry, all right!"

"Actually," I point out, "you didn't."

"Well, then, I'm sorry, okay?"

"Fine." I turn my attention back to my Rubik's cube, concentrating on the rotation of the coloured squares.

"Luc is taking me to dinner at *Bistrot Paul Bert* tonight," Madeleine offers gently, in a futile attempt to lighten the mood.

"I know, he mentioned it." I heave a sigh. Madeleine and I have excelled at bickering since the day we met — I don't know why it's so hard to keep the pace in this round. "I'm going away for a few days."

"I know, your brother told me."

I look up at my research partner. She looks up at me. "Well," we both say the words at the same time, "this is awkward."

"I'm sure we'll get used to it." Madeleine sounds positive, but there is an undertone of uncertainty in her words.

"Or maybe we won't have to," I mutter, gritting my teeth and glaring at my Rubik's cube. After all, Madeleine doesn't believe in love nonsense; there's no telling when her cavalier attitude towards passion will collide with Luc's hopeless romanticism.

And then Lauran walks in. I haven't even looked up — my eyes are focused on my Rubik's cube; the white side, still stubbornly refusing to accept its final square, sits face-up in the palm of my left hand — but that head of blonde hair appears in the corner of my eye and I just know. I would recognise it anywhere. He takes a seat at the front of the class without looking back. I take a deep breath and rotate my Rubik's cube again — and the ninth white square rolls into place. Shocked, I turn the cube over, searching for a mistake, but there is none. When I turn it over to the red side; all nine squares are neatly in place there, too. "Mado!" I jab my research partner in the arm.

"Ow! What is so important?"

"I solved my Rubik's cube! The one I've been working on since September!"

"Well," Madeleine grins, a mischievous twinkle in her dark eyes, "I guess you didn't need Lauran for that, after all…!"

"It was nothing I couldn't do with my own hands," I joke, and Madeleine has to cover her mouth with her hand to hold in her laughter.

"Good afternoon, class," the professor announces as he walks through the front door of the hall, silencing everyone but my research partner, who is so red in the face from laughing — or rather, from trying not to laugh — that she looks like she might burst, with just three words. "We will begin today on page two-hundred-and-fifty-four…"

§

When the lecture ends, Madeleine is in a rush to leave. "I don't want to be late to meet Luc, but I can't go out looking like *this*," she explains, gesturing to some undefined part of herself. It is impossible to guess exactly what she means, since she doesn't have even a single hair out of place.

But I humour her, our argument already long forgotten. "No big deal – I'm going to go out the front, anyway. It's closer to the metro."

Madeleine leans in to kiss me on both cheeks. "Stay safe."

"Be nice to my brother."

With a quick good-bye, my research partner disappears out the door. I put my textbooks away, check one last time to make sure that I still have my train ticket, and then make my way, slowly but purposefully, to the front of the lecture hall.

Lauran is still at his desk when I walk by; I can see him out of the corner of my eye, standing with a textbook in one hand and his jacket in the other. For an instant, I think I hear him start to say, "Sophie."

And I keep walking.

§

The train to Saint-Jean-de-Luz leaves from *Gare d'Austerlitz*. I arrive just in time for the last boarding call, and take my seat, alone by a foggy window, as the train begins to chug out of the station. As the thirteenth *arrondissement* passes by outside, gritty and gray, I close my eyes. The ride from the capital to my southwestern *commune* destination will take almost six hours – I need to rest; to prepare for the trying days that lie ahead of me. The tiny town of Urdazubi/Urdax is cold at this time of year. And if I get any sleep at all while I'm there, it will be in the back of a truck.

Instead, I find myself wondering if I will be the same way with the Euskadi liberation that I have been with Lauran. I was so sure of myself in the beginning, that day when I ran into him after our linguistics lecture. But the closer I got to what I wanted, the more the colours and lines began to blur, until I completely lost sight of it. I got scared. And then I lost him.

I heave a sigh and gaze up at the luggage rack above my head. There are days when I cannot be responsible enough to take my medication without prompting. I could not hold one man within my grasp. How can I be responsible for the fate of an entire people?

How can the earth keep spinning on a single axis?

How can the sky be blue and the leaves know precisely when to fall from the trees?

There are answers to all of these questions — just because I don't have them at my fingertips doesn't mean they don't exist. I am responsible for the fate of my people — and when they are free, I can explain how they came to be that way.

I run my fingers through my hair, sigh one last time, and then close my eyes to sleep.

§

It's dark when the train pulls into the station at Saint-Jean-de-Luz. I stay in my seat, pretending to read the tired SNCF advertising bill that I have been using to mark my page in *Gorbachev*, while exhausted passengers shuffle off the train, yawning and rubbing their eyes.

When the train car is empty, I stand, gather my things and walk out onto the dimly lit platform. The concrete walkway is damp under my feet, small pools of water reflecting fluorescent lamplight. I stride as if I were a giant, stepping in the pools but pretending that they are lakes that I am emptying under my crushing weight and taking villainous delight in the small splashes of water that spray upward, soaking my stilettos. To the dark suited conductor who watches me leave, I am just another young woman walking towards the station door. But I am on my own private war path; these steps are taking me to a battleground that only my *anaia* and I will recognise when we stand on it. I need to feel like a giant in these moments more than anything. When I face dangerous young men, I feel no fear – they are young and cowardly, far more afraid of me than I could ever be of them. And they have reason to be. But left alone with myself, even I am wary of me; I can be unpredictable.

When I step out into the night, the streets of Saint-Jean-de-Luz are silent. I turn left and walk two blocks, my footsteps echoing on the cobblestones. *Mirari*'s black shadow is barely discernible in the moonlight, but I would know the old, hulking creature in any light – we have seen so much together, the old truck is like a silent family member. I knock twice, softly, on her back door and take three steps to the passenger side, letting myself in.

My *anaia* sits behind the wheel, his bright eyes the only part of him that the night has not obscured. "Amaia."

"Ilari."

He hands me my gun, a small Smith & Wesson model 22A, fat with bullets. "Are you ready?"

I inhale, long and slow. The metal parts of my gun make a faint crashing sound in my unsteady hands, banging into each other with every tremor. The scar on my shoulder throbs, a dull, aching reminder of why I am sitting in the dark in the old truck in an unfamiliar town, preparing to stare an unknown danger in the face and hoping against hope that the danger is unarmed. I put my pistol down on the seat beside me and reach up with my strong hand, rubbing the pocked skin through my sweater. My mind rushes back so fast that I can hear wind in my ears. I find myself on that dirt road in the dark, face to face with Gab, his bullet halfway between us.

And then it hits me. Part of me dies on impact.

I shudder back to reality. A few more circles with my fingers and the pain in my shoulder fades away. This is it. I pick up my gun again, and lock the safety in place with my thumb. The metallic click has a ring of finality. "I'm ready."

Ilari starts the engine and we drive into the darkness.

# French Glossary

| *Word* | *Definition* |
|---|---|
| à bientôt | see you soon |
| addition | bill |
| allo | hello |
| arrivées | arrivals |
| baccalauréat | High School diploma |
| basilique | basilica |
| belle | pretty |
| bien sùr | of course |
| bijoux | jewels |
| bisous | kisses |
| bonjour | hello |
| bon après-midi | good afternoon |
| bon soir | good night |
| bordelais(e) | Person from Bordeaux |
| boulevard | boulevard |
| bourse | stock exchange |
| café noisette | hazelnut espresso |
| caramel au beurre salé | salted butter caramel |
| carrefour | intersection |
| centime | one-cent coin |
| chèr(e) | dear |
| chéri(e) | darling |
| chocolat | chocolate |
| chou | sweetheart |
| chou à la crème | cream-filled pastry |
| choupinette | dearie |
| citron | lemon |

| | |
|---|---|
| classe préparatoire | Junior College |
| commune | small town |
| cosmétique | cosmetics |
| cours | avenue |
| croissant aux amandes | almond croissant |
| d'accord | okay |
| défense de fumer | no smoking |
| départs | departures |
| deux | two |
| docteur | doctor |
| doctorat | Doctorate |
| école de conduite | Driving School |
| école normale supérieure | College |
| épicerie | grocery store |
| escargots | snails |
| et | and |
| ferme ta gueule | shut up |
| gare | station |
| gars | boys |
| grand(e) | big |
| grandes écoles | College |
| ile | island |
| jardin | garden |
| j'arrive | I'm coming |
| je m'appelle | My name is |
| la/le/les | the |
| langage | language |
| licence | Bachelor's Degree |
| lycée | High School |
| ma/mon/mes | my |

| | |
|---|---|
| madame | Mrs. |
| mademoiselle | Miss |
| maîtrise | Master's degree |
| maman | Mom |
| mamie | Grandma |
| mais, c'est affreux | but, it's awful |
| merde | shit |
| minette | bumpkin |
| moelleux au chocolat | chocolate cake |
| monsieur | Mr. |
| musée | museum |
| n'est-ce pas ? | right? |
| niais(e) | idiot |
| non | no |
| orphelin(e) | orphan |
| où sont les toilettes ? | where are the washrooms? |
| pain au chocolat | chocolate croissant |
| papa | Dad |
| papie | Grandpa |
| parisien(ne) | Parisian |
| pâtisserie | pastry shop |
| place | place |
| pont | bridge |
| portable | cell phone |
| poulette | chick (endearment) |
| primaire | grade eleven |
| professionnel | professional |
| public | public |
| putain | fuck |
| quai | quay |

| | |
|---|---|
| quatrième | grade eight |
| réflexions | reflections |
| rive gauche | Left Bank |
| rue | street |
| salon | living room |
| salope | bitch |
| seconde | grade ten |
| s'il vous plait | please |
| sur | on |
| tabarnac | damn |
| tarte | pie |
| théâtre | theatre |
| verre | drink |

# Euskara Glossary

| *Word* | *Definition* |
|---|---|
| aita | Dad |
| aitaita | Grandpa |
| alaba | Sister |
| ama | Mom |
| anaia | Brother |
| barkatu | I'm sorry |
| beitan jarrai | keep up on both (greeting/slogan) |
| da ados | that's okay |
| Ertzaintza | Basque secret police |
| euskadi | Basque person |
| Euskal Herria | Basque Country |
| euskara | Basque language |
| gau on | good night |
| jai alai | Basque sport |
| kafea | coffee |
| kaixo | hello |
| maitatu | I love you |
| maite | my love |
| mirari | miracle |
| potxa | cunt |
| printzesa | princess |
| sasikume | bastard |
| suge | snake |
| txakurra | dog (pejorative) |
| txipirones | squid |
| xistera | jai alai instrument |

# Spanish Glossary

| *Word* | *Definition* |
|---|---|
| bandido | bandit |
| carnaval | carnaval |
| civil | civilian |
| de | of |
| despachos | offices |
| hospital | hospital |
| pelota | jai alai |
| señor | Mr. |
| señora | Mrs. |

Made in the USA
Charleston, SC
08 February 2014